MW01332341

Asian Wife - Series of 14 Books

Cuckold Game Wife Sharing

By Dante

Contents

Asian Wife Series

- The First Time to a Fetish Swinger Club
- First Time with a Stranger
- First Time Dogging with Asian Wife
- Asian Wife starts Webcam Work
- Adventures in the Swinger clubs
- Dogging after the Fetish Swinger club
- Dogging with Dave
- I Shared my Wife at the Penthouse Party
- The Girl with a Tattoo on her Neck
- Lost my Wife in the Fetish Club
- Touched by a stranger (Coach and Cinema)
- Asian Wife went with her Dads Friend
- Sex, Drugs & Wife Watching in the Fetish / Swinger clubs

- Cuckold Sexting with a Shared wife

First Time to a Fetish Swinger Club

Adult Erotica True Stories

By Dante

Contents

Introduction

Chapter 1 - Our Introduction to the Fetish club scene

Chapter 2 - Wandering around the club

Chapter 3 - The couples room

Chapter 4 - On the way home

Introduction

So before I get into our story, I need to outline what happened to me and how I ended up meeting Jane, my sexy little Asian wife from the Philippines.

Previously, I'd been living in Thailand with a Thai girlfriend but things took a turn for the worse and my life went a bit crazy... or more accurately... She went crazy... Anyway, that latest Thai experience scared the hell out of me, especially when she was telling lies in the police station and I thought they were going to throw me in a Thai jail... So the next morning, I packed my case, left everything behind in my newly furnished apartment, and flew back to Bangkok, changed my UK flight ticket and flew out of Thailand a couple of days later. I must have lost at least a couple of grand, deposit, rent and all the furniture I'd bought. So I returned back the UK... vowing never to return to Thailand again... I'd seriously had enough of Thai women.

Fast forward 5 months and I was not happy... Living alone back in the land of grey skies and the ever increasing cost of living in the UK... I'd started my own business and was messaging quite a few girls in the Philippines from an online dating website. I'd heard that Filipinos were much less demanding and more loving to their partners, and to a Filipino, marriage is forever and divorce is frowned upon. Well, I decided I needed to meet some of the girls I was in contact with, so I flew off to Cebu in the Philippines for another adventure.

On arrival, I checked into a down-town hotel and started meeting some of the girls I'd been chatting to online... and one of them was Jane.... We hit it off immediately... she was attractive, reserved, never even been in a bar... had no kids, was only 24 and wasn't even allowed out at night without a chaperon (sister, cousin or some other family member). I'd purchased a 3 month return air ticket so was able to get to know her and her family quite well.

As for myself, I'm Dave, was 46, been married and divorced a couple of times and had lived in Thailand for some 10 years with my ex Thai wife. That was a couple of years before meeting my crazy Thai girlfriend that I mentioned above. I'd also started my own business on my return to England and one of my old friends and business associates was also married to a Thai so we both had a lot in common, Farang horror stories and "Thai wife" experiences...

Jane soon found a job and got involved with all the other Filipinos in our town, especially the cooking and weekend get together's at each others houses. Our sex life was very good and nothing to complain about. Most evenings she enjoyed making love and especially liked having her breasts touched and caressed, this always seemed to turn her on quickly and made her want more. They were an amazing curved shape, 34B with perfect little ¼ inch nipples when aroused, usually shaved smooth, slim to average build, very attractive, 4' 11" and 110 lbs, so quite a small girl really.

Chapter 1

Our Introduction to the Fetish club scene

So... one day I was in London having a business meeting with my old mate of mine Barry and he started telling me, all about about the UK Fetish and swinger club scene. He told me he'd been going for about a year with his wife and I was really intrigued. After a good long chat about the various clubs and what went on, he said...

"Why don't you and Jane come with us next week and see if you like it? You'll need to buy some leather or rubber fetish gear to get in, but there's a shop in Camden market or you can borrow some of mine."

"Well, I'm definitely up for it mate but not sure if Jane would go, she's never even been in a sexy bar let alone somewhere like that.... But I'll ask her tonight and see what happens."

I mentioned it to Jane that evening and she seemed OK about it, so told her that we had to buy some leather or rubber fetish club outfits to get admitted but didn't tell her much about what went on in the club... just in case she flat out refused to go. Barry had already told me various stories about the clubs he went to and how there were virtually naked girls walking around and there were many opportunities to join in with couples who were playing and having sex in various rooms or the BDSM dungeon areas etc.

Anyway, as you can imagine, I was game and had no idea this type of thing was going on in the UK. Previously, I'd had many experiences with my ex Thai wife while living and working in Bangkok over the years. We had threesomes, foursomes and some pretty wild sessions, even with Ladyboys or Katoys as they are called in Thailand. But never ever found anything like the Adult Disneyland experiences of Thailand in the UK... I will be writing those stories under different titles.

So the Saturday evening approached and Jane and I got our gear together in a holdall and drove up to London. The Club was called Club Rub and it was held once a month, and on this occasion it was held in a two story pub in Houndsditch in center of the financial district of London. But they also used several other locations all in central London.

By the time we arrived it was about 10.15 pm and the club had just opened so was still fairly quiet. We met up with Barry and his Thai wife Mae and were shown where to get changed into our gear. I had a black Lycra T shirt and some small black leather shorts with a front zip and black biker type boots. Jane had a silky black dress that was fairly short and laced up at the front showing her breasts if she loosened the ties or she could pull it down completely leaving just the bottom part on, small black G string and black hold up stockings.

She looked amazing and was as shy as hell dressed like that, wanting to just sit in the corner and not walk around. So we sat in the bar area having a drink while watching the place slowly fill up, having a drink with Barry and his wife. There was also a TV up in the corner of the bar area showing some hard-core sex movies.

Jane was really shocked at the movie's being shown in bar

but with all the new people arriving in really interesting costumes and a few were walking around virtually naked. She soon got used to it and after a couple of drinks and was much more relaxed. About 11 PM it was getting very busy and Barry asked us, If we wanted any sweets?

"Sweets...! What do you mean?" I said seriously not knowing what he was on about.

He laughed and said, “Sweets is the street name for E's or Ecstasy or molly.”

Now up to this point in my life, I'd never taken any party drugs, I used to smoke joints and weed in my younger days, and had the occasional spliff in Amsterdam at the marijuana cafes all around the red light area and canals but never taken any hard drugs like cocaine, heroin or whatever.

Barry then said, “It’s totally different to the hard stuff all the junkies take and most clubbers take E’s at the raves and clubs every weekend.”

I said to Jane,

“What do you think babe, you want to try one...?”

She looked at me and said,

"I don't know, what do you think...?”

She was totally inexperienced, so I said to Barry,

“Are you sure mate... it's not gonna send us into some weird trip or anything...?”

He laughed and said “Of course not, just try one and see how you feel later, then if you like them, I can give you some more.”

He handed us a couple of tiny pink pills and we apprehensively took one each, he said better drink water for the rest of the evening as alcohol numbs the effect.

After about 30 minutes, Barry asked us how we felt...?

"OK... but can't say as I feel any different," I answered.

"It usually takes about an hour or so to kick in, we're going to have a walk around, do you want me to show you around...?"

"OK", I answered and grabbed Jane's hand as we followed Barry and Mae out of the bar area into a curtained off play room dungeon area.

"This is where people like to play on that BDSM stuff later," Barry said, pointing to all the weird contraptions. There were all kinds of equipment there from whipping benches to stocks and crosses with hand restraints, love swings, cages and the grope box etc. Barry then pulled a curtain open and we all peered into a dark room or area with benches around the side and huge cushions all over the floor...

"And in here is the couples room, a bit quiet now, but will be full up later, single guys not allowed in here, only couples."

Jane and I looked at each other and her face was a bit apprehensive. I told her not to worry as we were only here to look around and see what goes on. About an hour had passed and we were still feeling the same so we sat down in a different bar area up some stairs called the chill out room.

Barry wanders over and sits down next to us,

"Are you feeling the sweets yet or do you want another one each? Me and Mae had a couple each earlier and they are pretty good but just one may not be enough."

"OK... give us another couple please mate, I don't think one's strong enough, not feeling any different to be honest."

He gave us two more and we took one each... The club was really getting full now and it must have been about 12. 30 am. The music was loud and pumping and we started walking around again and were amused to see, Barry and Mae dancing away to the heavy Techno music with a big smile on both their faces as they were stroking each other on the face and body. I looked at Jane and she had this strange look on her face and was squeezing my hand and saying,

"I feel all tingly and hot... you will look after me... you will look after me won't you...?"

"Of course I will babe."

I was feeling quite warm but then this wave of euphoria and a strong but extremely pleasurable tingly feeling came over me... Fucking hell, I thought... is this why it's called ecstasy...! I felt calm and relaxed and so horny... I swear I could feel my cock tingling and when I touched it... it felt so... well different, like the feeling was enhanced, and it was really pleasurable to be touched anywhere on my body.

I looked around the club and several girls were walking around with their tits out or wearing just stockings and a Basque and some had virtually nothing on at all, just a G-string. Some guy was being led past us with a tall sexy vision of girl holding on to his huge exposed and erect cock. I put my arm around Jane and she immediately hugged me and went to squeeze my cock. My God... she must be feeling horny as she'd never done that before, anywhere...! Her eyes were looking all around the room as there were so many couples and single guys starting to dance or snog and even touch each other up in corners and on the dance floor.

I started rubbing Jane's back while she was dancing and she was still squeezing my cock through the leather shorts. I had my hand up her dress at the back and was cupping her sexy soft bum cheeks, then another incredible wave of pleasure came over me and made me feel so uninhibited and really fucking horny.

While we were watching all the people dancing, I slid my finger down the cleft of her bum and slipped the tip of my finger in her tight little hole from behind.

Jane let out a loud sigh and said,

“Oh My God... that feels incredible...!” and then unzipped my shorts and pulled my cock out. It was already hard and she was rubbing and pulling it and started leading me across the room holding onto it, just like the couple we saw earlier. She’d definitely lost all her inhibitions and was really getting into the scene. The dance floor was heaving, so we went towards the curtained off dungeon play area and saw various people playing or maybe I should say, being used and abused with whips and canes on the BDSM equipment and toys.

There was this tall and very attractive Indian girl bent over a horse box and was being whipped by this weird looking older fat guy who had a case full of different whips and straps. Each time he lashed her bum and upper thighs with a few strokes, he would then stop and caress her bum softly with his hand and then delve in between her legs and finger her. Then he pulled her knickers to one side so we could all see him fingering her arse and pussy together with 2 fingers before he went back to using a different whip on her. Fuck me that girl was an absolute vision and it was such a turn on to watch with Jane holding and squeezing my cock the whole time.

I was groping Jane's arse and pussy from behind and playing with her tits with my other hand. I don't remember when, but at some point I must have undone the front part of Jane's dress as her tits were out and fully exposed for everyone near us to see. She didn't even try to cover herself up... she just let me touch and caress her tits as other couples stood nearby and watched. A couple of guys standing next to us were also staring and I noticed they had their hard cocks out and were stroking them, then one of them asked me if he could touch her?

"No, sorry mate we're new here and it's her first time," I told him.

We moved over to another bench where a crowd was gathering around and there was this, at least 6 foot tall, beautiful amazon looking girl with fantastic 38C tits... wearing a big black strap on dildo and about to fuck this equally stunning girl that was laying down on the bench. We squeezed to the front and Jane was in front of me directly next to the bench as the Amazon girl (I later found out her nickname was "Strap on Jane" and she has her own website) pushed the huge black dildo into the girl and started fucking her. Jane was in the best position to see everything and I was playing with her exposed tits from behind while also rubbing her butt and legs.

The sweets were really taking effect now and I was seeing all sorts of beautiful shapes and patterns in the darkness and when I looked at certain people, they seemed to shape shift, their skin turned all like a fine spiders web. Waves of tingling sensations kept sweeping over me but I was still very much aware of everything going on around us.

Jane then turned around and said, "Let's go look around some more," so she led me by the cock again and we walked out of the dungeon area back into the dance area with her dress down around her waist. Her stunning 34B tits were on show for all to see and even when we saw Barry and Mae again on the dance floor, she didn't even attempt to cover up. It was truly unbelievable and she was really enjoying the club and started chatting away with Mae as if she was full dressed.

Mae then turned to Jane and said,

"Your tits are great, can I feel them...?"

Jane just let her have a good feel her tits, pushing them out proudly and then Barry leaned over and said,

"Let's have a feel Jane," and just grabbed her other tit.

This went on for about 10 - 15 seconds and then they started dancing again, Jane and I were also bopping away next to them to the Techno beat. I couldn't believe Jane was letting them feel her tits, she was just standing there letting them grope her...!

Chapter 2

Wandering around the club

There was so much action going on around us in different rooms with girls, couples and single guys that I can't remember all the details because when on the sweets, the next day all my memories seemed to disappear quite quickly. So what I am writing here, is only a small fraction of all the things that happened that first night in the club.

Next thing I remember was Jane and I sitting on some chairs around the side of the dance floor, Jane had got between my knees on the floor and was wanking and sucking my cock. On my right, was a European looking couple just watching her suck me and smiling at me and to my left, was this absolutely stunning Asian girl... We found out later she was Korean and was with her English husband, we became good friends later as they were nearly always at all the subsequent club events. Anyway, she was sitting there with literally just a tiny G-string on... no bra, smallish 32B tits but her 1/2 inch long nipples had tiny elastic bands on, so as to make them stick out permanently all night long. Her legs were long and smooth and she was sitting directly next to me with her husband on her other side. And as I opened my legs more, to let Jane get in closer, my leg touched hers and instead of her moving it away, she just left her leg there and I could swear, she was rubbing her beautiful smooth long leg up and down mine as she watched Jane giving me a blow job.

I really wanted to reach down and caress her leg but decided not to... in case her husband didn't approve. We were told there's this "code of conduct" in the clubs that you must always ask permission from the girl or couple before actually touching or joining in with them.

Later on, in another part of the club, I remember Jane and I, sitting in a corner somewhere and we were watching this guy fingering his wife as she sat up on the bar. She must have been about 36, and quite attractive, just wearing a tiny white skirt and blouse with no bra. She was laying back on the bar, resting on her elbows while her much older husband had pulled her white knickers to the side and was fingering her quite hard and fast. About 5 guys and a few couples were standing around watching and playing with each other while the single guys were openly stroking their exposed erections.

I was standing right next to her and my arm and hand was directly next to her leg and touching it discretely. Her blouse was undone to the waist and her bare 34B tits were sort of half exposed but not hanging out completely. From where was standing, I could see right into her blouse and watch them swinging, so I asked the husband, if I could open her blouse a bit more and he nodded OK. So I undid a couple more buttons then her blouse was wide open exposing her beautiful breasts to the audience that had gathered around. This lasted about 5 minutes and eventually she had a huge orgasm shuddering and shaking on the bar and squirted all over his hand, chest and the floor. The audience applauded and several came over and thanked the couple for a really good show. A while later, we were sitting on a bench in a fairly dark corner, I was fingering Jane and her tits were still exposed... but the top of her dress had been put back on her shoulders. Her legs were wide open, hold up stockings covering her thighs and legs and I had pulled her G string to one side showing a group of 5 or 6 guys and couples, her smooth and shaven pussy. My finger was going up and down her slit and occasionally dipping in and out of her very wet and glistening pussy.

All the attention was now on Jane as she must have looked stunning sitting there with me... a 26 year old, sexy young Asian girl and me a much older guy playing with her tits and fingering between her legs. The group had crowded around us quite close and one couple was stood right next to me... the guy was fingering his wife virtually next to my head. When I turned around, my face was level with her pussy and I could have physically tasted her if he just moved his hand away.

Anyway, Jane was watching all the guys in front of us wanking their cocks slowly while they were all watching me finger her and playing with her tits. I remember there was this old guy of about 60 years of age. he stepped forward still holding his erect cock and said to me,

"I'm about to cum now, so would you mind asking the young lady to watch me please?"

I was amazed but turned to Jane and told her what he said, so she looked directly at his cock and watched as he stepped even closer and brought himself to orgasm right in front her, shooting his jizz all over the floor.

She just stared at him ejaculating and then to my surprise... reached out to touch him as he stood there in front of her going limp. She stroked and squeezed his cock a little and then reached under to cup and feel his balls. Although I was shocked to see Jane touching him, I was incredibly excited at the same time.

The other much younger and hunkier guys moved in closer as they must have thought Jane was game for some live action and playing. Then this big black guy was kneeling down right in front of her staring between her legs at her pussy while my fingers were going in and out. He reached up and put a hand on her leg but Jane looked at me and shook her head, so I told him,

"Sorry mate, she's new here..."

He then pulled his hand back and wanked himself a while longer until he came on the floor directly between Jane's legs... Another couple of guys were so close, they were almost on top of us and if they shot their load, would have sprayed all over Jane and myself. So we decided to get away from the fairly large group forming around us and have a walk around and see what else was going on.

Chapter 3

The couples room

The couple's only room was just across the dance floor so we decided to go in there and see what was going on. Inside the curtained off area, it was nearly pitch black, just a very dim red bulb in the ceiling. There were couples on the benches and bodies all over the floor on the big cushions and I think some kind of mattress in the middle. We found a space and slid down to the floor next to a wall and tried to see what was going on but it was so dark.

As my eyes got used to the darkness, I could see a guy right next to me being sucked off by his wife or girlfriend who was on all fours between his legs. Her tits were hanging down and he motioned for me that it was OK to feel them... so I reached out under her and started feeling her tits. The girl looked up from sucking the guy and then grabbed my cock through my leather shorts and gave it a quick squeeze before resuming the action with her man.

Jane was watching this and even encouraged me to continue, she told me it was really turning her on watching me play with her tits. Jane then decided to get my cock out again and started unzipping me. I carried on playing with the girl's tits and then reached down a bit lower and started rubbing her clit while the guy just smiled at me and egged me on. Jane now had my erect cock out and again, I can't describe the incredible feeling as she was squeezing and wanking it, then I saw this other guy with his wife.... stroking Jane's leg on the other side of her...!

It was hard to see exactly what was going on but I kept watching and the guy was whispering something to Jane but I couldn't hear due to the loud Techno... Then I saw the girl move in front of Jane and start to chat with her while they both touched Jane's legs and then the girl started playing with Jane's tits. I was still rubbing the girl's clit next to me and she was seriously wet, her juice was running down my fingers. Then she stopped sucking her man and leaned across my leg, grabbed my cock and started sucking me.... Oh fuck I thought... what's Jane gonna do!

Jane just stared down at her head boobing up and down, she still had hold of my cock... looked me in the eyes and smiled. I smiled back and shrugged my shoulders... Jane then looked back down at the girl in front of her kneeling down and me rubbing her tits. Her husband now had his hand going up the inside of Jane's thigh and was obviously getting closer to her pussy. Then Jane closed her eyes and grabbed his hand.... as he must have fingered her... then she let go of his hand and let him continue exploring her horny little smooth slit.

Fucking hell, here we are in this dark room with two couples doing things we would never have dreamed of previously each side of us, and because of the atmosphere and virtually everyone highly sexed up and on ecstasy or whatever... it was like a non-stop sex party with stuff going on everywhere. Jane was now being well and truly fingered by this guy next to her and his wife was playing with Jane's tits and then... she started kissing Jane on the mouth.

The girl sucking my cock was also wanking her husband on my

right and Jane was getting fingered on my left with that guy's wife snogging her. Jane suddenly orgasmed and the couple sort of backed off smiling as Jane gripped my arm trembling and saying,

"Oh My God... they made me cum... She was kissing me and they were both fingering me at the same time...!"

The girl sucking my cock had moved back to sucking her husband and we had decided to get up and go get some water from the bar. At the bar we saw Barry and Mae again and they asked how we were doing? We had a quick chat and told them what just happened in the couples room, then off they went back dancing in the middle of the dance floor.

In the corner of the room was another crowd of people, so I said to Jane,

"Let's go see what's going on over there."

I couldn't believe it... In the corner was the Korean girl who we sat next to earlier, she was bent over a chair and her G-string had been pulled down to her knees. Her husband, the English guy was standing next to her head and was stroking her head and occasionally feeling her tits underneath. By her arse was a guy dressed like a Roman warrior with a chained chest harness and some Roman looking kilt thing covering his cock but his arse was completely bare. He was fingering the Korean girl and by the look of it, he was alternating from her pussy to her arse. She was absolutely beautiful about 6 ft tall, slim, long legs, smallish 32B tits with the nipples sticking out, really long legs and a perfect arse.

The crowd was thick but I managed to push Jane through to the front and I could see over her head. The guy had the Korean girls bum cheeks parted and was licking and slurping her arse hole in between fingering her. Then I realized... he was actually fisting her in her arse... Fucking hell, what a sight, he had his whole fucking fist in her arse and she was moaning while her husband held her head down and was caressing her tits. Jane was looking wide eyed at the scene and then the husband looked over and saw us standing and watching in the crowd, so he waved for us to come over to him.

I told Jane and we somehow managed to get closer to them and Jane was standing right next to the Korean girl. The husband then said,

"Ginn really likes your wife, Can you get her to play with her tits while that guy is fisting her...?"

I told Jane and she looked at me with this really strange look... and then the guy repeated the request to Jane himself... Jane smiled and looked at me before reaching down under Ginn and started feeling her tits... I started caressing Jane's tits as we watched and I opened the ties on the front of her dress again as the Korean girl's husband Steve looked on smiling. He then reached out and also started feeling Jane's tits inside her dress. This went on for a good few minutes until suddenly... Ginn started to cum, her husband held her head as she let out a long loud moan then started jerking and trembling and when she calmed down, the guy fisting her pulled his hand out and stood back to let her pull her G-string back up.

Ginn and Jane started chatting and they seemed to be getting on really well and then suddenly, the lights all went out in the club and the music stopped... The lights came back on again and everyone started filling up the stairs towards the cloak room and toilets to get changed.

Time was about 4.30 AM and Ginn and Steve had became our new clubbing friends so we all said our goodbyes and were about to leave. Barry and Mae caught up with us and told us, there was an after party at someone's flat in London and did we want to go?

We declined as the effects of the sweets were wearing off but I was still feeling more than horny... and surprisingly, had not even cum yet...! I found out later that one of the side effects of guys taking E's is that, it makes it hard for guys to ejaculate and after long term usage, many guys can't even get a hard on.

Chapter 4

On the way home

In the car, I was amazed to find that I was perfectly aware and OK to drive, it was nothing like smoking weed or being drunk... That, I never ever do, especially if more than a couple of drinks, but never ever if I'd had a joint.

On the way home, I couldn't help but continue playing with Jane... I had her breasts out again and her dress was pulled up... fingering her while she sat there in the passenger seat with her legs parted, half sleeping and rolling her head around just letting me play, she was caressing her own breast with one hand and occasionally squeezing and wanking my cock as we drove through the middle of London at 5 AM.

Then I remember seeing a bus full of people staring down at Jane from the bus while sitting at the traffic lights. She was lying with her seat reclined, eyes closed, tits exposed and legs wide open, totally oblivious to the audience staring down at her in the bus. I was playing between her legs all the way home when we hit the motorway and also had my own cock and balls out, squeezing and stroking myself all the way home. It was such an amazing feeling and I just couldn't stop playing with either Jane or myself...

When we exited the motorway, I remember I was rubbing

Jane's stockinged thighs and pussy but then the traffic lights turned to red, so as we sat there, I pushed two fingers deep inside her and started to frig her really fast. This is one of the things that brings Jane off quickly and sure enough, she started to wail and cum, just as the lights changed to green... but this was a first because she also squirted all over my hand and it was spraying up in the air.... I had to hold my hand over her pussy to stop it going all over the dashboard... A car started honking it's horn behind me so I had to continue driving as she just lay there panting and holding her pussy.

"Oh My God" she said after a few minutes... "That was incredible, I've never ever cum like that before... It was... It was so intense and I just couldn't stop the pee coming. Sorry babe I made a mess in the car," she sighed.

We both laughed and I told her,

"No problem babe, I can't wait to get you home.... I want to kiss and lick and fuck you properly in the bed".

We couldn't get into the house fast enough and as soon as we were on the bed, I pulled her dress and knickers off and just left the hold ups on. I was naked in no time and dived between her legs and started licking away.... She never ever let me near her anus previously, but tonight she was like a bitch on heat and I was the same. I started to recount to her, how the guy in the couple's room was fingering her with his wife and then we talked about a few other encounters and soon I was inside her fucking like crazy. I had a finger in her anus and she was really getting into it. I pulled her over on top of me and fucked her as hard as I could... pushing my finger in as deep as I could into her tight little brown hole... This made her wail out loud and start cumming again... which at last sent me over the edge and I exploded shooting my pent up cum deep inside her. It was absolutely incredible and I spurted far longer than normal, must have been at least twice as much.

We made love and fucked for hours and eventually fell asleep in a 69 position until the late afternoon. That was our very first time at a Swinger and Fetish club and I have so many more stories about our clubbing experiences in clubs in the UK and Thailand.

I hope you enjoyed this story.

If you like my writing style, and stories about Husband or Wife sharing, Wife watching, BDSM, Cuckold, Swinger and Fetish clubs, Dogging and many other fetishes...

Why not check out my other stories on Amazon and sign up to my newsletter to get the heads up on all my new releases.

Dante x

Authors Website – Contact and Newsletter sign up

www.DantesErotica.uk

First Time with a Stranger

Wife Watching and Sharing

by Dante

Contents

Two short stories

Story 1 - Arousal

Story 2 – Torture Garden

Story 1

Arousal

This first story happened at Arousal a Fetish and Swinger club in the UK when we were very new to the scene. My wife Jane is a slim 4 foot 11 inches Filipino, 26 years at the time and has stunning 34B breasts with nice 1/4 inch sensitive nipples. On this particular evening she was wearing a black satin mini dress with front lace ups, tiny black silky G-string and black hold up stockings. I had my usual, tiny black leather shorts and a black Lycra T-shirt and we had both taken a couple of sweets (Ecstasy) an hour before arriving.

As we were walking around and looking at all the various things going on in different rooms we came across a side room with a curtain across the door and a girl standing there holding it closed. As she saw us looking, she said

"Couples only" and pulled open the curtain a bit, so we could see inside.

It was a very dark room with bench seats around the sides and the room only had a very dim red light in the ceiling and you could just make out that there were couples sitting on the bench seats and as we stood in the doorway trying to see if there was anything going on.... a couple got up and squeezed past us in the doorway.

I then said to Jane,

"Come on babe, let's go in and sit where they were."

So in we went and the curtain behind us closed making it

even darker than before. As we sat there, our eyes started to adjust to the darkness and I could just make out that there were about 6 couples in the room and they were all watching a couple in one corner where it looked like the woman was being licked out by her partner, he was kneeling down between her legs and she was laying back onto another couple of which, the woman was kissing her on the mouth and her husband was playing with her tits and then stroking down her belly and onto her legs and inner thighs.

We were both trying to see what was going on and I could just about make out, because of the darkness, that all the other couples in the room were all kissing and playing with each other. I then saw that right next to us, a very slim girl with tiny tits was being fingered by her partner and she had placed her head against Jane's shoulder... and Jane was watching them intently.

Jane must have been getting quite horny watching the couple so close to her, that she had reached over and pulled my cock out and was slowly, squeezing and wanking me with her left hand, while watching the guy sliding his hand up and down the slim girls legs. He also seemed to be whispering something into his girlfriends ear.

I then saw... she had her hand on Jane's right leg and was now leaning across her... rather than sitting next to her... Jane looked at me and I started deep kissing her on the mouth as the sweets had started working and I was feeling really hot and tingly with her squeezing my exposed cock and balls. The girl was gripping her leg as the guy was clearly giving her a really good fingering and then she started to moan and slide her hand... higher up Jane's stockinged thigh.

I saw Jane tense up a bit, as she'd never had a girl so close and touching her like this, and then the girls hand went up under her skirt towards her bare inner thigh... The girl then turned her head to look up at Jane.

Jane just looked down at her face and then the girl moved up and started kissing her on the lips really slowly and gently. The guy who was fingering her had now also seen what was happening... he had moved his hand up to expose his girlfriends smallish breasts by opening up her white blouse. As he slid his hand inside, I saw the girls hand had now slid right up between Jane's inner thighs and must have been touching her pussy through the little black satin thong she was wearing.

Jane's legs were now slightly apart and the girl was seriously snogging her and had pulled her head down more with her other hand. Jane still had hold of my cock and was rubbing it up and down and I then noticed the guy was moving his hand onto Jane's tits and had slid his hand inside her thin black dress which had string ties at the front and was very low.

Jane broke away from the kiss and was looking at the girls hand between her legs and her partner feeling her tits... I then placed my hand on Jane's left leg and slowly inched my way up her inner thigh to find the girl next to her, was already inside her thong and was fingering Jane.

Jane's head was back and the guy feeling her tits had moved around and was now on the floor in front of Jane and watching his wife fingering Jane. He placed his hands on her thighs and slowly eased her legs apart a bit more so he could see what was going on. The girl was now pushing Jane back so she was laying with her back on my chest and I was feeling her breasts from behind, while the girl bent forward and started to open her dress ties and get her tits all out.

Jane was just letting all this happen... I think, because it was so dark and she and I were both were so fucking horny now on the sweets. The guy between her legs had now moved his head closer and I could see his girlfriend, offering her fingers to her man and he was sucking them.

Jane was now laying right back into me and her legs were wide open, when I saw another couple, standing up right in front of us and the woman was wanking a black guy's cock. He was massive to say the least and they were both staring down at the guy who was about to start licking and sucking on Jane's smooth, tight shaved pussy.

The girl laying next to Jane was now fingering Jane in between her husband licking her and then offering her fingers up to him to suck again... Jane's pussy must have been soaking wet and I just started kissing her mouth while the guy and girl worked on making her cum.

I then looked up and saw that the black guy, who was standing in front had stepped over the guy between her legs and his wife was offering this huge long cock to the slim girl fingering Jane. As she leaned forward to take the end of his cock in her mouth, I saw Jane had her right hand between the slim girl's legs and was fingering her too... This nearly made me cum... but I managed to hold back and moved Jane's hand off my cock and up to the monster black cock that the girl was sucking.

Jane gripped the base and it must have been at least 10 inches long and so fat that... her little hand couldn't go right around it. All of a sudden Jane started to cum... she lifted her pussy up from the seat and arched her back as she screamed out in pleasure. The guy between her legs still had his head buried between her legs and was what seemed to be trying to hold her pussy to his mouth. Then he had to release her as Jane gushed a massive amount of liquid all over his face and the floor.

He moved to the side to let Jane recover and was now watching his wife suck on the end of the massive black cock. Jane had let go and was laying on me legs wide apart and looking absolutely exhausted. The black guy had now stepped forward and reaching down between Jane's legs... he started fingering her again. His partner who was white and looked like a real sexy slut with a tattoo on her belly, had kneeled down onto the floor in front of me and was wanking my cock... I moved Jane over a bit so the girl could come in a bit closer, because she had started sucking on my cock...

Jane was now watching the girl on the right sucking the monster cock and the girl on the floor sucking mine... The black guy must have had two or even more fingers inside Jane's pussy and she was gripping his hand... to either make him slow down or pull it in more as she looked like she was so fucking turned on. The ecstasy we took earlier was definitely working now and making Jane do things she would never have done on wine or alcohol.

The girl sucking my cock looked up at me and said,

"Do you think she can take his cock in her tiny tight pussy?"

I looked at Jane and she was just laying back with her head rolling from side to side as if to say, No way... it's too big. But was then clearly pulling the black guys hand closer to her pussy so it looked like she wanted more... The girl got up and went to the other side of the room into the darkness and then came back a couple of minutes later with something in her hand.

She then looked at her guy and he pulled his hand out from between Jane's legs and his girl squeezed something onto his hand. She then squeezed some more out and was putting it all over my cock, then she just climbed onto the bench, crouched over my cock and slide straight down. Fuck me this was girl was incredible and I looked down at Jane to see her reaction.

Jane was laying on the bench beside me and the girl who was playing with her before had now straddled her face and was lowering her pussy onto Jane's mouth...

It didn't look like Jane saw what I was doing, but the girl started to move up and down on Jane's face, so I can only imagine, Jane was tasting her first ever pussy. The black guy was now kneeling down in between Jane's legs and was looking me in the eyes... As if to ask for permission, to try to get his huge cock in Jane's pussy.

I smiled and nodded... as his wife of girlfriend was already on my cock and I had hold of her arse and was slowly pushing a finger into her tight bum hole as the gel had totally lubricated her up. Jane was now having his huge cock head, rubbing up and down her slit, while everyone else in this small and very dark room, were crowding around us, trying to see what was happening.

Jane then gripped my arm and screamed,

"Oh My GOOOOD... He's inside me... and... it feels amazing. OMG OMG."

She panted a few times, then she was wailing and orgasmed

like I'd never seen her before. The black guy was holding her thighs and had stopped moving till she calmed down, then continued sliding in and out very slowly so she could get used to his girth.

Jane must have been well high on the sweets to try this, and was taking at least half of his massive cock. Then he was speeding up and Jane's arms were round his neck... and he then stood up with Jane still hanging round his neck and placed her back against the wall.

I could now see various other couples all groping her tits and another guy was kissing her on the mouth and had his hand somewhere between her legs. Another guy had his wife get between the black guys legs on the floor and was licking his balls and Jane's pussy. Her husband had also somehow squeezed his hand between Jane and the black guy.

I couldn't hold back any longer and came deep inside the black guys wife... She just smiled and hugged me while we both watched all the couples and her man fuck and grope Jane for another few minutes and then he shouted, he was cumming, and pulled out of Jane. His cock was shooting spunk all up her belly and over her tits.

All the hands moved away as he lowered Jane back down onto the bench and he and his wife slid away into the blackness of the room... Jane and I kissed and then got up to go outside and get a drink and reflect on what just happened. We had both crossed another boundary and had fucked with different partners but we both hugged and kissed and fondled each other while telling each other... how much we both loved each other.

I remember Jane asking for us to go home early that night as we both wanted to home get into our own bed and make love properly... I was so on heat that night after seeing Jane taken like that and what really turned me on even mire was watching her with the other slim girl, kissing her and then licking and kissing her pussy... We made love for hours and I just couldn't stop going down and snogging her pussy... Jane was so tired that she fell asleep while I was lapping away between her legs...

Story 2

Torture Garden

The following week, we had decided to go to TG in London (Torture Garden) for a night out. They were holding a large Fetish event and there were well over a 1000 people in a huge venue under the arches near Kings Cross in London. Jane was wearing a black see through blouse with buttons and no bra so her amazing breasts and nipples could just be seen through the thin fabric. A black PVC skirt and sheer thin black tights with no knickers. I wore my leather trousers and black Lycra T shirt. We'd taken a couple of E's just before leaving home and brought a few more for later on... they just make us both as horny as fuck.
We 'd wandered around for about an hour or so and were getting really horny watching all the near naked couples and there was this one totally naked guy with his girlfriend who was topless... and she just had a tiny G string dancing to the Techno music. This guy's cock must have been 10 inches long, fully erect and wide with a big bulbous cock head and a cock ring.

As he danced with his girlfriend, who was laughing and grabbing it all the time, it just swung around and stood at attention. We thought he must surely have taken some Viagra or something for it to stay so hard. Everyone was staring at it and his girlfriend just kept holding it and dancing next to him and he in turn was fingering her from behind...

Jane saw stunned at the sight and couldn't stop staring at his cock as we were dancing very close to them. The girl then grabbed Jane's hand and placed it on her boyfriend's huge cock!

At first Jane pulled her hand away as she was scared and nervous but as the girl held her hand again and the guy kept dancing, Jane kept her hand on it and started dancing while holding his cock... I was amazed and wish I had my phone to take a picture but phones were banned in the club so I had to just keep the memory...

The guy then puts his arm around Jane and his other arm around his girlfriend while the girls danced with him... both of them holding his giant erect cock. I could see the guy running his hands up and down Jane's back and at one point saw him groping Jane's arse while he was watching her breasts bouncing up and down.

After a few minutes, Jane let go and we smiled at our new friends and went to sit down for a while and have another drink. About an hour later, we were wandering around the dungeon / play area and watched a tall and very stunning Eastern European girl being canned and groped by an old guy that was demonstrating the art...

Every now and then he would stop canning her... her beautiful arse and back was covered in long red weal's... and stroke her arse slowly, giving her I assume, pleasure and pain but she was clearly really turned on... As when he fingered her, (she was tied to the whipping horse) his fingers were soaking with her juices.

Jane said to me, "She's so beautiful why does she like being canned...?"

I just smiled and led Jane over to the couples only door and joined the queue to get in.

Jane asked, "What's in there babe...?"

"It's a couples only room I think, like the one we were in last week..."

The couples room is basically a sanctuary, away from all the single guys that can be a real pain when any action between couples start. They are like packs of wolves and crowd round any couple trying to have fun and start groping until the couple either go with the flow and let 5 or more rough guys all finger and grope her or they get pissed off and stop playing and walk away.

When we got into the couples room we saw a free corner and sat down. Looking around we saw several couples all playing together so Jane reached for my zip and unleashed my cock again. I lay back and let her play while watching this black girl being licked out by another guys wife right next to us and the two husbands or whatever were watching and wanking over them.

Then who should come and squeeze onto the corner sofa next to us but the girl and big cock who were on the dance floor!

The girl sat next to Jane and big cock (still erect and looking massive) sat next to his girlfriend. They immediately started snogging and he was fondling her tits. Jane was looking at them while wanking my cock so I started fondling her tits too. The guy looks over at me and smiles and nodded at Jane's tits... I knew what he was asking, so I undid a few buttons so he could see them better.

Jane was really turned on and was staring at his cock again and watching the girl. I opened the rest of the buttons on Jane's blouse and let it fall open. And because of how we were all cramped into the corner, her left breast was almost touching the other girl's breast. I saw the guy brush Jane's tits several times and each time he touched her... I felt her shudder and heard her sigh... Then I saw the girl was holding Jane's hand while she was still snogging and letting her man play with her.

The guy was now running his hand up his girlfriends inner thigh and was fingering her as she opened her legs more so they were now also touching Jane's leg. He then whispered something to her and she turned her head to Jane and started kissing Jane on the mouth while moving her hand up onto Jane's tits.

I moved my hands away and watched her play with Jane's tits and nipples while her man was seriously giving his girlfriend a really good fingering while she was snogging Jane. I slid my hand down and started stroking Jane's legs and soon... Jane her opened her legs and let me finger her too. The girl then took Jane's hand and placed it on her guy's huge cock again... Jane stopped kissing and looked at what was happening... and then me with my hand between her legs... then she started wanking the big cock and snogging the girl again.

"Are you OK babe...?"

She stops snogging and just turns to me and says

"Yes babe are you...?"

The big cock guy now kneels between his girlfriend and Jane. Jane is still wanking his huge cock and his girlfriend is seriously fingering Jane. Big cock then makes his move and dives between Jane's legs and is licking away at her pussy while the girlfriend has moved to Jane's tits. Jane was lay-ed down onto her back... just letting this all happen, so I decided to let it continue and see where it goes. The girlfriend reached over to me and started fondling my cock, so I willingly let her while watching what they are doing to Jane. Then Jane starts panting like a dog... the guy was fingering her while giving her the best licking of her life.

Then he stopped...looked up me and asks,

"You want me to fuck her for you...?"

After last week, I wasn't sure so I asked,

"Babe... You up for trying his big cock...?"

She didn't answer me as I think she didn't want to come across as too slutty but I could see she was well horny and the girl was clearly doing something to her she loved.

I nodded to the guy and just hoped Jane would be willing to try his massive cock. The crowd around us was now thick and there were several couples standing next to us and already fucking while watching us. He positioned himself in front of Jane's pussy and started to rub the head up and down her tiny slit. His girlfriend was talking to Jane and stroking her face, tits and kissing her mouth. Then he pushed the head in and Jane arched up... she looked at me and bit her bottom lip.... He eased in a bit more and she was holding onto the girl... and then he made her moan out loud and was inside her. Not all the way but about ½ way because his girth was stretching her pussy really wide.

Jane stares at me and then the huge cock between her legs, still panting and the guy fondles her tits and starts to push in and out slowly. Jane is somehow taking it and I am wanking like crazy watching this going on in front of me. Then he starts to get faster and Jane is grunting and shouting

"Oh my god... Oh my god... Oh my god...!"

His girlfriend has her hand between them frigging Jane's clit and kissing her mouth again. He goes on for about 3 or 4 minutes and his cock is now at least ¾ of the way in.... Fucking hell... how can she take that monster cock... it must be the sweets... Then he pulls out really slowly to show everyone her gaping pussy. He holds it open for us all to see and then pushes his huge cock back in...

More fucking and then Jane starts to shake and cum violently.... screaming and shaking and the guy just pulls out fast.... and shoots his load all over her exposed tits. The girlfriend slid down and grabbed his cock then starts cleaning it up with her mouth.

I reached down and clamped my hand over Jane's pussy and 4 of my fingers slip inside with no effort at all. ... So I frigged her fast and made her squirt all over the bench and floor to finish her off.

The crowd was still watching and clapping and hanging around but I got Jane up and we made our way out of the couples room and back to the main play area to see what else was going on.

Truly a really great night out at T G's.

I hope you enjoyed this story.

If you like my writing style, and stories about Husband or Wife sharing, Wife watching, BDSM, Cuckold, Swinger and Fetish clubs, Dogging and many other fetishes...

Why not check out my other stories on Amazon and sign up to my newsletter to get the heads up on all my new releases.

Dante X

Authors Website – Contact and Newsletter sign up

www.DantesErotica.uk

First Time Dogging with Asian Wife

By Dante

Chapter 1

This story is about the very first time I ever took Jane out dogging, we had both only been exposed to the London Fetish and Swinger club scene for about 6 months and to be perfectly honest, we both of us really enjoyed it and had started attending other clubs as well. Jane had only been in the UK for a year and had never even heard about dogging at the time.

So, we were on our way home from Club Rub a Fetish club in London and it was about 4 o'clock in the morning and my sexy young Filipino wife Jane was wearing her silky black short dress with a zip at the front. We chose this dress because when she would be walking around in the club we could pull the zip up or down so as to expose her beautiful 34B tits with lovely hard nipples, while playing with another couple or sometimes single guys....

Jane was 26 at the time and she had the passenger seat reclined as we drove home through the near deserted streets on London in the early hours as I used to love playing with her on the way home. We were also feeling incredibly horny after the club that evening due to the ecstasy we had taken earlier. As we pulled up at some traffic lights, a woman in the bus looked really shocked as she looked down into our car and saw me fingering Jane as she lay there with her eyes closed and the zip of her dress was pulled down also exposing her breasts....

Shortly after that, we came off north circular road and joined the motorway and I was able to release my cock and moved Jane's hand onto it to start playing with me as we drove home to Dunstable.

As we drove along, we touched and played with each other and talked about the events of the evening.... Jane used to love me recounting what we had done in the club with either single guys or another couple and on this particular evening we had played with a new couple from Poland... Jane had let the guy play with her tits and eventually finger her while I did the same to his wife while standing in a corner of the play room surrounded by single guys watching and wanking and trying to get in on the action. Jane always drew lots of attention because she was young and her figure, especially her breasts were absolutely stunning when exposed... and when she was on ecstasy, she turned from being really shy to an exhibitionist and really loved walking around the club with her tits on show...

As I told her what I did to the Polish girl... it made her cum for about the 4th time that evening as we were driving along.... We were nearly at junction 9 of the motorway when I asked Jane if she fancied driving to a dogging spot at the Downs I'd heard about, to see if there was anything going on going on.... it was about 4.45 AM.

Jane was confused and replied, "What's dogging...?"

So I briefly explained it was people in car parks and wooded areas that like to watch others playing, like in the club.

She looked at me and said, "If you like, I want to see."

I said, "OK let's see if anyone is out this early in the morning."

I pulled off at J 9 and we took the A5 to Studham and then

the back road to the downs. I knew of a small dogging car park going down the hill just after the Zoo so headed there first. When we pulled in, I could see 3 cars but nobody in sight. So we pulled up opposite the other 3 cars so we could watch if anything happened. Engine off and we sat there in the dark for about 10 minutes, Jane started playing with my cock again and I had exposed her tits and was playing with them as we stared into the darkness outside.

Then a light goes on in one of the cars and we watched as guys got out of the other two cars and wandered over to the passenger side of the car that just turned its interior light on. They were looking in the passenger window and it was obvious something was going on in the car. Jane's eyes were wide and staring into the dark but from where we were we parked, we couldn't see anything.

"Shall we go take a look...?"

Jane looked at me nervously and said, "NO... I'm too scared."

"What about if I put our light on and they come and watch us?"

No she said again, "I'm too shy and someone might recognise me."

"OK then we can watch from here."

I then moved my hand down to her leg and slid it up between her thighs. She parted her legs slightly and I had a quick feel of her pussy... she was clearly really turned on and soaking wet... my finger slid up the side of her knickers right into her.

"My god you're so wet babe..."

She just moaned and said, "I want to see what's going on in the car."

"OK... let's go and see." I opened my door to get out....

Jane said, "You go first and see what's happening."

"OK", and I wandered over to where the two guys were standing.

As I approached them I could see there was a couple in the car and the guys outside were watching and wanking as the guy in the car was fingering his girlfriend. She had her legs open and her blouse was open with her small tits exposed. He was sucking on her tit while fingering her with his other hand. She looked Indian and about 18 or 19 but very slim with tiny tits. Her legs were open and knickers pulled to one side as she held them over allowing the guys outside to watch. The guy in the car was white and was telling her to watch the guys wanking outside.

Chapter 2

I walked back over to Jane and told her what was going on and opened her door. She got out and held my hand as we walked back to the other car. The two guys wanking outside looked at us and I could see on their faces they couldn't believe their luck. I've been out many a night in the past and sat for hours and nights on end never seeing any action, just guys in cars or two guys walking into the woods together but never a couple. So as we approached Jane stood behind me and the guys could see that she was shy and wanted to look in the car.
One of the guys moved to the side and said to me,

"There you go mate, let her get in there."

I motioned to Jane to take his place and I stood right behind her so as to protect her in case he tried to touch her. I said to the guys,

"It's her first time and just curious, she's never been dogging before."

They just nodded and smiled at each other. Jane was now right by the window and could see the Indian girl with her legs open and getting fingered by her boyfriend. I held Jane from behind on her waist as the two guys moved in closer still wanking their cocks. Jane had her arms held in front of herself as if trying to protect herself in case anyone tried to touch her.

Inside the car the guy had taken his cock out and the skinny girl was wanking him while he got her to put one leg up on the dash board to finger her deeper and give us all a better view. He must have had 3 fingers in her but she looked so small and tight and he was now pushing 2 in her pussy and 2 in her arse. She was clearly loving it and the guys either side of us were getting really close. Jane was watching the couple in the car and also the guys wanking next to us outside, so I started to feel her tits from behind....

The girl in the car told her boyfriend we were also outside and he must have told her to open the window because she pressed a button and the window went down. We could all see much better now and the girl asked Jane what her name was?

Jane replied and the girl said, "I'm Rupa and this is Simon."

He says hi and then the girl asks Jane if she likes to watch?

Jane looked at me nervously and then just nodded and the Indian girl took Jane's hand and placed it on her small breast nearest the window. Jane was hesitant but because we had played in the clubs with other couples and occasionally let single guys play or suck on her tits she was up for it. So Jane started fondling the Indian girl's breasts while I was doing the same to Jane from behind. The Indian girl then reached out and slowly pulled Jane's zip down and I could now pull her tits out into the cold night air for everyone to see.

The guy to my right was looking really excited and looked like he was about to cum but stopped wanking and asked me, If he could touch?

I said, "Not yet mate, my missus will run away if you do anything now."

After I said that, I could feel the Indian girl pulling my hand off Jane's tit and fondling them herself.

Jane looked at me and said, Oh My God... she's touching me."

I slid my hand down her lower belly and then up under her skirt and into the top of her tiny black g string. Her hold up stockings were now exposed and the guys were staring wide eyed at the sight in front of them. The guy on our left had a massive cock and I could see he was so close to Jane's arm he was trying to get Jane to look.... He then started wanking really close to her arm and must have been touching her with it because Jane looked round and smiled at him. He must have took that as a sign it was OK to continue.... Then he started rubbing his cock up and down Jane's arm as the girl in the car was playing with both her tits. My finger was inside her G string and rubbing her clit.

"Open your legs a bit babe,"

Jane moved her leg and had her hands on the roof of the car, the Indian girl's boyfriend was fingering away as the Indian girls legs were wide open and I saw the guy to my left, had put his arm in the window and was stroking her leg. Jane saw this and started watching the guy sliding his hand closer to the Indian girls pussy. The guy in the car stopped fingering her and let the guy next to me touch her pussy. He was stroking her inner thigh and then slid a finger inside, then Simon asked us if we would like to get in the car?

Jane immediately said, "Can we...?"

I think she was feeling very exposed standing outside and a bit scared of the two guys either side. We opened the back door and Simon said to me, let Jane sit in the front with Rupa, as he climbed into the back seat behind his girlfriend. We then went to the other side and I told Jane to sit in the front seat while I got in the back.

Simon reclined Rupa's seat back so he could still play with her tits. I did the same to Jane's seat as the steering wheel was on her side and then Rupa turned to face Jane and reached over and slid her hand into Jane's open zip and started playing with her tits again. Jane lay back as I kissed her on the mouth and she closed her eyes while Rupa explored her breasts and then pulled the zip down further so she could slide her hand down her belly and then between her legs... She started sucking on Jane's nipple while fingering her... Jane looked more relaxed now and opened her legs more so Rupa could explore her properly.

The guys outside were wanking furiously and I then saw more figures outside gathering around the car in the darkness. Rupa now had 2 fingers in Jane and was kneeling up in the passenger seat. Her window was still open and I could see several arms in the window groping her between her legs. Simon also had his arm under her and was fingering her as he said to Rupa,

"You want one to fuck you babe...?"

She lifted her head and said, "Yes..... if you want me to."

"You got a rubber?"

He said to the guy closest to the window wanking his huge cock next to Rupa's ass.

"I do..." said another guy next to him.

Simon pulled Rupa's knickers to one side and said,

"Go on then mate, get in her and give her a good fucking."

Rupa parted her legs as wide as she could and pushed her ass out of the window so he could enter her. He was inside her in a flash and holding her hips from behind as he started to fuck her tiny little pussy and skinny ass. Clearly horny and worked up Rupa pulled Simon closer and started snogging him while saying,

"He's fucking my pussy babe OOOhhhh...God he's gonna make me cum..."

Hands were in the window groping her little tits hanging down, Simon was also groping Jane's tits while Jane was watching all this in shock and amusement. Jane didn't stop Simon touching her and Rupa was still fingering Jane. I now had my own cock out and was wanking and touching Jane and then Rupa's tits, when I could, because hands were everywhere. The guy behind Rupa must have cum because he pulled out and big cock was now behind her trying to enter her. Rupa looked around and saw who it was and said,

"That's too big..."

So she turned around and grabbed it with her hand and started wanking it. Her ass was now facing us inside the car and Simon was between her legs... licking and fingering her pussy. Jane's window was closed but several guys were outside knocking on the window offering their cocks and motioning her to open the window.

She looked at me and said, "NO WAY....!"

So I offered her my cock to suck and she leaned across so as to get in a better position. Rupa was now sucking the huge cock thrust into her window and I saw Simon squeezing the guy's balls at the same time. I started fingering Rupa as Jane was sucking on my cock and then the big cock started to shoot his load... Rupa pulled away and his jizz was shooting all over her face. She pushed the guy away and wiped her face laughing and wound up the window. Back in the car it was now just the 4 of us and Simon and Rupa turned their attention to Jane. Jane sat back down and Rupa turned around and went straight down on her pussy. Jane was laying back so Rupa slid on top of her and Jane's head was now between her legs.

Simon was already stroking Rupa's ass and pushing a finger in, while I also was stroking her ass and pussy. Jane's face was inches away and Rupa just teased her by holding her pussy and ass up just out of reach but then dropped down onto Jane's face and Jane instinctively started licking her... Oh My God... this was amazing as I never saw Jane do that before.

So the girls were 69ing in the car and I was now squeezing Rupa's ass and pushing a finger into her pussy and then her ass while Jane watched and licked. I then felt Simon's hand on my cock and I thought this couple must be really into everything... so hesitantly I let him continue and whispered to Jane,

"He's wanking my cock."

Jane let out a sigh and then said, "I want to see..."

I looked at Simon and he smiled so I got in position on my knees in the back seat so my cock was between Rupa's legs and Jane could see him wanking me. I was stroking Rupa's ass and legs and Jane was licking her slit with eyes on my cock and his hand. I tried a finger in Rupa's slit and then poked the tip of my finger into her tight little anus. She must have liked that as she pushed her ass back so more of my finger went inside. Jane was watching me finger her ass and then said,

"I want to suck your cock."

The guy wanking my cock aimed it at Jane's face and she could just get the head in her mouth as she was trapped under Rupa. My finger was still in Rupa's ass but really deep now and I wanted to cum...

I told Jane, "I'm gonna cum babe... where do you want it?"

She pulled off and said, "Put it in her ass..."

"Really....!" I said

Simon looked at me and said, "Go for it mate. I never seen her this worked up before."

Rupa lifted her head and said, "Yeh fuck my tight little ass while I make your wife cum..."

She went back to licking Jane's pussy so I positioned myself right over her ass, Jane watched as I lubricated her up with some of her pussy juice and then pushed in slowly... a cry of pain and ecstasy came from the skinny Indian girl as I pushed in as deep as I could. The boyfriend was now playing and squeezing my balls and started pushing a finger in my ass! I couldn't hold back and started shooting my load deep inside Rupa's tight little ass...

Jane was also bucking and arching her back as Rupa's fingers were frigging her fast and she moaned into Rupa's pussy as the wave of feelings overcame her. The boyfriend pulled his finger out and I pulled my cock out of Rupa as Jane just stared... my cock came out all covered in my own cum and it was still dribbling out of her ass... Rupa slid off Jane and we all said how great it was and we should all meet up again. Outside we could see about 5 guys all shooting their spunk over the windows as they all watched the show and another 2 guys were fucking at the driver's side door. We said our goodbyes and exited the car to go to our own car and drive home.

As we left, one of the guys outside said, "Fucking ace mate. Bring her again OK."

Jane and I smiled and drove home laughing and chatting about what just happened.

I hope you enjoyed this story.

If you like my writing style, and stories about Husband or Wife sharing, Wife watching, BDSM, Cuckold, Swinger and Fetish clubs, Dogging and many other fetishes...

Why not check out my other stories on my Amazon Author page or sign up to my newsletter to get the heads up on all my new releases.

Dante

Authors Website – BLOG – Contact – Comments and Newsletter sign up

www.DantesErotica.uk

Asian Wife Starts Webcam Work

First time shared with a stranger

By Dante

Chapter 1

It all started out part time as my new Filipino wife Jane could not find a job. She's very attractive, small and petite with a stunning set of breasts. She was only 25 years and about 4' 10" and 110 lbs with very shapely 34B breasts but her pussy was smooth and had virtually no hair, just a thin slit with no outer pussy lips like western girls.

We had been married about 6 months and when I first mentioned the adult webcam work that she could do from home but she said she was too shy. So life went on as usual and she kept trying to find a part time job but couldn't seem to find anything suitable. She didn't really need to earn money but was basically bored. She had only been in England for about 6 months and still getting used to her new environment. She'd met a few other Filipino friends and everything was looking good. After a few weeks of watching sexy videos together, playing around and making love, I found she didn't have a lot of previous experience and loved trying new things. Anyway, one evening I clicked on the webcam section of videos and we watched a few girls and couples doing all kinds of things on cam.

Jane then asked me how much she could make doing the webcam work and how it all worked. I didn't really know myself so we logged on to the site I'd found offering the adult work and we read all about it. Apparently, she could log on at the times she was available and choose the things she was willing to do and not to do. These included all kinds of stuff on cam with toys, anal, pissing, scat, insertions and if she had a partner, male or female for various acts like fucking, domination, slave training etc.

One webcam video we saw was really weird as the girl on cam loved having her tits slapped and squeezed, she even tied them up until they looked red and about to burst. Then the guy was slapping and even punching them... Really weird stuff... It ended with him putting strong clamps on her nipples and pulling them off to make her scream but this beautiful girl was clearly loving it and a very willing participant.

Another one that I am pretty sure got Jane interested was this couple, where the husband or boyfriend was tied up on the floor and this really sexy stunning girl sat in a chair and started playing with her pussy and then inserting this long sex toy that was designed to make girls squirt. Well she started squirting streams of pee and then it ended up with her pissing all over him as he lay on the floor.... she was trying to aim the long stream of piss into his mouth. Then she crouched down over his face and let him lick her pussy clean while she then used the sex toy on herself again... but this time she made him open his mouth and drink it all as she squirted directly in his mouth.... When she finished, she started playing with his cock and got him hard and rode him until he orgasmed.

Jane seemed to get really turned on with the squirting movies but she'd never done anything like that before. Then there was phone chat, sexting and escort work all from the same webcam company. We obviously decided together that Jane should just do the webcam work and we filled in the online form. The next step was an ID check and provide bank details etc. It all seemed above board and a few days later when approved, we set up the webcam in the bedroom and created a profile with a few sexy pictures and what services Jane was prepared to do on cam. Obviously escort work was out of the question, as was any kind of weird domination stuff but she did leave water sports, insertions, sexting and live phone chat ticked… I asked her if she was sure about the live phone chat and she said she would like to try it…. But if it was too weird, she could delete that as a service.

We logged on and we both couldn't believe it... about 30 minutes later she had a message saying someone has paid for a 20 minute live webcam session. We looked at each other and my gut was feeling really strange.... My sexy new wife was about to do something on cam with a stranger who had just paid money for webcam sex. I was excited yet also really apprehensive and said to Jane…

"I really don't know if I want you to do this Jane?"

"It's OK … I think I can do this but please can you not watch me and wait outside?"

"What! You mean you don't even want me in the room while you do stuff on cam with some guy we don't even know!"

Jane replied, "You can leave the door open a bit but please let me see how it goes with this first one by myself."

I reluctantly agreed and she opened her cam and started messaging the viewer. He started messaging back and Jane lay back on the bed and opened her legs for him. She looked so fucking sexy, I was getting hard watching her already. She was wearing a white low cut bra that made her tits stick out more and matching white knickers.

She looked at me and motioned me to go out of the room, so

I closed the door but left a small gap about 1 inch wide so I could still see her on the bed. She starts typing on the laptop by the side of the bed and then UN-hooked her bra. I assumed the guy paying for the session asked her to remove her bra. She lay back looking at the screen and then started rubbing her tits and smiling at the screen.

Another message comes through and she is kneeling up on the bed and rubbing her pussy over the top of her knickers with her tits on show. She squeezes her tits again and then her hand goes down inside her knickers and is rubbing her pussy and fingering herself for the viewer. My gut was in turmoil and I am sure this was the start of my own cuckold fetish I have had since this all began. I had my cock out and was stroking it slowly watching Jane perform for some strange guy on web-cam.

Then Jane gets another message and she pulls the side of her knickers over and is showing him her smooth pussy. She re positions herself on the bed, really close to the webcam and parts her knees more so he can see her little slit in close up.

Next she was rubbing a finger up and down her slit and then slid a finger inside herself and moaned out quite loudly.... I re-member thinking, was she really turned on watching the guy on her screen probably also wanking and showing her his cock or was she simply putting on a good show for him...?

She parts her pussy lips and is showing him the close up inside of her cunt... fucking hell this is so horny I want to cum but held back. Then she was on all fours with her bum towards the camera and easing down her knickers to expose her naked bum and smooth slit from behind. She types something on the computer and resumes her position. Knickers are off now and she is holding her arse cheeks apart and her tiny slit must be parted open as well...

I couldn't help it... she pushed a finger in her tight little arse... I was wanking furiously and started shooting my load all over the door and the floor. I had never cum so much in my life and I was still watching...

Jane was rubbing her pussy with one hand and had a finger in her arse from her other hand and she started masturbating herself faster until she collapsed on the bed shaking and orgasmed like I had never seen before... She rolled over and moved closer to the cam and had her legs wide open, obviously showing the guy she had come and how wet and sticky she was. Then she waved at the cam and said thank you and clicked the cam off.

I was in the bedroom and on the bed in a flash and went straight down on Jane's pussy licking and fingering her, she even let me finger her arse... She just held my head and started telling me about the guy on screen.

It was a young guy in his 30's and he was already hard and wanking as soon as she opened the cam. She said, he kept telling her to do things via the messaging and she felt so horny when he told her to do things.

She said, "It was like I had to do it because he told me... and I felt I couldn't refuse. When he told me to finger my bum I didn't want to but I knew he was paying for the session and did it, but I felt so... I can't explain... I wanted him to make me do really naughty stuff like put something inside me... like a bottle or something. He asked me if I had any toys, I said no but will get some for next time as this was my first time on cam. That made him really excited and he made me watch him cum all over his hands and belly as he was laying on his bed too. He also told me to get a glass beer or coke bottle next time, as he wants to see me fuck myself with it... That's when I cum babe and he wanted me to show him a close up of my pussy all sticky and wet."

I was now on top of Jane and had my cock inside her and was fucking her nice and slowly as she recounted what happened. I pulled her over on top of me and hugged her close and started kissing her on her mouth. She was also really turned on and was kissing me back and had her hand behind her reaching round to squeeze my balls so I placed a finger at her anus and started to rub it around the edge. Jane moaned into my mouth, so I assumed she liked what I was doing and then I sped up my pace and just before she cum, I pushed my finger as far as I could... deep into her little bum hole. As she came she arched her back and I shot my second load of jizz deep inside her pussy.

Chapter 2

The webcaming really turned her on and she started doing it every day and again in the evenings when I got home from work. She would tell me all about who she had webcam-ed with and what they made her do. We'd bought various sex toys and a couple of really big ones. One was a huge black dildo (10 inches long and wide) that she couldn't even get inside her... We tried with gel and even after a week or so, she could only just get the head of it inside her and about 2 inches. Her pussy was simply too small and we had even tried to get my hand inside her but I could only just get 4 fingers in and I have fairly small hands for a guy.

The other big insert toy was a butt plug set that came with 5 different sizes. The smallest was easy and we progressed up the sizes until she could get the number 4 inside, she would then put her knickers back on and start the webcaming with it still inside her. This always made the guys and even girls and women who paid to webcam with her really excited. I even got her to wear the number 3 butt plug during the day in the house and we even went to Asda one day to do our general shopping with it in....

Then a few weeks later, Jane told me one evening after I came home from work, that some guy had offered her £200 to meet him and all he wanted to do was play with her tits! I was really surprised to say the least, and although she refused, we did both find the idea turned us both on and considered it... We sort of played with the idea that, if I was there with her and she just let him play with her tits in the back of our car and with me as the driver...

So that's how it all started and after a month or so, Jane was webcaming twice a day, 12 pm to 3 pm and 6 pm to 9 pm and money was being deposited in her bank. She was making about 100 pounds a day more or less because the webcam company kept 60% and Jane got 40%. I had also started being included in the evenings, as some guys wanted to direct the action, to see Jane being fingered and fucked by me (the husband) and some even wanted me to fuck her in the throat, but we both didn't want to do that, so she refused those requests.

However over the next few months things changed a lot and Jane became much more daring... we also had to get a cheap waterproof mattress cover as Jane and I, really got into the water sports. Some of the things we did were unbelievable when I look back now. In fact some of the things they asked Jane to do on cam were so disgusting, she sometimes even wore a mask, just in case she was being videoed from their end.

So it started with the water sports and Jane pissing on cam, sometime close up shots or wetting herself in tight jeans or tights, and sometimes I was included and was instructed to make her squirt while fingering her, or me laying on the floor while Jane crouched over my face and squirted in my mouth really close to the webcam. We then decided to get a heavy duty mattress cover so we could do our water sports on the bed and just change the sheets daily.

Once, this guy wanted me to act out his fantasy... Where Jane was dressed in a pair of jeans and a t-shirt and the webcam was set up in the living room, aimed at the front door and sofa.

I had to pretend to be a delivery guy and when Jane opened the door, I was instructed to chat her up and seduced her. He wanted her to act like a very shy surprised housewife and as soon as she was touched on her tits... she got really turned on and let me suck her tits and nipples and then finger her down her jeans. He wanted her to squirt in her jeans as I fingered her to orgasm.

That session turned Jane and myself on so much, we started doing stuff we would never have dreamed of before. One couple asked us to fuck on cam while they fucked on their cam. We were all really turned on watching each other... and then this couple asked, if could I pee on Jane and then in her mouth? They started copying us and doing it themselves and this woman on cam was drinking her husbands pee and then he tossed himself off in her mouth till he came bucket loads... We copied them and I found that Jane was OK with it and although she told me she was nearly sick, she told me afterwards, it really turned her on.

We were always getting offers of live meetings with either Jane meeting a guy alone or as a couple where I could just watch or join in. But we declined all offers until one day Jane told me a guy had offered... £500 to play with Jane in the back of our car... and I could drive her and watch.

Well, we chatted about it for quite a while and as our sex life was out of this world for the last few months, we decided to take it to the next level. We had done virtually everything we could have dreamed up ourselves on cam but there were some requests we were not ready to do.... yet.... but we did later.

So we arranged to meet this guy who was in his late 50's, about 250 Lbs and quite fat but he had a fairly big cock. We had webcam-ed with him previously and he seemed fairly normal but he was amazed at Jane's small body and really loved her tits and her anal insertions... he said was willing to pay anything.... to meet her in person!

On the day, he'd asked Jane to wear a short skirt, tights and no bra.. just a t-shirt or tight top with her nipples showing through and to wear her butt plug. So on the evening arranged, we met the guy in a pub near the river in Bedford and we went for drink and chat to break the ice. We explained that although Jane had done webcam work for a few months, he was the first person we had decided to meet in real life... We explained that 500 pounds was too good an offer to turn down and after mentioning the money he handed me an envelope and said, "Here you are, I'm deadly serious and I find your beautiful wife Jane to be the sexiest girl on the whole webcam website."

And there were 100's if not a 1000+ girls on that website. He then asked if he could touch Jane's legs under the table? I looked at Jane who just stared at me like a deer trapped in a cars headlights. The pub was quite full but we were not being overlooked... So I nodded the OK to him and he reached down and started stroking Jane's legs and tights.

"I really have this thing for tights", he said.

"Me too", I replied and told him,

"I just love seeing her in tights with no knickers underneath. We went shopping for shoes once and Jane flashed this young shoe shop assistant, she opened her legs and he saw her knickers-less pussy through the tights.... He couldn't stop staring and Jane just looked around the shop and then opened her legs even more, giving him a really good show. I loved it and we sometimes do it on the train to London."

The fat guy was stroking Jane's leg and she had her arms leaning on the table in front and staring at me.

"What's he doing babe?" I asked looking back into her eyes.

"He's between my legs and rubbing the top of my pussy over the tights."

"She's so beautiful and sexy… she's getting wet already." the fat guy says..

Then he pulls his hand out from under the table and shows me his sticky wet fingers. I got that strange feeling in my gut again and said to Jane,

"You sure you want to do this babe?"

She just nodded and asked,"Where are we going to go?"

The fat guy answered,

"I know a place that's fairly quiet and safe. It's a dogging spot near a lake. Don't worry, if any doggers are out today, they won't do anything unless invited to play. If you keep the windows closed they will just watch and play with themselves outside."

We left the pub and went to our car and the fat guy got in the back with Jane. I started to drive and was being directed by the fat guy in the back, who has now got his arm around Jane and already fondling her tits. Jane was looking a bit scared, so I reassured her that it's only a bit of fun and if she really wants to go home, we can call it a night and give the guy his money back.

She responded, "No it's OK babe, but please stay with me OK?"

"Yes of course babe, I'm here, just relax and let him play."

The fat guy said, “Yes, No problem, I just want to play with you and won’t do anything weird.”

Jane relaxed and the fat guy put his hand up her top and started playing with her tits and nipples. I adjusted my mirror so I could watch and saw he was now sucking on her nipple and had a hand up her skirt feeling her legs and pussy over the tights. Jane started making moaning sounds as he was obviously making her feel horny. He told me to drive for another 2 miles and then turn into the car park near the lake on the left. When we arrived I turned around and saw, he had got his hand inside Jane's tights and she was laying back on the rear seat with her legs open.

“She's nice and wet.... Can you take some pictures for me”, the fat guy said and hands me his phone.”

Jane looked so fucking sexy laying there as his fat fingers were going in and out of her, with his hand still inside the tights.

“I can feel her butt plug is in”, he said.

Then Jane moaned again as he pulled it in and out a bit. Jane's tits were out as he had pulled her top right up and her skirt was up around her waist. It was fairly dark outside and I thought I saw some movement as I started taking the pictures. The flash must have been attracting them.

“Don't worry”, the fat guy said... “Its only the regular doggers. They won't do anything so just keep the doors locked and windows closed... Unless you want a bit of group action or groping”

He was peeling Jane's tights down and he left them around her thighs, then started to finger her again, pushing her legs apart.

But she could only open them so far because the tights restricted her.... so he told her to take one leg out but keep the tights on.

"I love tights... and her pussy is amazing and so fucking wet mate."

He said as I watched with my gut turning over and my cock rock hard in the front passenger seat.

"I want to taste her and take her but plug out now, so take some more pictures while I do her OK."

Jane sighs as he holds her legs open and then reaches down to remove her butt plug.

"Fucking awesome!",

He says as he pulls it out and starts to lick and sniff it. He starts sucking the plug like it was a cock and then puts in on the seat and goes down on Jane to lick her pussy. Jane was squirming and moaning and started saying,

"Oh My God his tongue is in my bum.... OOOOHHHH ... He's fingering my pussy and bum together... OOOOOHHHHH..."

I could see about 3 guys outside the car trying to look in the windows and they all had their cocks out and wanking. I couldn't believe it but Jane had reached forward and was squeezing the fat guys cock while he kept fingering her... and then he told her to take his cock out.... Jane undid his belt and unbuttoned his trousers and then pulled his cock out.

She said, "Oh My God babe... It's huge... it's so much bigger than on cam."

She started wanking him and I took a few more pictures.

He asked me, "Are you gonna let me fuck her mate?"

I responded, "I thought you just wanted to play in the car... We've never done this before and she's not a hooker mate."

"I understand... he answered, "But tell you what, let me fuck her pussy and arse and I'll give you another £200."

Jane looked at me... She was clearly turned on and was still wanking his cock.

"I'm OK" she said... "He can do it."

"OK mate, you got a rubber?"

"Yes I got one", he said and reached into his trouser pocket.

I told Jane there were three more guys outside watching and this made her even more turned on. I was also so turned on, that I got my own cock out and was also wanking and watching as the fat guy rolled the condom on his big fat cock.

"Sure you can take that babe? It looks a lot bigger than mine.!"

No answer but Jane started moaning as he started to push it in her tight little slit.

"Fuck me she's tight"

"Yes mate, she's from the Philippines and their all pretty small over there."

I kept watching and wanking.... Then he was in her and pumping up and down. Jane looked at me and started moaning and closed her eyes. He started mauling her tits and then he said,

"Why don't you open the window and let the lads have a better look."

I looked at Jane and she seemed to be OK with it, so I pressed the window button on her side and let it down half way. There were 2 guys standing there, both with their cocks out and wanking... they came closer and peered inside.

"I'm gonna fuck her in the arse now so let's get her legs up."

He pulled her back on the back seat and pushed her knees apart and towards her head. I looked down and her pussy was gaping wide open as he withdrew his fat cock. He fingered her a bit then rubbed her juice all around her butt hole... he pushed one and then two fingers in, then rubbed his cock head on her anal hole.... Jane looked so fucking sexy laying there and holding her own legs back so he could push his cock into her arse. It slid in no problem, probably due to her wearing the butt plug all evening. He pushed his fat cock in and held her legs back, then started pumping in and out.

One of the guys from outside had reached in the window and was caressing Jane's tits. I just watched and carried on wanking as this was such an amazing horny sight. Jane looked up and thought it was me rubbing her tits... and when she saw it was stranger from outside the car, she started to moan loudly and reached down to rub her own pussy and clit really fast. She was cumming...and it sent me over the edge as well... as it did with the fat guy inside her arse..

Jane wailed, "He's coming in my arse...I can feel his cock pumping".

The guys outside were all wanking furiously now and must have also shot their loads because they soon disappeared into the darkness.

I said, "Fuck me babe... that was one horny session."

The fat guy pulled his condom off and also said.

"Yes Jane, that was fucking awesome. Thanks for a really good fuck and I will remember this for a long long time."

Jane pulled her tights off and sat up. Then we started driving back to the pub where we met the guy earlier. On the way he gave Jane the extra £200 and we dropped him off and went home. We had many more offers of live meet ups and although we enjoyed that first time, we declined most of the offers, unless it was a nice, normal looking guy.

Chapter 3

On another occasion, we met a couple, where the guys wife wanted to try her first lesbian experience. We went to their house which was a big expensive pad in Kettering. They invited us for dinner and after we ate a sumptuous meal (served by a waitress and they even had a cook) and had several bottles of wine. We were all feeling nice and relaxed and Jane was sitting next to his wife.

Avril and Evan, I think their names were, both in their early 40's, rich and attractive. They had offered Jane £500 again, as she had declined £200 and told them she had never done it with another girl before. This made them even keener to meet Jane. They had already watched us fucking on cam and wanted to meet us both in person.

So during the dinner, Avril and Jane got fairly tipsy as they were sitting close to each other, whispering and giggling like a couple of school girls. Evan and I just watched and soon they were touching each other under the table.

“Hey girls, why don't we send the staff home and let the games begin.” Evan said.

We all retired to their lounge where we had another drink and let Jane and Avril get to know each other. Evan dimmed the lights and put some music on and then said to his wife,

"Have a dance with Jane and we will sit back and watch."

Avril giggled again and grabbed Jane's hand and pulled her up. They held each other around the waist and started swaying together... Jane was looking quite shy but the bottles of wine had definitely loosened her up. Soon they were snogging each other and rubbing each other's back and then Avril was inside Jane's blouse and fondling her tits. The blouses were discarded and the two girls were dancing in just their skirts and bras, next was Jane's bra as Avril UN-clipped it and started sucking on Jane's breasts. Jane held Avril's head and was clearly enjoying it, when Avril puts her hand up Jane's skirt and was rubbing her legs and pussy over her knickers.

Jane undid Avril's bra and I noticed she had really big auroras and nipples with well hung 36C breasts.

"Wow... Really nice tits your wife has", I commented to Evan.

"Yes mate, and she has a pussy and arse to die for as well." Evan replied.

Evan was already wanking his cock while sitting back in his armchair, so I released my own and got back into watching the lesbian show. The girls had discarded their bras and skirts now and were now just in their knickers, but Avril still had stockings and suspenders on. She looked really stunning. Jane was sucking Avril's tits now and Avril was inside Jane's knickers and fingering her. They sunk to the floor snogging each other and lay down on the deep pile white carpet as Avril peeled Jane's knickers off and went down on her to taste her naked little Asian pussy. Evan got up and went over to start a video camera that was already set up in the corner.

"Should have done this before but forgot",

he said and then went over to Avril and peeled her knickers down from behind.

"Come and see this beautiful arse and pussy", he said to me.

I got up and keeled down next to him behind his wife, whose bum was up in the air as she was licking and fingering Jane. He started fingering his wife and soon had 4 fingers sliding in and out of her very juiced up pussy. Then Avril moaned and opened her legs a bit more to let him get in deeper. He was pushing his fingers and thumb in her and soon... his whole fist was inside her and he smiled at me and said.

"She loves this in her pussy and arse and when she is ready to come she squirts like a woman possessed screaming for more."

Fucking hell, this woman was hot and I could see she was also trying to get her hand and fist inside Jane. Jane was laying on her back just letting her do it and then Avril reached over by the sofa and had grabbed a bottle of lube. She squirted it on Jane's pussy and then coated her whole hand and then pushed all 4 fingers into Jane. Her fingers and hand were going in and out as the lubricating gel made it much easier. Avril had very small hands and was soon pushing her thumb in as well. Jane arched her back and moaned out loudly as Avril's fist went right in and she experienced her first fist and orgasm of the evening. She gripped Avril's hand and was trembling and moaning like I have never seen her do before.

Evan was still fisting his wife from behind and was now alternating between her pussy and her arse with his whole fist going in and out of each hole in turn.

"Come on", he said to me, "Try this and see if you can make her cum. I'm going underneath cos when she cums she squirts a lot and we can't have it ruin the carpet." he laughs.

I watched as he clambered down between his wife's legs and started licking and slurping at her pussy. I needed no second invitation, as Avril was truly stunning and I wanted to see what it was like to get my whole fist inside a pussy. It slid in like a fish into water and I was even able to turn my fist inside her. I did this for a while and realised that Jane was also being fisted properly for the first time and was clearly loving it.

Then I pulled it out and went back in faster, Avril moaned out load and her husband said,

“That's it mate, in and out fast and alternate between her pussy and arse. Do if fast and she will cum and squirt.”

I pulled out of her pussy and tried her arse, fuck me... her arse was even looser than her pussy. I fisted it... in and out a few times and then pulled out and went back in her pussy. Avril had her whole fist in Jane and was licking away at her clit. I went into her arse again and felt I could go deeper so pushed in more... Avril let out this long guttural moan and my fucking arm was inside her arse up to my elbow. I pulled in and out slowly and was amazed at how deep I could go.

“Go on mate”, Evan says from between her legs, “Push it all in, she can take it.”

I pulled out and did her pussy again and then back into her arse but this time I went even deeper... I could get in up to my middle upper arm!

Avril screamed “I'm CUUUUUMMMMING.”

So I pumped in and out faster then she shook and moaned really deeply while squirting all over her husband's face. He was trying to catch it all but it was going all over him and the carpet.

When Avril calmed down, she got Jane up and they both sat next to each other on the sofa. Jane told Avril she had never had a whole hand inside her before and Avril said she hoped she enjoyed it as much as she did.

"Tell you what I would love to see", Evan said. "You girls in a 69 with Jane on top. Do you think you can make Jane squirt?" he said to Avril.

"I don't know but I'm willing to try."

Jane smiled and said, "OK we can try."

Avril lay down on the carpet again on her back and Jane mounted her with her pussy over Avril's face. Avril started licking Jane's clit and slit holding Jane's bum cheeks open. I could not resist and had to get behind Jane and finger her arse. I soon had two then 3 fingers inside and knew that we were going to be doing some arse fisting in the future. Then I felt Avril playing with my cock so looked down and she was trying to suck me and lick Jane at the same time.

Evan had moved behind Avril and was pushing his cock inside and fucking her. I suspect he offered his cock to Jane's mouth in between but this was turning into a really nice experience. I managed to get 3 fingers in Jane's arse but it was far too tight, so I went back to 2 fingers going in and out faster and faster.

Within minutes... Jane shouted out, "I'm CUUUUUMMM-MING" and Avril pulled her pussy down on to her open mouth while Jane let go.... shuddering and spurting pee into Avril's mouth.

What a great night that was....

Jane got more and more daring over the next few months and we even fucked on cam with a coke bottle in her pussy while

I fucked her arse. She really started to get into anal and many times she would ask me to fuck her arse while she stimulated her own clit and squirt streams of pee on cam for the punters and also when we made love together in private.

I hope you enjoyed this story.

If you like my writing style, and stories about Husband or Wife sharing, Wife watching, BDSM, Cuckold, Swinger and Fetish clubs, Dogging and many other fetishes...

Why not check out my other stories on Amazon and sign up to my newsletter to get the heads up on all my new releases.

Dante

Authors Website – BLOG - Contact – Comments and Newsletter sign up

www.DantesErotica.uk

Adventures in the Swinger clubs

Dante

Contents

Chapter 1 - On the Way to an After Party With a Friend

Chapter 2 - Gary's wife joins us

Chapter 3 - Arousal

Chapter 4 - Squirting for the first time

Chapter 1

On the Way to an After Party With a Friend

This was an interesting evening as Jane my 27 year old Filipino wife of 2 years and myself were at a London Fetish club and this time, we were with a mate of mine Gary. Jane is a slim, 4' 11" feet tall and has amazing nipples on young firm 34b tits.
She was wearing a small black mini skirt and a white boob tube that can be pulled up and down easily when playing in the club. Anyway, on this specific evening, we were leaving the club to go to an after party that someone had told Gary about and we were all still wearing our club gear, male G string and roman style chain and leather harness over the chest for me and Gary had a very small tight pair of shorts with a front zip that he could pull down and expose his huge wide cock and balls.

His wife Vicki is Thai but was not with us in the club on this particular evening as she was at her friends birthday party, so Gary had phoned her we were going to pick her up on the way.....

We had our street gear in a bag and just had our coats over ourselves as we left the club for the car. When we got to the car, I let Jane sit in the front seat and Gary was driving with me in the back of his nice big Mercedes saloon. We'd had some E's earlier in the evening like we normally did on club nights and although the main buzz had worn off we were still feeling pretty horny to say the least...

It was about 4am and still dark, we were off to some village location about 10 miles outside London. So as we were driving on the dual carriageway, I got Jane to put her seat back about half way and was playing with her tits and snogging her. Poor Gary was trying to drive but was more interested in watching me and Jane... He kept staring at her tits as I had her top pulled down and was playing with her nipples while kissing her and we were also watching Gary.

It really turns Jane and I on... to see guys watching us play and I could tell that Jane was feeling a little bit embarrassed and exposed as we were driving through London but as her seat was down, nobody could really see her tits or what was going on inside the car.

I could also see Gary squeezing his cock every now and then and thought I would take things a bit further. Jane was still well horny after leaving the club... I had let two guys play with her tits while we were in the club while she was laying in a sex swing and I was licking her pussy... She also had their cocks in her hands one each side and she even let one guy finger her for a while...

Jane was laying back and her tits were out, Gary was now looking between her legs, as her tiny skirt had risen up and was exposing her shaved pussy.

Most Asian women don't have big pussy lips, they usually just have a lovely thin slit and this was clearly on show as she was laying back in the seat. I winked at Gary and he unzipped his shorts and let his cock free... he also pulled his huge balls out, so as he was driving, he could play with his cock and watch me and Jane.

I said to Jane to look at Gary's cock, so she turned her head and was stunned to see his cock at full erection and him rubbing it up and down while he was driving.

He then placed his hand on her leg and looked her in the eyes and then slowly pulled her leg open... so he could see her exposed slit better. His hand was now rubbing up and down her inner thigh and she was looking at his cock... while I was caressing her tits and making her nipples erect.

His hand slid up further and brushed against her pussy and she went to close her legs... but I whispered in her ear to let him play a bit... She relaxed and I slid my hand down over her belly and dipped a finger into her little wet slit.

She started to moan into my ear, then I moved Gary's hand onto her pussy and let him finger her as he drove along... After a few minutes he said to me,

"There's a lay-by coming up soon, shall we stop for a bit?"

I looked at him and smiled and he pushed another finger into Jane... she closed her eyes and grabbed his hand... I was now sitting back and watching him finger her and she was playing with one of her tits, stroking my own cock in the back watching this erotic situation unfold.

Gary then said to Jane,

"Can you open the glove box and get me that tube of lube?"

She looked at him and then opened the box and found the tube of Super-lube. He then said,

"Can you open it and put some on my cock please?"

She looked at me smiling like a Cheshire cat... I smiled back and said,

"Go on babe, he can't do that while he's driving."

So she opened the top and squeezed some onto her right hand and then smeared it all over his cock and balls. It was so erotic and I could see that Gary was having trouble concentrating on the road... Jane was really getting into squeezing his cock and rubbing the gel all over his big swollen balls.

She kept saying,

"It's so wide... Oh My God Gary... how does your wife get that in her pussy... Oh My God."

She was now really getting turned on so I started to finger her as she wanked Gary while he was driving. Then luckily for us all, the lay-by appeared and Gary pulled in. He parked up under some trees so we couldn't be seen from the road. As soon as we stopped I started to kiss Jane again, Gary turned sideways and slid his hand up her leg and started to finger her some more.

This was so horny to watch and then she started to say, she was going to pee and to let her out of the car so she could pee.

I said to her,

"Listen babe, we want to see you pee too... so why don't you just open the door and pee on the floor..."

She asked how... So I opened my door and went outside to open her door. I grabbed her legs and moved her so she was still in the car but her feet were outside and on the floor and her pussy facing the open door.

Gary was now standing next to me and then he just knelt down and was between her legs licking her pussy... Oh My God this was such a sight to see... Jane was laying back while he was fondling her tits and licking her at the same time.

I then reached over them and said to Gary,

"Watch this mate"

I put 2 fingers inside her and started to frig her fast...

"This is what we do in the club... It makes her cum and squirt at the same time..."

All of a sudden she let out a long moan and started to squirt all over Gary... as he was kneeling between her legs and this young shy Filipino was pissing all over his chest and cock... He just knelt there wanking his cock while she squirted all over him... When the stream subsided, he went straight back onto her pussy and was sucking and licking away like his life depended on it...

Jane was in heaven and I'd noticed another guy standing in the shadows wanking his cock and watching what had just happened.

He saw that I' d seen him and started to come a little closer, so I nodded to him it was OK... He came up and stood right behind Gary and leaned over to caress her right breast while wanking his cock.

Jane looked up and saw this other man... but was enjoying what Gary was doing so much, I said,

“It’s OK babe... We‘ ll be going soon, so let’s just enjoy the moment.”

I was now back in the car and had Jane’s head in my hands and was feeding my cock into her mouth. Gary was still sucking away at her pussy and had a tried pushing a finger in her arse... as she said to me between sucking...

“He’s fingering my bum babe...”

This was too much for me and made me cum... so I just held her head tight as she took it all in her mouth.

The guy standing over her was now shooting his load all over her tits and Gary had pulled back and watched the two of us cumming in her mouth and on her tits. Gary still had not cum yet but we decided to drive on. We lifted Jane’s legs back in the car and shut the door. Gary went round to the drivers side and asked,

“Are we going home or to the after party?”

I looked at Jane and she smiled so I answered him,

“To the after party of course”

and placed her hand back on his cock as he started to drive away...

Chapter 2

Gary's wife joins us

Gary had already told me what usually happens at the after parties and although I had mentioned it to Jane, I only told her a little bit about it as I didn't want to scare her from going so played it down and just said it was probably couples only and Gary's Thai wife Vicki will be there as well.

"Where is she now then...?"

Gary answered,

"We're picking her up now at the house... she was at party with all her Thai friends. I think they've all been to the Casino as well, she sounded a bit drunk when we spoke."

When we arrived at Gary's house, we all went in as Jane wanted to use the rest room, then she was in the bedroom with Vicki for ages trying on all kinds of outfits, so Gary told them to hurry up as it was already 4.30 am...

When Jane appeared, she'd changed into a sexy short white silky skirt, white button up blouse and a tiny black knickers and bra set that were so thin and skin tight her nipples poked through and her little camel toe slit was showing. We all jumped back in the car and were on our way at last to the address Gary's mate had given him.

We arrived eventually and it was a big house in the West End of London, there must have been about 12 other couples and a few single guys wandering around. We were invited in and offered a large glass of punch by the woman who owned the house I think. It tasted a bit weird but could see everyone else drinking it so we had a glass. In the kitchen there was a finger buffet and a small bowl of sweets (Ecstasy). Of course we all had another couple each as the night... well almost morning now.... was just beginning. Gary told us these after parties can go on for 2 or 3 days...

Vicki started to chat with Jane and I noticed she was wearing a fishnet body suit with nipples poking through the mesh and nothing underneath. I couldn't help staring at her shaved pussy through the mesh.

Gary was smiling as he saw me staring and said,

"Wait till you see what happens later in the playroom..."

Jane and Vicki were in deep chat so Gary said,

"Come on let's give you a tour of the house so you can see what goes on in the various rooms".

The lounge was incredible with a huge white round leather pouffe in the middle of the room surrounded by another 3 long curved white sofas and it was really dark except for a red light hanging down over the center pouffe.

A few couples were sitting around watching and cuddling, then we went into another room that was set up like a dungeon, just like the club with various BDSM benches and stocks, a whipping cross and a cage. Upstairs we were told, there were 5 bedrooms which could be used but normally the doors were to be kept open for voyeurs to see inside.

More couples arrived and we were offered more punch.... I was starting to suspect something else was in the drink as I was starting to get more than aroused just watching the girls especially Vicki walking along in front of us.

Gary then reached out and grabbed his wife's arse and she looked back and just smiled at me ... I thought hmm ... maybe I could have a grope too. I nodded to Gary to do the same to Jane and I grabbed his wife's arse as he did the same to Jane.

She just let him grope her so I slid my hand between Vicki's arse cheeks and could feel she was already wet and nearly managed to finger her. Fucking hell I thought, this is gonna be an interesting evening. I then moved forward and put my arm around Jane's shoulders to reassure her all was OK, she responded by grabbing my cock and said,

"Why are you so hard already?" and smiled.

We went into the lounge and sat on one of the sofas just as two girls had climbed onto the center pouffe. They were starting to kiss and touch each other and a few more couples quickly took up any free spaces on the sofa. We looked around and could just see, in the dim red light, several couples either playing together or playing with the couple next to them as a group.

All eyes were on the two girls on the white pouffe and one was now completely naked on her back while the other was straddling her face making her lick her pussy while fingering and licking the girl underneath... Jane was staring with wide eyes, while Vicki had slid in next to her and I could see her hand on Jane's leg. Gary was the other side of her and had started fondling her breasts and Vicki's other hand was wanking his cock that he had already let out. Jane looked over and saw what Vicki was doing and then Vicki was whispering something into Jane's ear. Vicki's hand slid up Jane's leg a bit more and then she moved in and kissed Jane on the mouth.

I was loving the show and started to feel Jane's tits while also watching all the action starting up around us. There was a lot of attention on Jane and Vicki as they were clearly the youngest and best looking girls in the room and because Jane was so small.

Vicki now had her hand between Jane's legs and was clearly fingering her and was clamped onto her mouth French kissing her. I moved my hand down onto her other leg and slid my hand up her inner thigh to see how wet she was and met Vicki's hand. She grabbed my hand and pushed it into Jane's pussy to show me how wet she was... soon we were both fingering her at the same time and her legs were wide open with several couples crowding round to watch.

Gary had peeled his wife's body stocking down from the top and her 34 c tits were on show and he was letting another guy fondle them while he was fingering her pussy. I grabbed Jane's hand and moved it onto my exposed cock and she started rubbing me while looking at all the people watching us on the sofa. Gary had now got between Vicki's legs and was licking her pussy through the body stocking and the guy who was playing with her tits was now openly wanking while his wife was sucking on her tits.

I turned Jane round and started kissing her on the mouth and pulled her onto my lap while still fingering her. She had hold of my cock and as I pulled her knickers to the side she slid down onto my cock and started to fuck me really slowly. I lifted her skirt at the back to expose her bum and to let the watchers see my cock going in and out of her tight little shaved slit. I then pushed a finger in her arse and she started to pump faster, then another girl was kneeling down on the floor and stroking her legs and arse.

Jane stood up and let this new girl peel down her knickers and then climbed back onto my cock while the girl started to put her tongue into Jane's arse... Jane was bouncing up and down and then moaning into my mouth as I tried to kiss her and then said...

"She was fingering and licking my arse."

Jane griped me hard and started to cum ... she was trembling while I held her down on my cock.

For the next hour or so we wandered around watching everyone in the various rooms. Gary and Vicki had disappeared into one of the bedrooms and last time we looked, there were 3 couples in there with them... a mass of bodies doing everything and anything to whoever was near.

The sweets we took earlier were making us feel nice and relaxed and we found ourselves standing in a group of couples and single guys in a dark room with a big circular bed in the middle. We were all watching a slim girl in her late 20's and two guys on the bed. They were the center of attention as the two guys, one her husband and the other was one of the single guys that I had seen before in the club... This guy had a huge cock and the husband was getting him to fuck his wife in front of us all, while he had his cock in her mouth and fondling her breasts.

It was hard to see what was going on, as it was pretty dark but the room was electric and we could just see a few single guys wanking their cocks and couples touching each other near to us. I noticed a guy standing to the right of Jane and he kept staring between her tits and the action on the bed in front of us. He also had his cock out and was slowly wanking so I started to touch Jane's tits a bit and made her nipples stand out. I then undid a couple of the buttons on her blouse and slid my hand inside, watching the guy who was watching Jane.

He smiled at me... so I smiled back and saw that he was really close to Jane's arm and she turned to me and said,

"The guy next to me is rubbing his cock against my arm..."

"Just stand still babe and see what he does."

I continued to play with her tits as that always turned her on and she started to moan and hugged me tightly. Another guy moved in closer behind Jane and his cock was occasionally touching her back so I put my arm around her waist to reassure her all was OK and that I was there to stop any action that she was not comfortable with. I undid another few buttons and let the blouse fall open and her 34b tits were half out and her nipples were already really erect.

The guy next to Jane was trying to see more so I undid the last two buttons and Jane's blouse fell completely open... and her tits were fully exposed and on show. She looked at the guys wanking and sighed as I started to caress them again in front of the guy to her right. He was staring intently while holding his very long cock against her arm. I then nodded to him and motioned with my eyes that he could touch her tits...

As he raised his hand and caressed her right breast, I though

Jane was going to cum as she shivered and grabbed my arm....

I whispered to her, "It's OK babe, just let him have a feel..."

The threesome on the bed was getting even more heated as the girl was now in a 69 with the single guy while the husband was letting another couple fondle his wife... The woman from the couple was stroking his wife's arse. The guy underneath was slurping and licking away at her pussy. She then moved round and parted her arse cheeks and went down on her licking away between her arse cheeks from the top. The husband was felling her tits in between the 69ers and the husband of the girl was now behind the new girl licking his wife and fingering her from behind.

Jane was now gasping... as the guy was fondling both her tits now and had his cock pressed against her side as she had moved her arm up and was gripping me.

I said to her, "Go on babe, touch his cock..."

I saw the guy was looking at us so I motioned to his cock and then to Jane... He moved his hand from her breast and held her arm, then lowered it down so her hand was resting on his cock...

She looked at me with an open mouth as if surprised and then I saw she'd gripped it and was standing there with her tits exposed, holding this guys cock while he resumed caressing her tits.

I stood back a bit so I could take in the scene and then told Jane,

"Open your legs a bit babe..."

So I could finger her from behind... She parted her legs slightly and I slid my hand down at the back and pulled her little skirt up exposing her arse and started to stroke her legs and the soft skin between her pussy and just under her bum.

The guy behind us was now seriously interested as he could see the other guy playing with Jane's tits and me fingering her pussy and teasing her little brown starfish bum hole. She was still holding the guys cock on her right and then the guy behind reached out and touched Jane on the shoulder.

He looked at me for the OK, so I nodded and watched as his hand slid down her back and over her hips onto her bum. I moved my hand and let him slid his hand down and into her tight little wet slit.

As I had moved my hand, I think Jane thought it was still me touching her from behind but as I turned her around to face me... and started kissing her on the mouth, she must have realized it was someone else... I held her tight and slid my hand down over her belly and started to finger her from the front and the guy to her right was still caressing her tits but from behind her now.

Jane placed her hands on my shoulders and as we kissed the two guys were feeling her up between her legs and her tits. I then turned her around so she was facing the guy to her right and let him finger her from the front. I saw her close her eyes and rest her head back onto my shoulder just letting him do it. The guy from behind was now down on his knees and trying to get his head between her legs but the guy fingering her was not giving up so easily... he must have had at least 2 or 3 fingers inside Jane now and was frigging her quite fast ... and then suddenly she moaned and came violently, shaking and trembling as I held her up still facing the guy who had just made her cum.

When her orgasm subsided, I held her in my arms and hugged her close then put my hand down to feel between her legs... She was absolutely soaking.

“Are you OK Babe? Do you want to go sit down somewhere or stay here a bit longer?”

She looked at the action on the bed and said,

“Lets stay here...”

There were about 3 single guys and 3 couples now all writhing around on the circular bed and the girl who was there from the beginning was being fucked in the arse by a black guy and her husband was laying underneath fucking her pussy.

There were two more guys taking turns feeding their cocks into her mouth and a group of 6 more guys had crowded round the bed groping and wanking making the room really full.

The guy from behind Jane was still on the floor, he had somehow managed to get in front of Jane... He looked up at me... as if to say, Can I lick her pussy... ?

I could see that Jane was still highly aroused, so I pulled up her Lycra skirt at the front and told her...

"Open your legs babe..."

She looked down and saw the guy laying on the floor and moved her hand to cover her pussy. I took her hand and brought it back up and said,

"Just open your legs and stand over him."

She took a step to the side and I reached down to pull her G string to the side... The guys mouth was on her pussy like a limpet. He reached behind her and pulled her bum closer so he could get his tongue deep inside her as she just gasped...

I was holding her skirt up around her waist and watching the guy licking Jane from underneath.

The guy who had made her come earlier was standing there, still wanking, his cock was rock hard watching the guy underneath and me holding her at the front. He then holds up a condom...

I could see that Jane was in a state of heightened sexual arousal and needed more and the extra E's we had taken a couple of hours earlier was making us both as horny as hell, so I asked Jane,

"Hey babe, do you want to try a big cock...?

She looked at the guy standing next to us and gave it a quick squeeze. I nodded to the guy and he rolls on the rubber... Jane just watched and smiled...

"Are you OK babe, you want me to...?"

I held Jane by the hips and started to kiss her on the mouth while bending her forward a bit. The guy underneath was now making her moan then she said,

"He's licking my arse and fingering me down there..."

The guy with the long cock took up position behind her and run his hand over her pussy.

The guy underneath could see what was happening so moved his mouth away as the guy rubbed his cock up and down Jane's slit and then he was in... Jane looked amazing as he entered her, Just staring into my eyes as I held her, I smiled and held her tight while the guy behind slid his cock in and out really slowly.

"He's too big babe ... its..... oooohhhh god..."

Jane reached down to my own cock which was also rock hard and sticking out from the open zip on my shorts. She was squeezing my balls and wanking me and then rested her head on my chest. The guy behind was getting faster and fucking Jane quite hard but Jane was really getting into it. She was somehow taking his extra long cock very well indeed...

Mine's only average sized but this guy must have been at least 9 inches. The guy underneath was still there and he was now fondling the guy's balls who was inside Jane. He then pulled out and we saw the guy underneath, grab his cock and started sucking it and squeezing his balls...

Jane looked down because she wondered why the cock came out of her pussy and saw what was going on... so I rubbed her clit slowly until the fucking resumed. There were hands groping Jane from all over the place and all I could do was to hold her close until she exploded again into another orgasm but this time... she was squirting all over the guy underneath.

Once she'd finished, we left the room and went to sit in the main lounge for a rest and saw that Gary and Vicki were also there. We were all pretty exhausted and after a brief chat decided it was time to go home, so that was the end of another very interesting experience.

Chapter 3

Arousal

One of the things I love most about Jane... is that when she's on ecstasy and gets really horny... (it usually happens while we're watching other couples playing and fucking in the fetish clubs), is that, when I finger her in a certain way... she has a massive orgasm and starts squirting... Well the following week it happened again while we were in "Arousal", our local swinger and fetish club. We'd decided to stay local as the last couple of weeks we had driven in to London and it's a bit of a long drive home at 5 am still buzzing on the sweets.... Anyway, in Arousal we were sitting in the cinema room with 5 or 6 single guys hovering around and 3 other couples on sofas and benches all around the room. In the center was a big round padded bed thing, a bit like a round stage and occasionally a girl or couple would get on it and play in front of all the cinema watchers.

On this occasion, a slim girl was being fingered by her boyfriend while on all fours and there were a few single guys sitting close by and trying to touch her tits and her legs while the boyfriend was only letting them have quick feels but not allowing any full on engagement.

We were on a sofa to the side and were watching while I had Jane's tits out and was caressing them in front of a single guy that had sat on the end of our sofa. Jane was wearing her silky black dress with a slit at the front showing the cleavage of her beautiful 34 B tits with nice long nipples. No bra so I could just slide my hand in and ease them out. Tiny black G string with black hold up stockings...

While she was watching the girl get touched and fingered, my hand went down to her pussy and she instinctively opened her legs to let me finger her. She was already a little wet, so I slid my hand down the top of her g string and pushed a couple of fingers deep inside her... She arched her back and moaned as they went in and I started to pleasure her giving our watcher a show...

Still watching the girl getting fingered on the big round bed in front of us, Jane lay back on the sofa and I started sucking on one of her nipples.

Then I saw another guy watching us... he'd been following us around earlier and was white but not English abut I could tell he really liked Jane... He was standing by the door but as soon as he saw a space he quickly moved closer to us and was then sitting right next to Jane's legs on the other side. He looked at me for approval and I nodded as he started to stroke Jane's feet. This made her jump but I said, to let him play while we watch the action on the round stage.

Now the girl on the round stage was laying on her back and her husband was letting another guy finger her while he was stroking her hair and kissing her deeply on the mouth. More hands were groping her and she was arching her back as another guy was sucking and playing with her breasts.

The guy stroking Jane's feet had now started running his hand up her leg and had his cock out... wanking slowly with his other hand. I saw him slide closer and let his cock touch her leg every now and then, while he was stroking her inner thigh with his free hand.

I kissed Jane again and asked,

"Can you feel his cock on your leg? He's really hard and wanking while looking at your pussy... I'm gonna take your knickers off so he can get a better look OK...."

She looked up at me with a naughty smile and bit her bottom lip....

"Don't worry babe, we won't let him go too far, let's just get him all worked up and tease him a bit."

With that, she let me slide her g string down and I put them on the sofa next to her. The guy was now openly stroking his cock which was quite impressive at about 8 inches long and much fatter than mine...

Jane looked down and saw what he was doing and then moaned again as I slid my fingers back into her while she opened her legs a bit more. I was watching him and eased my fingers in and out slowly opening her up and giving him a really good look.

Next thing he did, was stand up and move to the side while holding his cock over Jane's belly and started to feel her tits. He kept looking at me for approval and I sort of nodded and motioned for him to come up closer to Jane's head so she could see his cock better.

He was now standing level with her head and his cock was directly over her face and Jane was staring at it as he wanked slowly, pulling the foreskin back to expose the shiny helmet. I was now fingering Jane quite vigorously with two fingers and the guy offered his cock to Jane's mouth...

She looked at me and then at the cock and to my disbelief... she opened her mouth....

The guy puts the head of his cock in her mouth and she started sucking it, then licking it around the head while he was squeezing her tits.... Suddenly she started to cum and a massive stream of pee was gushing all over my hand. I pulled my fingers out and the stream was still shooting up in the air so I quickly placed my hand over the stream and held it over her pussy till it slowed down.

She was shaking and gripping my arm and still had hold of this guy's cock while squirting all over the sofa and floor.

When she calmed down, she was so embarrassed... She jumped up and ran out of the cinema... So I went after her and found her waiting in a queue outside the rest room ...

"Hey babe... everything's OK... and that was incredible... what an amazing orgasm and there's nothing to feel embarrassed about..."

We hugged me and said how she couldn't help herself and with my fingers going fast in her pussy and the strangers big cock in her mouth, she just cum so fast and the pee came...

I reminded her of another time she squirted when we were in a couples room in Club Rub in London a few months ago. We had been wandering around and it was about 1am. The club was really busy and packed on this particular night and we'd squeezed into the couples room and were sitting on these huge cushions on the floor by a wall. Then this other couple who we had sort of played with before, (soft play only, I let her husband stroke Jane's legs as I played with his wife's tits) came and squeezed in next to us. As they sat down Jane watched me stroke her bum and then saw me fondling her tits with my other arm around her. Her husband had encouraged me to do it so he could also play with Jane.

Well, Jane wasn't having any of it... She jumped up and stormed out of the couples room and we all looked at each other in shock... I had to tell them, I 'd better go see what was up... I got up and started looking for her in the club but couldn't find her anywhere. It was heaving with people and I went through the club a couple of times, searched in all the dance areas and BDSM play room. Eventually, I saw her sitting on a small stool at the side of the dance area. Thank god I thought to myself, I was getting really worried as she'd never done that before...

She said she was OK but didn't want him to touch her. So I hugged her and we kissed as I had pulled up another stool so was sitting directly in front of her.

"I saw you playing with her tits and he was letting you"

"Yes babe, I think they wanted to play with us and he must fancy you. So you don't like them then?"

"No, it's not that, I like them but he is always trying to get between my legs and... you know.... finger me... It turns me on but I don't know... I didn't like watching you touch his wife...."

As Jane was talking, I was hugging her head into my shoulder and one hand was stroking her stocking-ed leg. She kissed me and said,

"Babe, I feel so horny... I'm so sorry I ran out... we can go back if you want."

"No problem babe, we can see them again later or another time."

She'd reached down and had pulled my cock out of my little leather shorts and was wanking me. I in turn had slipped my hand between her legs and was fingering her. We were surrounded by loads of people standing but as we were facing each other on the stools, nobody could really see what we were doing, it looked like we were just hugging, kissing and talking.

"Fuck me babe... your so fucking wet."

Jane just moaned into my ear and kept squeezing and playing with my cock and balls. I pushed two fingers in her and started to finger fuck her fast.

"That couple want to play with us and I know you want to watch me finger his wife, don't you babe?"

Jane squeezed my cock so hard I though she was gonna pull it off... She started to tremble and cum... she was pulling me towards her, then I felt her squirting all over my hand... It was gushing out like a fountain, so I kept my fingers inside her to stem the flow... the floor under our stools was a huge puddle.

When she eventually stopped, we hugged and laughed as nobody around us knew what she just did. We quickly got up and walked away to explore the club a bit more.

Another time was when we were in the same venue, Club Rub in London but on a different night. This time we were standing in the BDSM play room watching people getting tied up and whipped or whatever. We were in a crowd of people, single guys and couples and Jane had her back to a wall. We were watching a couple let several guys fondle and finger the wife while she was tied to these stocks.

I was playing with Jane's bum and fending off wandering hands from single guys standing close by and watching us. Then Jane grabbed my hand and placed it between her legs. She'd already got my cock out and I knew she wanted me to finger her again as we watched. I'd started to realize that she ... well we... We both loved to be watched and I'd mastered the technique of making her squirt... So I exposed her tits... so as the guys standing near us could have a good look and sure enough they started stroking their cocks and moved in closer.

Jane stared at all the guys wanking around us and I pushed my two fingers into her pussy. I started to frig her slowly at first to get her worked up. There were a couple of guys hands on her tits so I sped up my fingering... One guy started to cum and shot his jizz all over her leg...

I fingered her as deep and fast as I could and she exploded shaking and trembling and squirted all over the floor. I saw one guy had his hand behind her and was fingering her arse and after she told me, that was what made her cum and squirt so hard.

Chapter 4

Squirting for the first time

This story is about the time I made Jane squirt for the very first time and shared her for a bit of soft play with my mate in the club... We'd been going to a few different clubs over the last year or so and one night in Arousal, we bumped into a really good mate of mine Gary. In fact it was Gary that had introduced us to the swinger and fetish club scene with his wife Vicki. However, on this particular night, he turned up alone.... He told us, they'd had a row... so he had come out alone!! Usually when we saw them, his wife and mine would chat and Gary and I would wander round and watch some action.

Well as the night went on, it got really busy and as usual, we had all taken some sweets (ecstasy) earlier in the evening and Jane was already starting to feel horny and aroused as she had already unzipped me and was leading me around by my cock. Every now and then she would stop and push me into a corner or against the wall and wank me to keep it hard and erect.

At one point we were sitting in the dungeon BDSM play area on a bench and I was playing with her exposed tits... She liked them being on show when in the club and on that evening, she was wearing a short silver dress that could be opened at the front making it easy to expose her very shapely breasts and long nipples. Sheer black hold up stockings, tiny silver G string and high heeled shoes.

As we were playing with each other, I noticed a group of guys forming a semi circle around us, it was pretty dark and they all had their cocks out, wanking and watching us. Jane was getting really turned on as two of the guys were standing really close, just a few feet away and her eyes were fixated on their cocks. One of them was huge... at least 9 inches long and then I saw my mate Gary, hiding in the shadows, he was also watching and wanking.

It was such an arousing situation, I started to rub her thighs and told her to open her legs a bit... just so we could see the guys reactions. She parted her legs slightly and I run my hand up the inside of her thigh over the stocking to the soft flesh at the top. My god it felt so sexy and her inner thigh was so smooth and soft.

We were sitting on a bench in a corner and Jane was laying back with her eyes closed... she seemed to be really relaxed, the E's were working and really enjoying what we were doing. Her legs were parted and all these guys were standing around us, watching and wanking.

I started rubbing her pussy over the G string and then slid up inside dipping into her tight little wet pussy. The guys around us had now moved in even closer and were literally just a few feet away... so I pulled the G string to one side and exposed her beautiful newly shaved pussy for them all to see. I noticed Gary getting closer, peering over a guys shoulder in front of him, so he could see her naked pussy for the first time.

Then to my surprise, Jane opened her legs wide and let me finger her even deeper as the all guys around us were wanking and staring at her smooth pussy and exposed tits. The guy with the big cock was getting very close to Jane's face... She just stared at him wanking it...

Then this old guy leaned forward and said to me,

"Can you tell the young lady, I'm about to cum and if she could watch me ejaculate please".

I whispered to Jane and she turned her head to watch... The old guy stepped forward so he was standing directly in front of us... wanked his cock for another few seconds and then he cum ... shooting his spunk all over the floor in front of us.

The other guys standing nearby were also were wanking furiously now as I was alternating between her tits, legs and lightly fingering her, more like teasing her and the crowd, while she had her legs wide open, laying back and tits fully exposed.

The guy with a big cock stepped forward as the old guy retreated back into the crowd. He also shot his cum all over the floor in front of us. I can only imagine a few more guys did the same as Jane looked so fucking sexy laying there like that. It wasn't long before she also jerked and grabbed my hand... she had her 1st orgasm of the evening.

We then went to the bar and had another drink, then had a walk around the club to watch a few more couples in action. Later on that evening, we ended up sitting in the couples only room and somehow, my mate Gary had managed to get in there with another guys wife and was sitting next to us chatting and watching the action all around us.

I again had Jane's tits out and he kept staring at them... We could see he was really aroused as he had his fat cock out and was playing with it discreetly next to us. He was sitting really close to Jane and his leg was touching hers, he was also letting her see his cock as he was playing.

I then said to Jane,

"It's a shame about Gary being alone and nobody to play with tonight..."

She looked at me and smiled, so I said,

"Why don't we let him play with us for a while, I know he loves your tits, he can't stop staring at them."

Next thing I remember was asking Gary if he wanted to join us in some play... He didn't need to be convinced as he immediately reached over and started caressing her right breast as I was stroking her left. Then Jane reached over to his cock and started to squeeze and wank him. I was running my hand up her inside leg again... she parted her legs a bit to give me better access, so I slipped a finger inside and saw Gary watching me and going down to suck on her nipple. I was already sucking away on her other tit and had about 2 fingers inside her. He was running his hand up her other leg, so I moved my hand away and let him finger her for a while.

I asked her if she was OK and started kissing her on the mouth. This was amazing as she was letting us both play with her tits and pussy at the same time. I was so aroused at watching him touching and fingering Jane and her holding his big fat cock, I remember saying to her,

"Why don't you suck his cock?"

Jane must have been well aroused as she just looked at me... and then him and then without saying a word, just slid down into his lap and started to lick and try get the head of his cock in her mouth...

I couldn't believe she was actually going for it... I had my own cock out and could see that she was really struggling to get the head of his cock in her mouth, it was wide, not really long, probably 6 inches but really wide. This went on for a few minutes and then I remember her sitting up, my mate and I looked at each other and smiled as we both never thought Jane would go that far.

We sat there in this dark room and had an audience of 3 other couples, who were also involved in various acts with each other and watching us three at the same time.

I then tried to move my wife's legs up, so she would be laying across both our laps... but she somehow, ended up kneeling over Gary and he started sucking her tits. I was behind her watching and stroking her sexy bare arse... Then I saw he'd put his hand between her legs, so I sat back and watched as he fingered her and sucked on her nipples. This went on for a little while so I watched and wanked as they played.

Then I saw she was kissing him while he had about 2 or 3 fingers inside her... and she was grinding her hips down onto his hand. She also had hold of his big cock between them and he was whispering something into her ear.

She leaned over to me and said,

"He wants to put a condom on and put his cock in me."

"Up to you babe, do you think you can... It looks really big?"

She then slid off him and said,

"No we agreed we wouldn't go that far... but playing was OK."

We then all got up and went for a walk through the club to another dark room, this one was much larger with a glass viewing window that looked into another room, full of couples on a huge bed. I was walking in front and holding my wife's hand and she had hold of my cock. I could also see she was pulling my mate along by his cock too. I also found out months later that my mate was fingering her ... as she was walking along with us through the club UN-be-known to me at the time.

She was standing in front of the window and watching the action on the big bed and I was standing behind her playing with her tits. I could see she was still wanking my mate to the side. So I turned her around so they were facing each other and I was still at the back rubbing her tits and letting them have a good feel of each other...

It was so dark in there, that it was hard to see what was actually happening but the noises coming from my wife... it was obvious she was nearing an orgasm... So we all moved over to a bench against the wall, where we laid her down and I was fingering her with about 3 fingers very fast and deep. Gary was at her head and I couldn't see exactly what he was doing...

All of a sudden I felt her cum and for the very first time ever... she squirted... and it was shooting up in the air and all over my hand. I held my hand there to stop it going all over the couple next to us and felt the hot warm liquid gushing out for about 30 seconds...

It was such an amazing feeling when she did that and there were about another 4 - 5 times that I made her squirt in various situations but they are all in other stories.

The time was now about 4 am and we had decided to leave the club and head home. On the way to the car park we were chatting away and I asked Jane if she was OK with what we just did with Gary?

Jane said she was feeling really horny tonight and the E's were really nice... she then said to both Gary and myself,

"It was a great night but for fun only... but next time make sure you bring your wife OK..."

I hope you enjoyed this story.

If you like my writing style, and stories about Husband or Wife sharing, Wife watching, BDSM, Cuckold, Swinger and Fetish clubs, Dogging and many other fetishes...

Why not check out my other stories on Amazon and sign up to my newsletter to get the heads up on all my new releases.

Dante X

Authors Website – Contact and Newsletter sign up

www.DantesErotica.uk

Dogging after the Fetish Swinger Club

Wife Watching with a Stranger

by Dante

Contents

Introduction

Chapter 1 - Dogging on the way home

Chapter 2 - Jane comes over to look

Chapter 3 - Fun in the fetish club

Chapter 4 - Marrissa

Introduction

As this story is part of the "Asian wife series." I'll jump straight into what happened, as all the background information about Jane and Dave can be found in the previous books but for anyone brand new to my stories, here's a brief intro;

Jane is Filipino and has amazing 34 B tits on a slim size 8 body. A sexy and very attractive 26 years young, but very shy and reserved unless she has had a few drinks or some sweets (ecstasy) like we usually do on club nights. We'd been married about a year and was introduced to the fetish and swing club scene several months ago by a mate.

Ad because we were always still so horny on the way home from London, we decided to check out at a dogging location I'd heard about online.

Chapter 1

Dogging on the way home

It was 4 am and we were on the way back from a London Swinger / Fetish club... And on this particular evening, we'd been soft swing playing with another couple in the club and Jane had let the couple kiss and fondle her tits while I did the same to the other guys girlfriend but on the way home, she told me that the guy had also fingered her from behind and nearly made her cum... but I had not seen this at the time.
I was playing with Jane's exposed breasts and smoothly shaved pussy as we drove down the M1 motorway and as we approached the junction to the road which led to the dogging spot I knew about... I said to Jane,

"Shall we go and see if any doggers are out tonight?"

Jane had only seen dogging videos before this evening but because she was still really horny after soft playing with the new couple in the club and me playing with her in the car on the way home... so she agreed.

I turned off the motorway and drove to the car park I knew was a typical dogging location between Studham and Whipsnade and saw there were 2 cars parked up but all was quiet and dark. I parked up in a corner so we could watch, turned the lights and engine off.

Nothing was going on and it was pretty dark with very little moonlight because of all the trees but we could see that the other two drivers were still sitting in their cars. Jane asked why they were just sitting there? So I explained they were probably just single guys that were waiting for some one to turn up and give them the OK to watch or play. If a car pulls up and flashes the interior light or headlights it probably means they want some voyeurs or players. Also a lot of guys seem to be either Bi or gay and go off together into the woods or do things to each other in their cars.

As we were in a dark corner, I got Jane to put her seat back, not all the way down but just enough so she couldn't be seen... exposed her tits and started fondling and rubbing her little clit again making her sigh. She just sat there staring over the dashboard into the darkness letting me play... I got her pretty aroused by telling her I was going to put the light on... so the guys in the cars would come over and watch.... and I could show them her beautiful breasts and bare pussy... but she stopped me turning the light on so I told her I was only joking...

Then another car pulled into the car park and parked right next to the other two cars. It was a top of the range new Jaguar XJ and the driver was alone. He sat there assessing the situation and could obviously see the other two single guys but as we were on the other side of the car park under some trees it was too dark for anyone to see into our car.

He got out and wandered over to the drivers door of one of the other cars and seemed to be talking to the driver. After a few minutes the driver got out and they both walked over to the other car. Jane and I were watching with interest but I was still had my hand between her legs and she was wanking my cock while the top part of her dress was wide open.

The two guys were now chatting with the other driver, then one of the guys pointed towards us and the Jag driver started walking towards our car... Jane quickly covered herself up and pulled her skirt down and I held her hand over my cock. As he approached, I opened the window and he was surprised to see Jane in the car with me… He then smiled and said,

“Sorry mate, thought you were alone. I was just talking to the other 2 guys over there to find out if they were up for a bit of action tonight…. Is your girlfriend there up for a bit of fun then?”

“That’s my wife and she’s very new to all this… so to be honest mate, we’re only watchers tonight, Sorry.”

He then replied, “That’s OK... My wife is in the car too and we are out to play tonight, so you're welcome to join us over there and just watch if you want.”

“Sorry mate… I can’t see anyone else in your car, Where is she then?”

“She’s in the trunk at the back, we play this game you see... She likes to be tied up and blindfolded and stuff. Gets her really turned on when she can’t see who’s doing what and says she doesn’t want to see their faces or her face being seen. Anyway, come on over if you like.”

With that, he just smiled and walked back to his car where the other 2 guys were waiting and having a smoke. Jane looked at me and said,

“I’m not getting out the car. There’s nobody else in his car, can we go please?”

As we stared across at the 3 guys they were all looking over at us so I said to Jane,

“OK babe, they all know you’re here now so I suppose we’d better go.”

Then as we were watching... the rear boot of the Jaguar opened and all 3 guys were crowding around and staring inside. Jane looked at me in surprise and we both watched as the driver of the Jaguar stepped aside letting the other two guys reach into the boot.

“What are they doing babe, quick... let’s go… I’m scared”.

"No wait a minute babe, he said his wife was in the back and it looks like someone is in the boot of the car".

"What! ... his wife is in the boot?"

"Yes, I think so.... You wait here, I'll go over and take a look."

"NO.... NO.... PLEASE DON'T LEAVE ME HERE ALONE"

I calmed Jane down and told her to lock the doors when I got out, just to be safe. As I got out, Jane pressed the central locking button and I wandered over. In the trunk was a really stunning but totally naked older woman with very white skin and long dark brown hair. She was blindfolded with a sort of half leather mask, a bit like bat girl but the eyes were also covered and her hands tied up behind her back.

The driver stands next to me and said,

"Meet my wife, and feel free to have a feel or just watch if you prefer. We have another guy out here watching darling... and he has his wife in his car also... Say hello and tell him he can join in."

The blindfolded woman, still in the trunk answered,

"Hello, is your wife with you really?"

"Yes, she is but she's scared to get out the car."

The guys all laughed and I watched as the 2 strangers were groping her and one was between her legs trying to finger her. I waved for Jane to come over but she wouldn't get out of the car.

"Tell you what, let's get her out the trunk and put her on the back seat so we can all have a bit more room and fun with her... and she can suck your cock's... You want to suck their cocks don't you darling? Go on go get your wife mate, she can watch or sit in the front seat."

The 3 guys all help the woman out of the boot and she stood there totally naked and blindfolded with her hands tied behind her back. One guy was fingering her and the other was behind her cupping her breasts. The Jag driver holds his wife's arm and leads her round to the rear door and untied her hands... then she got in and sat down on the back seat of the Jaguar.

I walked back to Jane and could see her staring wide eyed at what had just happened and knocked on the window for her to open the door.

"What are they doing to her...? Why is she blindfolded and all tied up?"

"Apparently that's a game they like to play, she doesn't want to be recognised or see the guys touching her."

"WHAT...!" Jane says in disbelief.

"Come on babe, It's safe and they said we can just watch."

"Are you sure...?"

"Yes babe, I'm sure, come on... let's go and watch."

Chapter 2

Jane comes over to look

We walked over to the Jaguar and the 3 guys faces all lit up and several comments were made about how beautiful and sexy Jane looked. Jane was still wearing her club outfit which was black hold up stockings, a very short silky black dress with poppers at the front, so her tits could be exposed easily when we wanted to play...
One of the strangers had already opened the other rear door of the Jaguar and had climbed in... the woman was laying across the back seat sucking his exposed cock. The guy was groping and playing with her tits. The other guy was still fingering her from our side, so the husband moved to the side so Jane could get in closer for a better look.

I stood behind Jane as she stared in at the woman with the 2 strangers playing with her on the back seat. I held her waist then moved my hand down over her bum and started squeezing it while my other hand cupped her left tit over her dress.

She reached behind and started squeezing my cock so I quickly unzipped myself and got it out so she could play with me properly. The stranger in front of us got down on his knees and started licking between the woman's legs holding them wide open so we could all see her glistening wet pussy. She was obviously enjoying it as she was moaning out loud and saying,

"Yes, Yes, please make me come... Oh please fuck me someone... I need a cock inside me."

Jane was getting aroused and I'd managed to open a few of the poppers at the front of her dress and her tits were nearly out.... The Jag driver had released his own cock and was wanking slowly while watching his wife with the 2 strangers. He was also staring at Jane's exposed tits so I held them out and rubbed the nipples with my thumbs. Jane tried to cover them up, all embarrassed but I whispered in her ear to let him watch... so she moved her arm down again and stared at him wanking his pretty impressive cock.

I put one hand down behind, slid over her arse and cupped her bum cheek, you know the lovely little soft fleshy area just under the cheeks, then slipped a finger into her sticky little slit..

"Go on babe, you can touch his cock if you like. Just like you did that guy in the club tonight."

"No, I can't...!" she responded.

"Yes you can babe, look how hard he is and look at his wife being licked out in the car."

His wife was moaning away and pulling the guys head into her pussy. He stopped slurping for a second, looked up and asked the husband,

"Can I fuck her mate?"

"Yes mate... go for it... so long as you've got a rubber".

The stranger gets up and smiles as he sees me fingering Jane and her tits exposed. He reaches into his pocket and pulls out a rubber and rolls it onto his cock in front of Jane.

Jane was staring at the woman's open legs in the car and watched as she rubbed her own pussy and fingered herself.... waiting to be fucked by this stranger.

"Give me a cock... please get a cock inside me... I need to be fucked" she says again.

The guy pulls her legs out of the car to better position her and then pushes his cock straight in go the hilt. The woman let out a deep long moan and shouted,

"Yes.... Yes... fuck we with your big cock you bastard... my husband wants to see me take a strangers cock.... so fuck me hard and make me cum.... You dirty dogging bastards."

The guy started fucking her hard and fast and she was making a lot of noise, moaning and vocally telling them to use her and fuck her mouth and pussy... The guy at her head cums in her mouth and all over her face, she shouted to her husband,

"See darling, this dirty fucking dogger has cum in my mouth.... Is that what you wanted to see... it's all thick and... tastes really salty darling?

The husband is quiet but wanking really hard next to us and then the guy fucking his wife tells the woman he was about to cum. This sends her over the edge and she moans out loud while he shot his load into her pussy.

The husband shoots his jizz all over his wife's leg as he was holding it up while she was getting fucked. I could sense that Jane was ready to cum... so I pushed a couple of fingers inside her from the front and finger fucked her deep and fast. This always makes her cum quickly and squirt.... I like to do it to her like this in the club when we're watching other couples. She grabs my hand and moans that she's cumming then starts to squirt.... It was running all down her legs and splashed out from under my hand onto the ground, I kept fingering her deeply until she almost collapsed as her orgasm and squirt took over.

The two guys thanked the husband and his wife, still laying across the back seat, in her half mask blindfold and now fingering herself. She tells her husband to take her home now as she needs more cock and wants to have him fuck her all night while telling her what else was happening during their night out.

Jane and I said thanks for the show and the woman said,

"Please join us again, we are new to this as well and it was great to know another girl was watching... Did he touch you?"

Jane answered, "No but he wanked his cock next to me and I watched him come on your leg."

We said goodbye and walked back to our car.

"Oh My God, that was amazing!" Jane said as we drove out of the woods car park and headed home.

"Did you want to fuck her as well?" she asked me.

"No babe, I love to watch, like her husband... I would have touched her or let her play with my cock if you agreed but if not, I'm happy to see you cum and make you happy."

Jane was quiet on the way home and as our home was only 10 minutes away we arrived quickly and were fucking on the bed in no time. Next day Jane said, she wanted to go dogging again..... and asked me to buy her a blindfold.

Chapter 3

Fun in the fetish club

So last week I took Jane to see what happens at dogging locations and although she was scared and wouldn't let anyone else touch her, she was incredibly turned on and excited when we got home. She couldn't stop talking about the blindfolded and tied up woman in the boot of the car. Well we looked online and found a black leather half hood / mask just like the one the woman in the trunk was wearing but this one had a removable section for the eyes, so could be worn with or without the eye covers.

It arrived in the mail a couple days later so I suggested we go to Subversion, another fetish club in London on Saturday night so she could try it out.

Jane also ordered a one piece black fishnet body stocking, to wear with no bra or knickers and a short leather skirt to match the hood. We also bought a leather neck collar with a ring and chain like a dog lead. She looked absolutely stunning with her shapely young tits and nipples poking through the fishnet. Her smooth pussy was also visible when the short skirt was lifted and she was really excited because nobody could recognise her wearing the mask.

I wore a leather / chain chest harness and a black leather cock pouch that was basically a male G-string. I put my jeans and leather jacket on for the drive to London and Jane covered herself with her long ankle length coat.

When we entered the club we went straight to the changing area and put all our street clothes in a holdall and handed it in at the desk. Jane had the hood on but not the blindfold and I led her through club with the chain attached to her neck.

Jane got loads of attention and we were followed around by several single guys. After a few drinks, I suggested we go to the play area so Jane could try out the blindfold and we agreed people could touch her...so long as I was there... and to make sure they didn't go too far... no full sex or fucking.

I led her around the playroom blindfolded and we stood in a corner next to a tall white girl getting lashed on her naked arse and back with her knickers pulled down to her knees. She was tied to a big cross and every few minutes the guy whipping her stroked her arse softly and delved between her legs fingering her. He ordered her to push her bum out to accept more whipping and not to cum or else she would be punished severely with the pussy clamps and weights.

Another guy was standing next to her and groping her tits and down between her legs from the front while his girlfriend was kneeling on the floor like his slave.... He was making her suck his cock while he fondled the girl on the cross.

Then another guy stepped forward and caressed her face and whispered something to her, I assumed it was her husband. He told the guy whipping her to give her 5 hard strokes....The guy did what he asked... then the husband held her arse cheeks apart and told the guy to push his fist into her pussy.

I told Jane what was going on right next to her and asked her if she was OK? She said yes and it was really turning her on as she had felt people touching her arse and tits as I led her through the crowd. The club was very busy and there must have been 150 to 200 people in there. The play room was only 10 by 5 metres and the play equipment took up 1/2 of the room and about 20 single guys and 6 couples were standing around watching but it was like trying to get to the bar in a crowded pub with lots of pushing and squeezing past people.

As Jane was in the corner she was sort of protected but several guys had managed to squeeze in next to her. One guy started touching her arm and looked at me for the OK to continue... so I nodded and smiled.... Jane shivered as he explored her arms and belly and then her tits and nipples poking out through the fishnet. He squeezed her nipples that were sticking out and then started sucking on them.

Another guy moved in closer who was wanking his very impressive fat and long cock that had a ring pierced though the head. He asked me if he could join in, so I agreed. He lifted Jane's skirt and touched her pussy over the fishnets then pushed a finger up into her. She instinctively grabbed his hand... so he took hold of her hand and guided it on his cock... Jane initially pulled her hand away but when he moved it back she started feeling it and seemed to be exploring how big he was, then she felt the ring in the end and gasped...

She was being fingered and touched all over by these two strangers while I held her other hand. She asked me if the guy fingering her was the one with the ring in his cock? I told her yes... and someone else was fingering her from behind. I told her there were 3 guys touching her and the guy she was holding with the cock ring was a big muscle builder type guy with tribal tattoos up his arms and shoulder..

Jane was being well groped and the cock ring guy asked,

"Is this your wife mate? ... Where she from? She's fucking sexy as fuck."

"She's Filipino and yeah she's the wife."

"Fuck me mate she's got a stunning body and those fucking tits are beautiful, how old is she?"

"26 and we've only been into the club scene a few months."

"Can I taste her mate?" he asks.

“If she let’s you...” I responded.

He slid down onto the floor and got between Jane’s legs. I told Jane,

“The guy with the cock ring wants to lick your pussy babe, open your legs for him.”

Jane had a guy each side fondling her tits and their hands were between her legs but as the big guy slid down they moved their hands away so he could kiss and lick her pussy from underneath....

Jane grabbed my arm and asked me what the guy was doing between her legs and that he was going to make her wet herself...

“Just relax and let him lick and play with you babe, then if you do squirt when you cum, he’ll fucking love it.... I’m sure.”

I lifted up the front of her skirt so I could see him licking between her legs and saw he was having a problem with the fishnets.

“Lets make a hole mate” I told him,

I got down and ripped the fishnets open exposing her smooth bare pussy. Jane gasped and I saw her legs tremble as his hands gripped her bum and pulled her pussy towards his face, his tongue must have entered her pussy and he started snogging it.

“His tongue is inside me.... oh my God.... I can’t hold back.... babe it’s coming...”

Jane moaned out loud and held onto me as she had a massive orgasm on the guys face. Piss was gushing out all over the guys face and chest... She nearly collapsed but I managed to hold her up and the guy underneath held her up by her bum.

When she finished, he got up and kissed Jane on the cheek, thanking her for a great session, then told us he was available anytime if we ever wanted a private 3some or group play.

Jane asked me if I could take her blindfold off, so I undid the buckle at the back and took it off. When she saw the guys that were fondling her she went all shy and told me she wanted to go to the bar area for a rest and drink.

She smiled at the cock ring guy and even gave his cock another squeeze as we pushed our way through the crowd.

"So how was that babe…?"

I asked her when we were sitting down upstairs in the bar area.

"It was so nice feeling his cock... but all the other guys were a bit too pushy and rough, they were hurting me and two or three hands all trying to finger me at the same time. Then that guy made me cum really fast with his tongue and fingering me in my bum."

"Really babe, he was in your arse as well...!"

We walked around for the next few hours watching other couples play and Jane went into the grope box for a while and had 6 guys and myself groping her through all the holes. On the dance floor we were in the middle of a crowd and Jane told me after we sat down that 2 guys were dancing really close behind her and they had their cocks out and kept rubbing themselves on her bum and arms.

I asked her if she touched them or if they touched her? She said one guy was trying to get her to hold his cock so she gave it a quick squeeze... Then a short time after, she felt him ejaculate all over her arm as it was all sticky. Another guy kept touching her bum but she couldn't tell who.

The time was 3.30am, the action was slowing down and people were going home, we decided to get going and check out the dogging spot on the way home.

Chapter 3

Marrissa

As we drove down the motorway, I got Jane to open her coat and play with my cock while I played with her tits and pussy. She looked so fucking sexy with the ripped open fishnets exposing her naked hairless slit between her legs.

"Babe... I want to wear the mask and blindfold but don't let anyone let anyone fuck me... will you?"

"What about me babe, are you gonna let me fuck you in front of some doggers, if anyone's out tonight?"

"Yes babe... of course...you can... but promise to look after me OK?"

"Of course babe"

"Can we meet up with that couple from last week again? You took his number didn't you?"

"Yes we can ring them and arrange a meet I'm sure".

As we drove, Jane received a text on her phone.

"Who's that babe?... Strange time to be getting a message."

"It's Marrissa from Dunstable, she's had a big argument with her husband and he's stormed out the house. She's all upset, I better call her."

Marrissa was Jane's best friend, another Filipino and a real looker, tall and beautiful with long legs and a bum to die for.

Her husband is about 25 years older than her... and a right arsehole, always out drinking with his mates. She's 29 or 30ish I think and leaves her home alone.

Jane comes off the phone and said, "Can we pick her up, she can stay at our house tonight."

"Well if you must babe, so we're not going dogging tonight then?"

"I can't let Marrissa stay alone tonight, she's crying and says they are gonna get divorced."

"Wow that must have been a serious row, what's his problem... she's a really nice girl."

"She wants to have a baby but he doesn't. She also wants to come to the club but he's not interested, she thinks he's seeing his ex wife again behind her back."

"What... is he nuts!, Marrissa is beautiful and you've told her about the club?"

"Yes and what happened last week with the woman in the boot of the car and the doggers."

"So does she want to come dogging with us?"

"Maybe... but I need to be with her tonight, please let's go pick her up."

I couldn't believe my luck, Jane's best friend wants to come to the swingers club and dogging! As soon as we arrived at Marrissa's house she was waiting outside at 4.30 am with a holdall and it looked like she was really serious about leaving him. She jumps in the back and they start chatting away in their language Tagalog. I started driving towards our home and then Marrissa said to me...

"I'm so sorry, I ruined your night out."

"No problem Marrissa, we had a good time in the club so we can go out again another night."

Jane then said, "I told her we were gonna go dogging again and she said it's OK with her and she wants to watch".

"But I thought you were too upset with breaking up with your husband"

Marrissa responded, "He's fucking his ex wife and I don't want to be with him any more... We haven't had sex for over a year now and I want to see what goes on at your club and... well like what you and Jane are doing out in the car in the middle of the night."

"Well we were going to see if any doggers are still out but it's very late now, nearly 5 am and it will be getting light soon. We could still drive through Whipsnade on the way home and have a quick look."

"Jane... Have you shown Marrissa your new clubbing fishnet body stocking?"

"What! Are you wearing it now?" Marrissa said in surprise,

"Go on babe, open your coat and show her."

Jane opened her coat and they both burst out laughing... Marrissa couldn't believe Jane wore it at the club.

"But your tits and nipples are on show and..."

Jane lifts her skirt to show her bare pussy and ripped open fishnets.

"OH MY GOD ... Jane... you ... your pussy is shaved ... and..."

Marrissa cannot believe it...

"Put your mask on babe"

Jane pulls the mask out, puts it on and then shows her the eye cover attachment.

Marrissa stares open mouthed! Then they start going off in their language again. Luckily it was only a short drive to the dogging spot and we pulled into the car park to see only 1 car in the spot we parked in last week. I parked up opposite, facing the entrance so we could exit easily and also watch any new cars coming in. It was still dark and I couldn't see anyone in the other car.

It seemed a bit awkward for me and Jane so I told Marrissa how it all worked with the lights flashing and dogging rules etc.

Then said, "Do you mind if we play a bit and you can just watch in the back?"

"Do what you want... Just Go for it, I can't believe I out here doing this" She said giggling to herself in the back.

I opened Jane's coat and started caressing her tits, seriously not believing my luck at having Jane's friend in the back watching and really hoped something eventful would happen. Jane reached over and started squeezing my cock through my jeans so I opened the buttons and let her pull it out. Marrissa was watching intently from the back seat and I was well hard.

"Keep your mask on babe, do you want the blindfold on as well?"

"Yes put it on." Jane answered

Marrissa was staring at us in disbelief then said, "Look another car's coming".

I attached the eye covers to Jane's mask and buckled it up at the back. Then told Jane to open her legs so I could play and show off her legs and pussy to any doggers. I turned the light on and flashed my headlights.... In no time, the guy from the car came over holding a torch.

Then we saw 3 guys and young girl about 20ish appear... coming out from the woods walking towards the empty car. They saw the guy walking over to us with a torch and followed him to our car. Jane was sitting reclined in the passenger seat with her coat wide open and the mask covering her face and eyes. I was leaning over fingering her pussy with her erect nipples poking through the fishnet body stocking.

There was a bit of talking outside then I saw all 4 men and the girl by Jane's window shining the torch inside. One guy was touching the young girl outside between her legs. She only had a short skirt on and he was fingering her from behind as she stared into our car. The guy with the torch was shining it onto Jane through the window.

Marrissa was dead silent and still watching in disbelief in the back, then the girl knocked on the window. I opened it and she peered inside at Jane and asked why she was wearing a mask. I told her it was our game then she saw Marrissa in the back.

I asked the girl, “So what was going on in the woods then?”

She just replied casually, “My boyfriend likes to watch his mates with me.”

Jane then said, “Is that another girl outside?”

“Yes babe, there are also 4 guys out there so open your legs and let them see your nice little shaved pussy.”

She opened her legs a bit wider so I pushed a couple of fingers inside.

“They all have their cocks out now and wanking looking at your tits and me fingering you... does that turn you on babe?”

The girl outside starts moaning as one of the guys started fucking her from behind. She was holding on to the door and her head was almost in the passenger side window right next to Jane.

“I can hear them, what are they doing to her...?” Jane asks.

The girl answers, “That’s Len my boyfriends mate, he’s already had me in the woods but now he wants more. What’s wrong with her in the back then?”

“She’s just come to watch”, I answered.

“No she’s not, she’s wanking herself and watching the guys fucking me” she laughed.

I looked at Marrissa in the back, her jeans were open and her hand was inside rubbing her herself.

I smiled and said,

“Do you need some help Marrissa?... Open your window and

have a closer look at those guys wanking their cocks."

Marrissa looked at me and then said.

"Can I just open it a little bit?"

"Up to you Marrissa."

She buzzed it down halfway and immediately a cock was pushed through and wanking right in the window. She stared at it while still rubbing herself then the guy asked her,

"Can you take your jeans off and maybe your top so we can see your tits?"

Marrissa looked at me again, so I said,

"Go on.... it's OK, you're safe in the car."

She pulled her top off hesitantly and then took her jeans off. Then the guy still wanking said,

"That's it babe.... God your fuckin beautiful... Lay back and open your legs babe".

Marrissa lay back as I watched intently, she opened her legs and rubbed her pussy inside her knickers on the back seat.

Jane was now being kissed by the girl being fucked outside and she had a hand in the window between Jane's legs.

I was so turned on watching Marrissa in the back so I reached over and touched her leg. She looked at me.... then sighed and closed her eyes rubbing her pussy faster. I took that as an OK to continue so rubbed up her thigh working my way higher towards her pussy.

"Show him your pussy Marrissa... go on... just pull your knickers over and let him see it"

Marrissa looked at me again with a really naughty smile then slowly pulled her knickers to the side..... revealing herself to me for the first time and the strangers outside. What a sight, her pussy was really hairy and sopping wet.

"Wow... fucking hell Marrissa, your pussy is so beautiful, are you feeling horny?.... Can I touch it?"

Without an answer I moved my hand onto her belly and slid it down into her hairy bush and exposed pussy and slipped a finger inside.... She sighed as it went in and the guy at the window shouted,

“I’m fucking coming you fucking sexy bitch....”

He shot his load into the window... all over Marrissa’s open legs... She started panting then orgasmed just as another cock appeared at the window.

I looked over at Jane and she was being groped by... I don’t know how many arms and hands were reaching in the window.... between Jane’s legs and tits.

Marrissa moved closer to the cock being wanked in her window, she changed position and had got up and was kneeling on the back seat with her face inches away from it. She then reached out and touched the guys balls. He gave a long groan and said,

“Go on babe, play with my balls and suck my big fat hard cock, you know you want to.”

I couldn’t believe it but she opened her mouth and started licking the end of his cock still fondling his balls.

“My husband is fucking his ex so I’m gonna fuck some guys” she said all revengefully.

I reached into the back and felt Marrissa’s thighs and bum. She didn’t stop me so I carried on and delved between her legs feeling her lovely wet pussy from behind.

As I fingered Marrissa on the back seat, I heard Jane moan out loudly as she came... The old guy was fingering her really hard and fast and had his whole body squeezed in the window.... When she come down, he pulled his arm and body out and continued wanking until he shot his load all over the passenger side door, then said thanks and walked off towards his car.

It was getting light now so we all decided to call it a night and go home. Marrissa stayed the night in our bed and looks like she will be living with us for a while so more tales to tell I am sure. There's still so many more stories to tell so I will save it for another book.

I hope you enjoyed this story.

If you like my writing style, and stories about Husband or Wife sharing, Wife watching, BDSM, Cuckold, Swinger and Fetish clubs, Dogging and many other fetishes...

Why not check out my other stories on Amazon and sign up to my newsletter to get the heads up on all my new releases.

Dante

Authors Website – Contact and Newsletter sign up

www.DantesErotica.uk

Dogging with Dave

By Dante

Chapter 1

Here's a dogging story that happened a while ago but one I remember quite vividly. My wife and I had been to a London Swinger and Fetish club, (Those experiences are in other stories) and this is what happened on the way home and later when I went dogging alone.

We'd had a great night and were both still horny as hell driving home at 3 AM. We'd both taken some E's (ecstasy or sweets as we call them) as nearly everyone does in the clubs and I was playing with Jane on the way down the motorway. She was laying back in the passenger seat and letting me play with her exposed tits. Her legs were parted and her little black silky dress was up around her waist. Her knickers were pulled over and she was letting me finger her as we drove down along. She also had these black hold up stockings on and had hold of my cock which was covered in baby oil, as I keep a bottle in the car exactly for this type of play on the way home.

The sweets make you feel incredibly horny and want to have sex with virtually anyone, it also makes you enjoy deep penetration. Jane especially loved me trying to fist her while on sweets but the most I could ever manage was 4 fingers as her little Filipino pussy is too tight.

Anyway... she had oiled up my exposed cock and balls, as I had already released it from my tiny leather shorts (club gear) and the feeling was incredible as she slid her hand up and down and squeezing my balls.

I had a couple fingers in Jane and as we came off the motorway we were stopped at the traffic lights... I was finger fucking her quite fast and then she screamed out, she was gonna cum and had a huge orgasm.... squirting, jerking and shaking and gripping my hand. The lights had changed, so I had to continue driving... but Jane was still squirting in the car. It went everywhere... and because she was laying back in the seat , it went all over the dashboard, the floor and it even hit the windscreen. We both laughed and were soon back home and climbing the stairs to our bedroom.

On the bed we fucked like crazy, going over what happened. I went down on Jane and she pulled me around in a 69 and sucked my cock. We made love for a while but Jane was knackered and wanted to sleep, so I said I would go down and watch some porn on the internet. She knew I couldn't stop having sex while on sweets and was used to me watching porn and playing with myself after club nights like tonight.

So down I went and started watching some sexy movies but It wasn't doing it for me... I was still so horny and I looked at the clock, It was 4 AM, so I decided to drive to a dogging spot and see if there was any action going on. Now I'm not gay and not normally into guys in any way... but I am Bi-sexual I suppose, because I do like ladyboys (Katoys). I lived in the Far East for a long time and had several experiences with Katoys out there.

So off I went in the car to a dogging spot I knew about, not too far away.... and I have no idea why... well horny as fuck is a good reason I suppose. I went out still dressed in my club gear, small leather black shorts and black T shirt. My cock was still hard and poking out of the zip in my shorts as I drove. I'd also took a blue pill (Viagra) earlier in the evening as sweets alone, tend to make the old John Thomas go limp and not function properly, therefore, I always have a blue pill to compensate, then no problem... it stays hard all night.

So when I got to the car park it was still dark and there was only one car there. I parked up and turned off my engine and lights and sat there in the darkness watching and stroking my self. I grabbed the baby oil from the glove box and poured it all over my cock and balls but because of my shorts, it was getting a bit messy, so I slipped them off and sat there naked from the waist down.

As I rubbed the oil over my cock and balls, the feeling of pleasure was so... well it's hard to describe on the sweets... ultra sensitive... heightened pleasurable feelings.... well intense pleasure I suppose.... I continued stroking and squeezing and staring into the darkness and my mind was racing... I was thinking about all the horny stuff we did that evening in the club.

I was remembering how Jane was letting me caress her beautiful shapely 34 B tits in front of this single guy... We were in this dark room and there were several other couples in there having sex but we were standing behind another couple, watching some girl being fucked from behind as her husband held her at the front kissing her and fingering her. Several single guys were crowding around and groping her tits and I assumed one of them was fucking her.

Anyway, there was this young 30 something single guy right next to us, staring at Jane's tits as I was holding and fondling them from behind. He had his cock out and was wanking it almost in front of Jane. She just watched him as he stroked it, he was sort of showing it off to her. I had exposed her tits from the dress and was twirling her nipples and had turned her so she was facing him. He kept alternating from looking at me, then her tits, then her face and then me again... eventually he asked if he could touch?

I asked Jane... and she hesitantly nodded, so I gave the guy the OK to have a feel... He stepped forward and I moved my hands away, so he could caress and squeeze them. Jane must have obviously liked it as she moaned and rested her head on my shoulder. I cupped her bum cheeks and pulled them apart... then delved down lower.

I told her to part her legs a bit, then as she did so... I slipped two fingers in... This made her shudder and the guy in front leaned forward and started sucking on her one of her nipples. This was so fucking horny I got Jane to squeeze and wank my cock as I fingered her from behind....

Then a few more single guys appeared and were watching closely as the guy in front was having a good old feel and sucking Jane's nipples. Then I felt his fingers trying to enter Jane's pussy from the front. I thought for a few seconds if I should let it go this far but Jane seemed to be OK with it, so I pulled my fingers out and let him finger her for a while...

Jane was still wanking me as I held her facing the guy. Then the other guys all started groping her and there was a mass of hands on her tits and between her legs. Jane orgasmed suddenly and nearly collapsed... so I held her up and told the guys, that was enough... and to stop acting like animals, then we exited that play room.

Chapter 2

My cock was rock hard sitting in the car in the dark and I didn't know anyone was outside watching me... that was until... I heard a tap on the window. This English looking guy about 40ish was standing there looking in. I thought about driving away but something stopped me, so I opened the window a bit and he asked me if I was up for a bit of fun?

"What sort of fun?", I asked him as I couldn't think of anything else to say.

"Just a bit of mutual wanking mate, nothing heavy." he answered.

I saw he also had his cock out and was wanking it as he spoke. I looked at it and don't tell me why, but I felt so fucking horny watching him pull his foreskin back exposing a big pink head. He asked me if he could sit in my car, so I nodded and he walked around and got in the passenger side.

Fuck me, what am I doing, I'd never done this before... He got in and introduced himself as Trevor and we shook hands. He started talking about, how it was a quiet night and no action, he said he'd been out for 3 hours and only seen cars drive in and out.

Then he asked me,

"What are you into mate and why are you here wanking alone in your car?"

And then he noticed... I was naked from the waist down.

"Well mate, me and the missus have been clubbing in London last night and I wasn't tired enough to sleep, so I've left her in bed and come out dogging alone."

“Shame you didn’t bring your missus with you”, he said.

Yes... I know... but she was too tired... So what about you... You married then?"

“Yes mate, but she’s not into sex anymore, that’s why I come dogging.” he answered.

I looked at him wanking his very impressive cock, it must have been about 8 inches long and twice as fat as mine. He pulled the foreskin back and showed me the head. It was all red and glistening.

I told him, "I'm not gay mate but I must say, you've got a pretty impressive cock there..."

He looked at mine and said,

“Yours looks nice as well mate, what’s that you got all over it, you using some kind of lube or something?"

I showed him the bottle of baby oil and he said,

“Mind if I...”

"Sure, go for it mate, makes it feel nice and well... slippery and horny.”

He took the bottle and poured some onto his cock, then rubbed it up and down. I was wanking my own and I felt so fucking turned on it was making me wank even faster.

We watched each other and then... without saying a word... he reached over and cupped my balls. Fucking hell it felt amazing... so I just let him explore and moved my hand so he could wank my cock... I just let him do it... and it felt great, then he had his other hand on me... so one was squeezing my balls and the other wanking my cock. Then he lowered his head and took me in his mouth... sucking me and massaging my balls at the same time.

I was sitting back and watching him suck me... then I remembered staring at his cock... it was still hard and sticking up... so I decided to go for it. I reached over and held it... He let out a long moan and I felt it twitching in my hand. It felt quite unusual but really nice, soft yet hard and with the oil it was slick and pulsing. I slid my hand up and down and each time I stroked his bulbous cock head he let out another moan. He obviously liked that, so I concentrated more on the head.

Suddenly I felt him spurting his cum all over my hand and he let out a really long moan. He continued sucking me... and as you can imagine, I didn't even last another 30 seconds and started squirting my own cum into his mouth. He didn't even pull off but let me unload in his mouth. He then pushed a finger in my ass and I'm sure that made me orgasm again but I was totally out of sperm... My cock just jerked... as we both watched but nothing came out.

"You must be empty..." he joked

Well mate, we've been playing all night and yes... I suppose I've come a few times but we also had some sweets and a blue pill... so that's why I'm still so fucking hard and horny..."

"Sweets... what you mean... sweets?"

"E's mate.... ecstasy... everyone takes em in the club... that's probably why I'm out here playing with another guys cock for the first time... LOL They make you want to have sex with anyone..."

"Fuck me mate... I could do with getting some of them for the missus... she's a dead loss when it comes to sex..."

"Why not try taking her to one of the fetish clubs... no need to do anything, lots of couples keep themselves to themselves and get turned on by watching others I suppose."

"Well... talking of E's and stuff... I got this serious situation come up and I'm not sure if I should I call the police of something...

"Really... so whats that then...?" I asked

"Well... I'm not sure what to do about as my mate Davis who disappeared about 8 months ago. He was living in Chelmsford but met this really rich and sexy looking Chinese woman at a party in some London apartment. Anyway I get this long text message from him the other day claiming he has just managed to get access to a phone and needed to tell someone (me because I was his best mate) to assure his daughters he was OK... still alive and he hoped to get in touch again soon but for now he was abroad and had a few issues to sort out. He then went into detail about what happened."

While he was talking he was still wanking his cock... I was just holding mine but listening to his story.. He continued talking,

"So Davis was ecstatic when he met this Chinese woman at the party but what you need to know about Davis is... that he's a total sex addict and loved Coke, Ecstasy, crack, meth and in fact, any thing, drugs or otherwise that induced high states of sexual arousal... I've seen him fucking and playing with the most grotesquely old fat women, weird couples and literally anyone guys included that wanted sex when we went out dogging together. He also had a few regular older women well past their sell by date in their late 60's and one that was 74... that he used to service regularly... In a nut shell... he was a sexual animal that I've never ever encountered before. He's told me so many stories about his experiences that I could easily fill a book.

However, his main asset was the size of his cock..... It was fucking huge and whenever women, couples or anyone saw it, they wanted to try it for size. It was about 10 inches long with a pointy head and about 3 inches in diameter. It was fucking big to say the least....

Anyway, back to his text message

"He told me this really sexy Chinese woman he met was named Laichi and that they had become an item as he really fancied her and she had introduced him to all these other underground clubs and letting him do whatever he wanted with other women, girls and couples... in fact she seemed to get more turned on watching him fuck and play with other women than when they were together alone. Well 6 months ago he said they went on holiday to her home in China and he's sort of been stuck been there since... He says she keeps him in a big old house and they have sex parties nearly every evening... he is the in house freak show with the big cock...

"So what does he want you to do then...?" I asked

"I dunno cos he said he'll message me again soon but what the fuck can I do if he's in fucking China..."

Chapter 3

We were both still sitting there wanking and it was still dark outside when he reached over and started playing with me again...

"You don't mind if I... do you mate...?"

I let him stroke me again and watched as he brought me back to full hardness... he pushed a hand under my ass and was trying to push a finger in while squeezing my bollocks... Fuck it felt good and the sweets were still working... giving me waves and short bursts of pleasure and tiny little colored lights when I shut my eyes...

Then a white ford transit van drives into the car park and backs in right next to us. We both sat up and tried to see who was in the van then a short stocky white guy jumped out and walked around to my drivers side window. He peered in with a torch and we were both in an uncompromising situation as I was naked from the waist down and he was still holding onto my cock...

I could see he was alone so opened my window a bit... He said hello and smiled when he saw us with both our cocks out... Then asked if we were up for a bit of fun with a couple of birds....?

"What girls... what you got some in the van then...?" I asked..

"Yes mate I've got two birds in the back and they want to try some dogging we heard about this place on swinging heaven a dogging forum and chat site..."

"Who are they then mate... you ain't kidnapped them have ya...?"
Trevor the guy in my car says laughing out loud.

"No mate... ones the missus and the others her mate... her old man's a piss head and doesn't look after her in that department anymore so she stays at our place a lot... you know what I mean..."

"Well we can have a look can't we..."

Trevor then says to me and starts to put his cock away. I grabbed my shorts and was trying to put them on but my cock was still standing to attention...

We all walked to the back of his van and he opened the rear doors.. Inside was a mattress and two women... not the most attractive in the world but they at least were dressed up for the occasion in stockings and short skirts and must have been about 45 to 50ish... One was quite slim and size 10 I suppose with smallish tits and the other was plump and size 14 with huge tits and a big ass.. They were laying on the mattress and giggling as we all stared into the van..

"That's Vera the skinny one and this is Avril my missus, I'm Den by the way."

The guy who was in my car was already climbing in the van and said,

"I'm Trevor and not sure what his name is..." he said pointing towards me..

"Dave... nice to meet you all..."

Trevor lay down between the two women and had an arm around each one's waist...groping at their tits while the women were giggling and the fat one... Avril was pulling his cock out from his trousers...

"Ooohh look at this Vera... he's got a fucking snake in here... "

They were both laughing and grabbing his cock then the driver Den said,

"Jump in mate and I can close the doors..."

In we got and I was kneeling down next to the skinny one and Den closed the doors behind him. The skinny one Vera saw her chance and started gröping my cock as my tiny leather shorts were far too small to contain it... The head was sticking out through the leg and she giggled as she realized what I was wearing...

"I don't normally come out dressed like this... been clubbing in London...."

I tried to explain but the van was in hysterics and Vera had pulled the zip down and was trying to get it out... I pulled them down and off as it was far easier than trying to pull it out through the zipper...

Vera was onto me like a sucker fish and was trying to get it down her throat while I held her head... hoping she didn't have sharp teeth and had done this sort of thing before... Avril was on her back with her legs wide open and Trevor was almost fisting her as her husband Den was egging him on...

"That's it mate... get in there... give her a good seeing too mate... She's a dirty fucking slag and needs a big cock... you gonna fuck her with that fucking big cock are yer mate... Go on Avril... he's gonna give you what you need luv..."

Avril was moaning and sighing and to me... she looked like a big fat whale but Trevor was onto her like she was miss fucking Universe...

Vera was still sucking me so I reached down and had a grope of her tits and surprisingly they were quite nice, a bit loose and floppy but still nice to play with for sure...

Then Avril was screaming that she was cumming and Trevor had his whole fist in her and was licking her clit at the same time... As soon as she come down from her high... Trevor was between her legs rubbing his bell end up and down her soaking wet cunt... Yes it was a cunt... not a pussy... a pussy is beautiful... what she had between her legs was a horrible hairy looking wet cavern... He entered her and she wailed like a wounded animal... then the van was rocking as as he fucked her stupid for the next 15 minutes... I was feeling like I needed to pee so I told Vera I needed to go but she wouldn't stop...

Den then told me,

"She's a dirty slag mate, just do it in her mouth.... go on mate... piss in her mouth..."

She opened her eyes and looked up at me with wide eyes... she pulled my cock out of her mouth... Then aimed it into her wide open mouth while staring into my eyes as if to say.... Come on I'm waiting... do it in my mouth...

I started to let go and she clamped her mouth onto the end and started swallowing and drinking it... I was pissing into her mouth and she never spilled a drop... When I finished she licked her lips and lay back rubbing her pussy over her knickers... She had long skinny legs and wearing black hold up stockings.... I was still hard so I reached down and started to finger her through the leg of her knickers... Then Den was egging me on again saying...

"Go on mate... get in there... give her a good fucking seeing too... "

She pulled the leg of her knickers to one side and I saw her pretty nice looking snatch... well it was 10 x better looking than the whale Trevor was fucking next to us....

I moved forward on my knees between her legs and she reached out for my cock.... I let her aim it into her slit and then plunged in... God it was so warm and wet... we started to fuck as Den started up with his verbal abuse again... He was definitely one of these weird guys who get off on dirty talking as his wife and her mate were being fucked side by side on the mattress in his van...

She was really enjoying it and so was I but we then heard Trevor moaning and slapping Avril's ass... He was on his back and had pulled her on top of him and she was straddling his cock... while he was slapping her ass really hard... she was screaming for him to make her cum and then...

The van doors opened at the back...

Two policemen were smiling and shining their torches into the van...

"OK you lot... if it wasn't for the fact that your inside a van and not visible to the public you'd all be nicked... but as it is... we're letting you off with a warning this time... so get dressed and piss off home OK..."

We were all speechless and I for one, couldn't wait to get away from there... Trevor made his excuse and left within a minute or so and I quickly cleaned myself up with some tissues, put my little leather shorts back on and jumped out of the van.... The policemen didn't say a word but I heard them laughing their fucking heads off as I got in my car to drive away...

I climbed into bed next to Jane and held her beautiful soft breasts and nipples and fell asleep.

I hope you enjoyed this story.

If you like my writing style, and stories about Husband or Wife sharing, Wife watching, BDSM, Cuckold, Swinger and Fetish clubs, Dogging and many other fetishes...

Why not check out my other stories on my Amazon Author page or sign up to my newsletter to get the heads up on all my new releases.

Dante

Authors Website – BLOG - Contact – Comments and Newsletter sign up

www.DantesErotica.uk

I Shared my Wife at the Penthouse Party

First time swingers party

by Dante

Chapter 1

My mate Gary came to visit us in Thailand last week and told us he was invited to a "penthouse party" at Tony's new apartment in Bangkok.

He also told me, my wife Jane and I were invited as we had also met Tony a few times when we used to attend Club Rub and Decadence (Swinger / Fetish clubs) in London. Tony was an older guy in his late 50's and had a few properties in London and was quite well off. He used to go out with this beautiful Japanese girl but then we heard he married a Thai girl and moved to Bangkok, Thailand.

At the club, he was always trying to play with us or more with my wife Jane as he made it obvious he really fancied her and was always hugging, kissing and groping her whenever he saw us.

Gary had told him we also lived in Thailand now, hence the invitation. Now Gary knew him better than us as he had been involved in the club scene for a good few years before he introduced Jane and I. He also told us that Tony used to make Sex party videos in Thailand and I remember coming across one online and recognized Tony immediately. The party was in an apartment with his Thai wife, three more girls, two western guys and a stunning ladyboy. It was a real orgy and he was fucking this ladyboy over a chair while the ladyboy was screaming and his wife was wanking the ladyboy off and encouraging Tony to fuck her/him harder ... It was so funny.

Anyway, we all jumped in a taxi on the Saturday evening to Tony's Penthouse party and when we arrived we were stunned to see it was at the top of really high class apartment building with its own rooftop terrace overlooking the Bangkok skyline. The apartment was absolutely huge and the view was like overlooking down town Hong Kong with all the lights.

Tony was ecstatic to see us all arrive and even more so when he saw Jane was with us. He quickly explained that it was a special themed sex party and guys were to be fully naked and all the girls must wear pantyhose tights only and no bras. They can wear knickers over or under the tights and that was up to the girls.

He introduced us to a few other couples and said that more people would be arriving shortly. He then offered us all a blue cocktail drink from a punch bowl in the kitchen and mentioned that condoms are in bowls in all the rooms and here is a blue pill (viagra) so you don't get the limp after having a drink or two. He then whispered to Gary and me, to make sure the girls all have at least a couple of glasses of the blue cocktail, then laughed and said, it makes them horny as fuck. Jane had started chatting to Tony's wife and another couple of girls and their husbands or boyfriends were standing outside on the terrace admiring the view and having a beer.

"Can I have a beer mate?" I said to Tony just as he was walking away to let some more guests in.

"I would stick to the blue drink and water if I were you", he answered and nudged Gary in the arm.

"What's that all about mate?", I said to Gary.

"No idea, but I fucking love birds in tights, this is gonna be interesting" he answered.

Another 3 couples came in and were introduced and then the intercom buzzer went off again so Tony answered it and let another group enter the lift downstairs. About an hour later and the place was getting full so Tony came round handing all the girls a pack of pantyhose and told them to go and get changed in the bedrooms. Guys can strip off on the terrace and put our clothes in a small store room by the front door.

Jane looked over at me and giggled so I went over and said to her,

“Are you OK babe, we can leave if you’re not feeling comfortable with this?”

“No I want to see what happens and Lek, Tony’s wife said she will look after me.”

Gary smiles at me and winks then nodded to the terrace where 3 of the girls were walking out in just tights and nothing else.

“Fucking hell mate, they look so fucking sexy and this viagra making my cock go up already” Gary said

“Yes me too”

We wandered outside for a better look and the 3 really sexy young Thai girls had joined their partners and were giggling away pointing at all the naked guys sporting hard on’s just like me and Gary.

“Tony sure knows how to set up a party”, I said to Gary.

Gary’s cock is much fatter than mine and we are both about 6 inches in length but because of the girth he looked massive. I looked around and couldn’t see Jane anywhere, so said to Gary, I was going to find her. Then I saw she had just come out the bedroom with Lek and both had their tits exposed and wearing flesh coloured sheer tights.

“Fuck me babe you look so fucking sexy in them”,

then I squeezed her arse and put my arm around her waist. She looks down at my erection and said,

“Why have all the guys got hard on’s already?”

Lek laughed and replied,

“That’s Tony’s Idea, he gives them all a blue pill when they arrive.... (she laughed) Do you want another drink?”

Off they walked to the kitchen and just before I missed my chance, I stroked Lek’s arse and gave it a quick squeeze. There must have been about 30 people in the penthouse now and most were couples but a group of 3 single guys had arrived without their wives and a few girls that did not seem to be with anyone in particular.

The lights were down and people were groping each other in the darkness, then Gary waves me over and I saw he was watching a couple of girls doing a lesbian act with each other in a crowd of people. I tried to squeeze in for a better look and was surrounded by girls in tights with their naked tits pressing into me. I was in heaven and groped several girls and a couple of them even grabbed my cock while their husbands watched the two girls doing the show.

Then I saw this guy sitting on a sofa with his tiny skinny wife. She could only have been just over 4 ft tall and about 45 100lbs, tiny little tits with hard nipples sticking out and sitting there in just her tights. I assumed they were married as she had the gold wedding rings on and she looked like a typical young 18 - 20 year old Go Go dancer. I was starting to feel really hot and strange and realised that there must be something else in the blue cocktail drink. Why was he making everyone have a glass when they arrived!

I sat next to this couple and they had just started kissing each other. He had already made a rip in her tights and had a hand between her legs while pulling her on top of his lap. She had hold of his cock and was wanking it as he was fingering her little pussy from behind. It was such a horny sight, I couldn't help stroking my own cock as I watched.

The guy looked English so I said to him,

"Beautiful little wife you have there mate".

He smiled back and said,

"Yes mate, we met in Phuket 3 months ago and married a week ago, her names Ploy"

The girl looked over at me stroking my cock and smiled then slid down onto her husband's cock then started moaning and staring at me while riding him. He gripped her arse and fucked her hard and fast, then he slowed down and took her hand and moved it onto my cock.

Interesting I thought to myself, so I lay back and watched to see her reaction. She pulled her hand away at first and told him No, but he just kissed her and whispered in her ear and then moved it back onto my cock. This time she didn't pull back so I reached over and cupped one of her little breasts in my hand. She started stroking me, then exploring my cock and balls with her tiny little hands while her husband continued to fuck her slowly on his lap.

I looked around the room to see if Jane was coming back but no sign of her. The girl was really getting worked up as she was getting well fucked next to me then her husband told her to suck my cock. To my amazement she bent down and started sucking me like crazy.

I held her head as it bobbed up and down, then the guy starts pushing her head down hard and she started choking.

"She like it like that", he said to me.

"Do you wanna fuck her?, she's so fucking tight, that's why I married her, she loves fucking... morning till night".

I have no idea what was going on around me now as people were all around us watching us and groping each other. He hands me a rubber and said,

"there you go mate".

His wife was still trying to deep throat me so he pulled her up and said something to her. She pushed herself off his cock and stood up and grabbed the rubber from me. She ripped the pack open and put the rubber in her mouth then knelt down between my legs and put it on my cock using just her tongue and mouth.

I pulled her up and reached down between her legs to feel her soaking wet, tight little cunt and slipped a finger then two inside. God she was tight and his cock was bigger than mine by about another inch and fatter. She knelt over me with her legs either side of mine and aimed my cock straight into her little slit, rubbed it up and down a couple of times then she slid down and it was in... and started grinding up and down in my lap. She looked into my eyes and started running her tongue around her lips making a dirty suggestive gesture then she clamped her lips to mine and forced her tongue in my mouth.

Her husband was fingering her arse while I held her hips and fucked her on my rock hard cock. I couldn't cum yet and suspected it was the viagra or the blue cocktail but my whole body felt alive and tingling. Suddenly the lights came on and I heard Tony telling everyone to come out into the open air terrace.

He told all the girls to line up and face the city lights holding on to the chrome rail on top of the glass balcony wall. About 12 girls all in tights were standing there as Tony approached holding his massive cock. I'd never seen his cock before but it must have been the biggest in the room tonight, at least 10 inches with a big cock ring in the end.

I saw Jane and she came over and said to me,

"I saw you fucking that skinny Go Go slut back there!"

"Oh babe, he made me do it, they've only been married a week."

She laughed and said,

"It really turned me on watching you fuck her. Do you feel all weird and horny?"

"Yes babe, it's the blue drink I think."

"Oh My God... I've been drinking it all night and I keep seeing colours and lights flashing and people talking to me but my mind is somewhere else..."

"Whoa babe, better not drink any more, you look well out of it, come and sit with me over there."

Just then, Tony and his wife grab her arms and said,

"Oh No, not yet, we have to do the girls in tights line up first."

Jane just let's them walk her over to the other girls and she stands in line. Some of the girls still had knickers on over the tights and were covering their tits with their arms some had ripped tights and looked like they had already been well fucked.

Chapter 2

Tony tells the guys to stand behind the girls, but not your wife or girlfriend. He then gives all the guys a rubber and tells them they can fuck the girls... or if they don't want to be fucked... they can suck you off.

Jane collapses on the floor, so I run over to help her up. Lek and I take her back inside.... she said she felt all weird. I saw that Lek was groping her tits as we brought her inside and then she was rubbing herself as if she wanted to cum. Gary came over and asked if she was OK, then told us there are 3 stunning lady-boys getting fucked on the terrace.

"Are you OK with Lek for 10 minutes babe, I got to see this?"

She nods and smiles, so Gary and I went back outside. These 3 ladyboys were like models with long hair, big beautiful tits and tall with long legs and smooth bodies. They were even more attractive than many of the girls there tonight!

One was being fucked by a guy while standing at the rail with her tights and knickers pulled down around her knees, while the other two were in a 69 on a wooden padded sun-bed, with the crotches torn out of their tights and their cocks exposed while we all watched. Several other girls were also being fucked at the rail but the centre of attraction was the ladyboys.

One guy stepped forward holding his very impressive cock and mounted the ladyboy on top, on the sunbed. The one underneath was sucking her friends cock as the guy entered her arse above. Another guy stepped forward and was reaching between them and playing with their tits and another guy was making his girlfriend wank him right next to me as we all watched.

She then grabbed my cock and started wanking us both together. So I started groping his girlfriends tits and then I could see he wanted me to fuck her so he stood behind her holding her tits and pushed his hand down inside her tights and fingered her in front of me. She was facing me so I rubbed her legs and tits and then peeled her tights down to her knees. She stood there with her legs open and just let me finger her while her husband played with her tits from behind.

Then he turned her around and told me to fuck her while he kissed her on the mouth and held her tight. Just as I was about to slide inside, I saw Lek and Tony holding Jane's hands leading her I assumed, back to the kitchen. I managed to get away from this couple after about 15 minutes of playing when another couple started playing with them, so I started looking for Jane again.

I searched everywhere but Jane, Lek or Tony were nowhere to be seen... A good hour must have passed and I was asking people if they knew where Lek or Tony was? Then I saw Tony at the other side of the room., so I made my way over and asked where Jane was?

He just said, "She wanted to lay down so we took her to our bedroom, Lek is still with her I think, last door down the hallway or you can get in through the glass door on the terrace".

As we were next to the terrace, I walked outside and saw a large group watching something going on and quickly realised they were looking into Tony's bedroom.

I pushed through and the door was wide open, about 5 more couples were inside all watching Jane getting fucked by a big fat German guy. He was laying behind her, holding her leg up and fucking her from behind. Lek was kneeling on the bed snogging her face and playing with her tits. Another girl, the Fat Germans wife I think, was pulling Lek's tights down and licking her arse and pussy from behind.

Gary was in the room as well and was smiling at me as two girls were kneeling down taking turns trying to suck and deep throat his cock. I had to get over to Jane and see if she was OK, so pushed through. Gary leans over and told the fat German guy I was Jane's husband and he just laughed and said,

"She is so good yes ... Tony fucked her first and then said we can all have a go yes!"

I couldn't believe what the fat cunt was saying, but I was so aroused at everything going on around me, I couldn't help but smile and let him carry on.

Jane saw me sitting on the bed so I held her hand as the German guy was still pounding away then Tony appeared again and asked me if I had fucked Lek yet?

"Not yet mate", I replied

So he told Lek to come over to me as he motioned for the fat German guy to get up and Tony slid in where the German guy was behind Jane. Lek sat next to me and started wanking my cock, so I just lay back next to Jane and watched as Tony was getting ready to fuck Jane again from behind.

Lek then said to me,

"He wants you to see him fuck your wife and he told me, I have to let you have me, so lay down and let me get on top of you."

Jane was just laying there as Tony's massive cock entered her again and she started rubbing her own pussy and saying

"Good babe, Fuck her while Tony fucks me. His cock feels so big babe, he made me come twice before and now I want to come again but see you fucking his wife."

The bed was heaving and 3 couples were now fucking on the bed and more standing up fucking and watching. Jane started to come again and was rubbing herself like crazy as he held her leg up showing the crowd his cock sliding in and out of my wife's pussy. Lek leaned over me and started snogging Jane as she started coming and took over rubbing her clit until she calmed down and Tony pulled out.

On the way home we were hugging and groping each other and Jane told me Tony had fucked her at least 4 times that evening and one of his friends had also had her in the bathroom while she was trying to get cleaned up to come and find me... I asked her about the German guy and she said, Tony asked him to do it because he wanted to watch.

"So you just let the fat German guy take you while Tony watched?"

"Yes babe, I was feeling so horny and I needed another cock in me after him, I felt so hot and Lek told him to do it too. She was licking my pussy after Tony cum inside me and she was helping him and holding my legs open."

"What! You let Tony come inside you? Your pussy is still gaping babe and come is leaking out all over my hands and the seat. God I need to fuck you as soon as we get inside..."

The taxi driver must have been getting a real good show as I was virtually fisting Jane in the back seat and she was moaning so loud... When we got back to our place, we jumped in bed and lay there talking and playing for hours before eventually falling asleep in a 69 position with her on top of me.

I hope you enjoyed this story.

If you like my writing style, and stories about Husband or Wife sharing, Wife watching, BDSM, Cuckold, Swinger and Fetish clubs, Dogging and many other fetishes...

Why not check out my other stories on Amazon and sign up to my newsletter to get the heads up on all my new releases.

Dante X

Authors Website – Contact and Newsletter sign up

www.DantesErotica.uk

Tattoo Girl

Sexual Ecstasy, Fetish Club and Car Park Fun

By Dante

Contents

Introduction
Chapter 1 – Arousal
Chapter 2 – Tattoo Girl
Chapter 3 - Tatainia meets Jane
Chapter 4 – Fun in the afternoon
Chapter 5 - Webcam fun
Chapter 6 - Dogging at Whipsnade
Chapter 7 - Dogboy
Chapter 8 - Tatainia

Introduction

I usually go for a walk into town most days for a bit of exercise and to get out of the house, and there are several quite attractive MILF's and girls I see often, but there is one in particular that I really fancied and whom this story is all about.

Sometimes she has a couple of young kids with her, one about 4 years and a 1 year old and sometimes she is alone. She's quite tall and looks like she come from Russia or Eastern Europe, has short blond hair, but that changes a lot as she's always reinventing her look with different hair colours and styles.

Anyway, we do sort of fancy each other as I've caught her smiling to herself several times when our paths cross in the town. And on this particular occasion, I was in a health food shop and when I walked over to the till, she was in the queue directly in front of me. She hadn't seen me come in the shop and it was quite funny, because when she turned around, I was literally so close, she looked really surprised, so I just smiled... and as she was clearly embarrassed, I couldn't help noticing her smiling to herself as she turned away. We'd never spoken up to this point as she'd also seen me with my wife in town and I in turn had seen her with her husband and kids.

So, as I stood behind her in the queue, I noticed she had a barcode type tattoo on the back or her neck, and it made me think that she had at some point in the past, been a hooker or had an interesting underworld past in Russia or whatever country she came from. She was as tall as me, about 5' 10" and medium build but had really nice, sexy long legs and used to always dress up in a sexy outfit and wear fishnet tights like she was wearing today.

Chapter 1

Arousal

At the weekend, my wife Jane and I had decided to go to Arousal, the local swinger and fetish club in Dunstable, and on this particular evening, it was good because it was a couples only night and very limited single guys.

So when we arrived at about 10.30 pm, there were probably 20 couples and about 10 guys were wandering around, and then I saw her... she was sitting in the chill out area in a corner near the bar. It was the girl with the tattoo on her neck, with whom I assumed was her husband. She immediately saw me and was clearly embarrassed, but as we caught each other's eyes, I saw her smiling to herself as she quickly looked away.

Throughout the evening I kept looking out for her and hoped I could watch her playing in one of the rooms with another couple or some guys.

Jane is from the Philippines and was dressed in a short black skirt, hold up black stockings and a tiny black G-string. The tattoo girl was wearing a sort of one piece white swim suit, but her breasts were exposed and each time we passed in the club she looked shy and embarrassed. Her husband was leading her around by the hand, and I think they were fairly new to the scene as they didn't seem to engage with anyone, they were just watching and wandering around from room to room.

Jane and I were also fairly new to the scene and had only been attending the clubs for about 8 months or so, and back then, hadn't tried full swapping but we did let couples and the occasional guys touch and soft play with us and we'd had some very interesting group sessions.

I found myself following tattoo girl and her husband around and tried to get as close to her as possible, but this time they went into the cinema room and sat on a long sofa against the wall at the side of the room near the back. I stood with Jane in the doorway and watched as her partner started to play with her tits and moved her hand onto his cock. She immediately looked over at me, sort of embarrassed again as she knew I was watching her.

I then suggested to Jane we sit down for a while and went straight over to the sofa and sat next to the tattoo girl. She pretended not to know me, as I did also, being with our respective partners.

It wasn't long before Jane and I started to play as we watched the movie on the big screen, but it was a bit of a tight fit as there was another couple on Jane's other side that were also squeezed on the sofa. The twenty something girl was laying back against Jane and her boyfriend was kneeling on the floor with his head between her legs. Jane was far more interested in watching them than the hard core movie and I could see she was getting really turned on, so I ran my hand up and down her leg and started to finger her. Jane parted her legs to give me easier access, then reached over to undo my zip and expose my cock, I was wearing a pair of tight black leather shorts, so she pulled me out and started to play with it while we watched the couple next to her.

The tattoo girl was so close, that our arms and legs kept touching and I was moving my own leg closer to hers as Jane started stroking my rapidly growing erection. The tattoo girl was staring intently as Jane released my cock so I turned and looked directly at her, but her eyes were transfixed on my erection that Jane was now wanking with her tiny hands.

Tattoo girl was also playing with her husbands cock and he was fondling her tits, so I parted my legs a little more... so as my leg touched hers and to my surprise, she didn't move away. Fuck me, I was feeling so horny and it was electric as we touched as we'd never spoken before, but we both sort of knew, and dare I say, fancied each other from seeing each other often the town. And here we were, sitting next to each other, with her watching Jane stroking my cock and me watching her do the same to her husband as he was caressing her very nicely shaped tits.

It was quite dark and I moved my hand so it was resting on my thigh, but the back of my hand was also touching her thigh. As she lay back, I could see her nipples were really hard and her husband had put his hand on her other thigh, stroking and caressing her inner thigh and delving down between her legs. She nervously looked up at me, so I smiled back as he pushed a finger inside her, making her press her leg even more against mine...! I pushed back and we were as close as we could ever be, both playing with our unsuspecting partners. But Jane was now being touched on the leg by the guy licking out his girlfriend next to her, letting him caress her thigh and then looked over at me as I was caressing her other leg.

God it was turning me on so much, I slid my hand down between her legs and pulled her G-string to the side, giving the guy on the floor a perfect view of her beautiful smooth and newly shaved pussy. Jane covered it quickly with her hand but I moved her hand back onto my cock and whispered... to let him play.

The tattoo girl on my other side was now being fingered quite seriously by her husband and she'd turned her body so her exposed breast was pressing into my arm. Fucking hell, I really wanted to have a proper feel of her beautiful tits but her husband seemed like he was the really jealous type and not into playing with other couples. So I just pressed my arm back into her, rubbing up and down, slowly teasing her nipple so as he couldn't see. Surprisingly, she responded by pressing herself into my arm even more...! This went on for a few minutes and then I saw her start to tremble... she was cumming as her husband was still frigging away at her pussy... and I was rubbing her nipple with my arm...!

Fuck me, it was so naughty and sexy and after she'd calmed down, they were both watching Jane getting fingered by the guy on the floor and his girlfriend was kissing Jane on the mouth.

Jane was laying back now and I could see tattoo girl on my other side watching Jane's hand holding and squeezing my cock, so I also lay back so as she could get a better look. Jane was getting well excited and about to cum, and when the girl snogging her pushed her hand between Jane's legs as well, Jane let out a long moan and started jerking, she squeezed my cock so bloody hard that I had to grab her as it was so painful.

Another five minutes passed and the tattoo girl and her husband got up and left the cinema room, so I suggested to Jane we have a walk about and get another drink. Off we went and I was looking around trying to see where the tattoo girl and her husband were going, but I lost them in the crowd. We ended up in the bar area again, so I bought a couple of drinks and then saw them again on the other side of the room, they were in a group of people crowding around a girl getting groped by several guys while she was sucking off a guy in front of her as her partner was fingering her.

The tattoo girl and husband were watching the action and I saw a couple of guys try to touch her, but her husband said something to them and they backed off.

The husband then led her away by her hand and she caught me staring at her again and saw that inward smile to herself yet again. A while later, we walked into a dark play area and I saw them again, but this time they were looking through a shoulder high viewing window. The window looked into another room where there was a huge rubber coated mattress in a separate play room. It was about 4 meters square and had 3 couples on it, all fucking and touching each other.

I immediately stood next to her with Jane on my left and we were all watching the couples play through the window. The room behind us was nearly pitch black and there were various cubby holes with mattresses inside where couples were playing and guys trying to get in on the action.

I started to edge closer to the tattoo girl and I could see she was smiling to herself again... Jane had my cock out again and I had a hand behind her legs at the back fingering her as we watched the action in the other room. Tattoo girl was now pressing her tit into my arm again as her husband on the other side of her couldn't see. I rubbed my arm against her nipple again and saw her shiver with my secret touch... then moved my hand around her back and just stroked her back and the top of her hips, just to see her reaction. She sort of shivered but didn't move my hand away, so I went lower and gave her butt a quick squeeze.

I sensed she liked it... so ran my hand around to my side and gently stroked her thigh and then pressed my arm into her tit again.

Jane was getting really wet with my fingering but told me she needed the rest room, so I said I'd wait there as the rest room was literally just next door. As soon as she left, I placed my hand back on tattoo girl's butt and this time caressed it for a while longer to see her reaction... I love touching girls butts, especially the soft area at the top off the thighs just under the buttocks. As I slid my hand down, I noticed her husband was still staring through the window, so I pushed my hand more daringly between her legs from the back and to my amazement... felt her part her legs a little bit more... so as I could feel her more intimately.

Fuck me, what I was doing was so risqué, fingering her from behind with her husband right next to her... She turned and pressed her tits into my arm even more, I really wanted to caress them and suck her amazing erect nipples, she was obviously turned on and getting very wet, as her fluids were running down my fingers. I pulled my hand away and moved it up to my mouth... she was looking directly at me so I put my fingers in my mouth and sucked them clean. Staring with her mouth open in surprise, I slipped my hand back down, cupping her soft quivering bottom, then went back in between her legs.

Reaching out for her arm with my other hand, I slowly moved her hand onto my cock, she was a bit reluctant at first and pulled away... obviously scared in case her husband saw anything, but as it was so dark and that I was standing more or less to the side and behind her, it was virtually impossible for him to see, so I stepped back a little, so I was out of sight of her husband, tugged her hand again and placed it back on my hard cock. This time she didn't pull away and held it, then started to squeeze and explore, reaching down to rub my balls and then stroking me very slowly... obviously so he didn't notice what she was doing. She turned her head and looked me in the eye, then raised her eyebrows... giving me a questioning look that was meant to ask "where is your wife...?"

I smiled and nodded towards the doorway... she looked a bit apprehensive but was still holding my cock. I had two fingers inside her and nobody could see, and her husband was still looking through the window. I then realised that Jane would be back any minute, so I eased my fingers out and back in again but with one in her pussy and the other in her butt... That was all it took to sent her over the edge and she started shaking... I'm pretty sure, she squirted on the floor and as her husband turned around, she pretended to want to go to the loo and they quickly left the viewing room.

Jane appeared soon after so we went for a wander around to find some more action in the club. About an hour later, I saw the tattoo girl and her husband in another small play room where he had her bent over a horse box whilst her hands were tied down. He was behind her and trying out various whips and paddles on her lovely smooth bottom, a group of single guys had crowded around and were watching. I managed to push through and manoeuvred Jane near the front of the horse box... so as the tattoo girls head was directly in front of us. She looked up shocked to see me again... and as she did so... Jane had already pulled my cock out and was wanking it... this time directly in front of the tattoo girls head. Smiling at the tattoo girl, I placed my hand behind Jane and started to finger her from the back... just like I was doing to the tattoo girl earlier, so she could see what I was doing to Jane.

I knew how to make Jane squirt but needed some more stimulation to make her cum. A couple of guys were also standing behind us and were watching me finger Jane, so I motioned to one of them that he could touch her if he wanted, and soon he was caressing one of her breasts from the other side, then I let the other guy take my place with his hand between Jane's legs at the back. I moved my hand to the front, so the 3 of us were playing with Jane and the tattoo girl was watching Jane wank my cock just a few inches from her face.

I knew Jane was about ready to orgasm as she was squeezing my cock a bit too hard... she always does that when about to cum. I pushed two fingers deep into her pussy and started to finger her hard and fast to make her cum and hopefully squirt. The guy at the back was now wanking his cock and rubbing it on Jane's butt... the other guy was doing the same but now caressing and sucking on Jane's left nipple. I kept up the frigging and all of a sudden she moaned out loud and cum with a massive squirt. I kept my hand there as it gushing and streaming down her legs just to the side of the tattoo girls head. I was also ready to cum and Jane kept squeezing and pulling my cock until I just couldn't hold back any more. Tattoo girls face was directly in front of me and as a spurt of my sperm hit her directly on the cheek. She was staring up at me open mouthed as if to say... "what the fuck was I doing...!" I so wanted to put my cock in her mouth but Jane had let go of my cock and was gripping my arm holding herself up as the two guys were still working on her. So I moved forward a bit and as we turned to leave, I made sure my cock touched tattoo girls face.

I was sure I felt her tongue licking my cock head as I moved close to her face and then saw her licking her lips as we walked away.

When I looked back again, I saw tattoo girls husband had pulled her swimsuit aside and had her pussy exposed. Jane wanted to see, so we moved around behind them for a better view. Guys were wanking all around and he was fingering her arse with gel and looked like, he was trying to get his fist in her. She was unable to stop him as she was still tied down and although several guys tried to touch her and offer their cocks to her mouth, he was not letting anyone near her. He managed to get 4 fingers in, then made her cum in front of us all, trembling and shaking as she was tied to the horsebox.

The evening ended a while later and we went to get our coats to drive home. On the way, Jane mentioned to me about the guy with the tattoo girl and how they didn't want to play with anyone...!

I said I'd noticed and that they must have been newbies and maybe next time they would play a bit more then asked her if she liked the look of them.

Jane said she did, and that the girl had smiled at her a few times, like she wanted to be friends. So I told Jane, I'd seen her before in the town and we could try to chat to them if we ever saw them in the club again.

Chapter 2

Tattoo Girl

A week goes by and who do I end up bumping into in the queue at Tesco... the tattoo girl. She was in front of me and wearing a short stylish white leather jacket, knee length skirt and flesh coloured tights with high heeled shoes.. She saw me and looked really embarrassed, so I just leaned forward and whispered in her ear...
"Nice legs...!"

She looked back at me, smiled and then said,

"Thank you."

"You're not from here are you, where are you from...?" I asked

She was silent for a moment then answered,

"I from Odesa in Ukraine"

"I see... so that's why you look kind of Asian...so have you been to the club in Dunstable before then...?"

"No... our first time," she replied in her broken English.

"Well, my names Dave and my wife is Jane."

I didn't want to come across as trying to pick her up, so told her my wife's name. She smiled but didn't answer as she was about to get served, so I quickly asked,

"Would you like a lift home with your shopping...?"

I knew she always walked to the town centre and back as I'd seen her many times walking up or down the hill.

She said, OK and then waited for me to finish paying for my own groceries, then we were walking along on our way to the car park. I was thinking to myself, fucking hell this is a bit weird, we are alone and on my way to the car park.

"So what's your name then...?" I asked.

"Tatainia.

"And where are your kids today...?"

"Oh my friend... she take to nursery with her kids and tomorrow I do for her, so get free time... for shop... without kids run around."

She then asked me,

"So what you do... I see you many time driving when I on way home...?"

I told her, I had a couple of internet businesses and like to get out in the day-times for a while. We arrived at the car and I put all the bags in the back, we jumped in and drove to exit.

"So where do you live...?" I asked.

"I think you know... you always see me walk near my home...!"

"Yes, but I don't know exactly."

"I show you", she answered.

On the way I asked her,

"So what does your husband do...?"

"He work for computer company... in London."

"And did you enjoy the club the other night...?"

She looked at me all embarrassed and said,

"Of course... and I like when you touch me in dark room next to husband."

"Really...!" I exclaimed.

"Yes... you make me crazy and I cum... he nearly catch you with finger in me. He very strict... he crazy man and no let anyone touch me."

As we approached her road, she said,

"I live in house on corner but you cannot come in house with me, my friend live two house away... will see you... go to back of house... I open gate."

I had that feeling... this was going to be a very interesting afternoon, I stopped the car and she opened the back to get her shopping, then walked the rest of the way. I drove ahead and went around the back to the garages area. A few minutes later, she opened a gate and waved me over so I jumped out and followed her through the back garden and into the house.

The door led into the kitchen so as soon as we were inside I asked,

"What about your children...?"

"They home at 3.30."

"And how are you feeling now...?" I asked as she was looking increasingly nervous.

"Scared...!"she answered.

"Why... because of what happened in the club the other night...?"

"Your wife... she know...?"

"No... she's OK with us playing, but I didn't want her to see me touching you...!"

She smiled and I pulled her towards me, her jacket was open and I put an arm around her waist, kissing her on the mouth. She responded straight away by grabbing my cock through my jeans, so I slid my hand down between her legs whilst still snogging her and felt she was wearing tights. God she was so hot and sexy, I could feel the heat from her pussy as I rubbed the gusset over her knickers. Moaning into my mouth, I continued exploring between her legs when suddenly she broke the kiss and dropped to her knees, easing my zip down and pulled my erect cock out. She started licking and sucking and one hand was cupping my balls, caressing and then squeezing them really hard.

God she was so fucking horny... then she looked up at me and said,

"Why you cum on my face in club...?"

"Because you looked so beautiful in front of me and I wanted to put it in your mouth... but my wife was standing next to me and I don't think your husband would have let me."

"Of course.. he very possessive and no let anyone touch me"

She was trying to get my cock down her throat and I remember thinking, this was like an unbelievable fantasy coming true...

Grabbing her head I pulled her off me saying,

"Please stop you're gonna make me cum...!"

She giggled as I helped her up, then put my hand back between her legs and started to feel her pussy through the tights and knickers again. She started snogging me and I somehow got my hand into the top of the tights and was now going down into her knickers and fingering her wet slit. One finger at first... then two and then I pulled her dress up at the back and pushed my other hand down the tights from the back, trying to reach her anus. Easing the tip of my finger in she squirmed and sighed into my mouth.

"Fuck me.... you're so fucking sexy Tatainia... Get undressed."

She pulled away and went to close the curtains, then peeled off her jacket and white blouse then unhooked her bra... Her beautiful white and shapely 34B tits were released, standing there in just her tights and knickers I said,

"No leave them on for a while, I really love tights."

She kneels on the sofa, looking over her shoulder and looks me in the eyes, her hand was inside her tights, fingering herself while looking back at me. I stripped my jeans, pants and shirt off and walked to the sofa. My cock was sticking out like a flag pole and she must have had a couple of fingers inside herself, moaning and sighing as she pushed her butt out. She looked so fucking sexy, I bounced my cock on her sexy tights covered butt a few times and rubbed between her legs with my hand again. Then I slowly pulled her tights down to expose her beautiful tight arse and shaved pussy. Easing them down to her knees, I parted her cheeks to watch her fingering herself.

Then got down on my knees and held her cheeks apart while I started to lick her anus and sexy smooth slit from the back. I nearly made her cum with my tongue and fingers, but slowed down and then kneeled up and started to rub the head of my cock up and down her slit. Reaching down between her legs, she grabbed hold of my cock and pulled me straight into her pussy. It slid in and we started to fuck... What an amazing tight pussy, I fingered her arse while we were fucking which sent her wild... then pulled out and placed the head to her anus and slowly started to push in.

It slipped in no problem so I asked,

"So you like it in your butt then...?"

"My husband like... he try to get hand in... all...!"

"Really...!" I exclaimed.

I pulled out and pushed a two fingers in, they slipped in quite easily so I tried four and again, it was really easy, next I curled my fingers up and pushed my whole fist in and she started to moan... Reaching round she pulled my arm back and forth so as to fist fuck her arse.

It was incredible and she must have cum a couple of times as we were doing that for a good while, when all of a sudden, there was banging at the front door.

"OH NO... my friend.... come with kids... quick.... you go back door...!"

I quickly got dressed and before I slipped out to my car through the back garden I asked her,

"When are you going to the club next...?"

"My husband may go again... but he not want play... but he away business with job.... next week for 3 days. Can I come club with you and you wife...?"

"Well, I would love to... if I can somehow find a way to get you and my wife to become friends...!"

"Please Dave..." she said and I was out the door.

Chapter 3

Tatainia meets Jane

When I picked Jane up from her friends house later that evening, I mentioned to her I'd seen the girl with a tattoo on her neck from the club in town and she'd recognized me. I told her she was from Odesa in the Ukraine, had 2 kids and that it was her husband she was with that evening in the club. I also told Jane she wanted to be friends with us as her husband was a bit possessive, and asked if she could come to the club with us as he was working away next week.

Jane seemed a bit apprehensive and asked,

"How do you know all this...?"

"Because I was in Tesco and we started chatting in the queue."

I then suggested to Jane,

"Why don't we invite her round for a friendly chat, so we can get to know her a bit better... then if you like her and get on OK... maybe we could take her with us to the club next week."

Jane said she'd like to find out more about her, so I told her I'd ask her to come round on Saturday if she could get a babysitter. I rang her in front of Jane and told her,

"Hi Tatainia... I've told Jane about your situation and she said she'd love to meet up on Saturday if you're available...?"

Tatainia replied saying she would call us back tomorrow if she could arrange a babysitter.

That evening in bed, Jane was asking more questions about her, so I started recounting about what happened in the club last week, and how she was watching us play while sitting right next to us, and that her husband wouldn't let anyone touch her... Then as we made love, I got Jane to remember how we watched her cum while her husband was fingering her in the play room, and then fisting her in her arse when she was tied to the horsebox... This made Jane orgasm really quickly, so I continued talking about how we could play with her, if we took her with us to the club as a threesome without her husband.

"So do you want to do it with her then...?"

"Well babe, I would if you wanted me to but I don't care so much about fucking her as I get more turned on by seeing you and her play together... and if I could join in that would be even more fun... and having you both with me in the club would be amazing."

"Yes, I'm sure you would... and I bet you'd like her to play with your cock like I did with your friend Gary that time when his wife wasn't with him...!"

"Would you like to see her playing with my cock then...? I think that would really turn you on wouldn't it...?"

"I don't know... maybe... I'm not sure... maybe I'd get jealous but if I'm there as well... yes... I think it would be fun... do you love me babe...?"

"Of course Jane, I love you very much and you know I only want us to play together and I think you agree... it sure makes our sex life more exciting."

"Yes babe I understand and I really liked it when you and Gary were playing with me together... and when I was playing with both your cocks together in that dark room... His cock was so fat and he wanted to put it in me when I was sitting on his lap... but... you know... we agreed not to go all the way back then. I wonder if she likes taking the E's...?"

"Maybe you can find out on Saturday... What do you think

babe, should we all go out somewhere or stay at home and just... well you know... have a drink or if she does like the sweets...?"

Jane was nearing another orgasm, so I whispered in her ear about how I felt Tatainia's tits pressing against my arm while we let the other couple kiss and finger her in the club last week... This sent her over the edge, so I kissed her deeply and eased off rubbing her clit until her orgasm subsided.

Jane seemed really keen about meeting Tatainia and when Saturday arrived, she'd bought some wine and even got all dressed up in her new leather skirt and top that showed off her sexy tits in a low cut white bra. We thought she wasn't coming as we had arranged to meet at 10 am and by 10.30 we were thinking, maybe her husband was home or whatever.

Tatainia arrived at 11 am in a taxi, all apologetic and telling us her babysitter was late but everything was OK now and her husband was at a meeting with his work friend in London, so she was free till the evening.

Jane and Tatainia hit it off immediately and were chatting and giggling away with each other in the kitchen. I thought it best to let Jane spend some one on one time with her and get to know her a bit more. After an hour or so, they asked me if I wanted to go for a drive or would I prefer to open a bottle of wine and stay home?

I responded by saying, "I'd rather have some sweets...!"

Jane laughed and said to Tatainia,

"He loves ecstasy and we usually take them when we go to club but they're also nice when we're relaxing at home or walking in the countryside. Have you guys ever tried them...?"

Tatainia seemed a bit shy and asked Jane,

"What are they...? I never try before."

Jane told her they just make you feel really relaxed and makes your skin feels all tingly... and when someone touches you, it's like it feels more sensitive... and if your in the club, you feel all horny, especially when watching people play.

She told us her husband and was far too controlling and didn't think he would approve but she would love to try one.

"Tell you what girls, why don't we let Tatainia try one with us, were all nice and safe here at home, and then later, if you both feel like it, we can go out for a drive... maybe find a few doggers to watch."

They both burst into giggles and started chatting about things they saw couples doing in the club again.

Jane then said,

"Go on then, go get some so Tatainia can try."

Chapter 4

Fun in the afternoon

I left the room and let them chat while I went into the kitchen and returned with some coffee... I didn't want to open the wine in case we went for a drive later.

Tatainia seemed to be asking a lot of questions about us, and how long we'd been going to the club in Dunstable. I told her we'd been going to various clubs for about eight months and the clubs in London were much better with lots of good looking couples and always very busy. Whereas Arousal in Dunstable was a bit hit and miss, sometimes it was busy and other times it would be empty or full of single guys with only 2 or 3 couples, and we would end up coming home early as nothing much was going on.

I then asked her about her husband and how they got involved in the clubbing scene, so she told us, her husband had heard about Arousal from a friend at his company and he wanted to try it out last week.

"So that was your first time to a sexy fetish swinger club then Tatainia...?" I asked.

"Yes, but he say he no like many man try touch me and you know... they want join in... but he like them look at us and he look other couples... he say he want go again."

"But what about you Tatainia, did you like the idea of being touched or whatever, without him knowing...?"

She looked me directly in the eyes and smiled... she knew exactly what I meant, as I'd fingered her in the dark viewing room while her husband was watching through the glass window and Jane was in the rest room last week.

Tatainia replied,

"Yes, I saw lot couples play and we even watch you two... You let man and girl kiss and finger Jane, when we sit next you in movie room... I very turn on."

"Well maybe you should try a couples only night," I suggested.

Then I asked Jane if she fancied putting some clubbing music on as we'd taken the E's about half an hour previously and they'd be taking effect soon. I wanted to create a nice atmosphere as Jane was looking really sexy in her new black leather skirt and bare legs. Tatainia was wearing a mid thigh dark blue dress with an open back, tights, and it looked like she wasn't wearing a bra and her hair had been restyled quite short making the tattoo on her neck clearly visible.

About an hour and a quarter had passed and I was feeling the ecstasy kicking in with the warm tingly waves of pleasure creeping up my back, so I asked Tatainia how she felt...?

She had this big smile on her face and Jane was sitting next to her on the sofa holding her hand and stroking her arm. Jane started giggling and whispered something to Tatainia.

"What's going on with you two...?"

"Nothing...!" Jane answered... more giggling...

"Why don't you put a sexy movie on...?" Jane said.

"Really...! You want me to...? What do you say Tatainia...?"

"I OK... Yes I want."

I couldn't believe it... but quickly logged on to Xhamster and picked a threesome movie, plugged the HDMI lead into the TV then sat back in my chair. The movie started so I asked Tatainia again if she felt OK...?

She said she felt really nice, all warm and relaxed and Jane was still holding her hand. As the movie started, I was watching

Jane and Tatainia and I was pretty sure, after several clubbing experiences that Jane was bisexual. In my experience, I've found that many Asians seem to swing both ways. We'd had quite a few sessions in the clubs and Jane never stopped a girl touching of kissing her, in fact it seemed to make her even more horny.

Jane then told me,

"You can stay over there and just watch babe... Play with your cock if you want," she laughed teasingly.

They both burst into a giggling fit and were hugging each other.

So we all started watching the movie. It was quite good with a guy getting blown by two women. Jane and Tatainia were stroking each others arms and then to my surprise...they were kissing.

What a sight, they were snogging away like a couple of new lovers and Jane was stroking Tatainia's arm. Then she held her face with both hands before moving her hand onto Tatainia's breast. This continued for about 5 minutes as they both explored each others mouths and breasts.

I was already rock hard and decided to open my jeans and get the old John Thomas out. They were occasionally looking over at me, then the movie, and then back to playing with each other, copying the action of the two girls on screen. Jane saw me slowly stroking my cock so smiled and went back to snogging Tatainia.

Jane had placed her hand on Tatainia's leg and was rubbing her thigh over her tights and under her dress. Tatainia broke the kiss and looked over at me slowly stroking my exposed cock, then parted her legs giving me a lovely view up her skirt. Jane's hand was up between her legs and rubbing her pantyhose covered pussy as Tatainia moaned that she felt really nice and was feeling all shivery as the waves of pleasure swept up and down her back. Jane told her she felt the same, and snuggled up to her as they started snogging again.

It was the most incredible and horny thing to watch, the

movie was in full swing with a guy laying on the floor as his wife was riding his cock and her friend was straddling his face.

Tatainia was laying back on the sofa and Jane had pushed her dress up to her waist, her long legs were parted wide as Jane rubbed her pussy, then she was pushing her hand inside her pantyhose and knickers still snogging her face.

Jane was still dressed, but her tits were exposed and Tatainia was fondling them. Then I saw Tatainia put her hand down between Jane's legs and feel her pussy, I couldn't see much but was sure Jane was being fingered, just like she was doing to Tatainia.

The effects of the E's was quite strong now and I felt hot waves and an amazing feeling of euphoria and god I was so fucking horny, my cock was ultra sensitive so I stood up and went to get some gel lubricant.

On my return, Jane had taken her skirt, bra and blouse off and was kneeling on the floor in just her knickers. Tatainia had her pantyhose and knickers pulled down and out of one leg but they were still on her other leg, hanging around her knee and Jane was between them kissing and licking away at her pussy.

As I stood over them holding my cock, Jane stopped licking and looked up.

"Go back to your chair babe... Yes put some gel on your cock and let Tatainia watch you play with it."

Tatainia was laying back with her eyes closed, moaning and sighing while holding Jane's head with both hands. I could tell by her facial expressions, the ecstasy was clearly making her feel really relaxed and horny and enjoying what Jane was doing.

I stripped off the rest of my clothes then sat back down, opened the gel and rubbed it all over my cock and balls. Jane had started fingering Tatainia and her moans were getting louder, Jane was pushing in and out and turned to me all excited and told me she had four fingers inside her and to bring over the gel.

I was over there in a flash, kneeling behind Jane, I opened the gel and offered it to her hand, she rubbed it all over her fingers and pushed back in. Tatainia opened her eyes and looked down as Jane eased all her fingers and then her thumb into her pussy. Tatainia's eyes were wide as she said,

"Oooohhhh It feel so good... Oooohhh please no stop... I no do this before but it feel so nice."

I ran my hand down Jane's back and over her butt, then down between her legs. My fingers were all slimy and covered in gel as I pushed one then two up Jane's knickers leg into her pussy.

Jane's whole hand was inside Tatainia and slowly moving in and out so I reached over with my other hand and had a feel of Tatainia's tits which were still inside her dress, but her nipples were clearly poking through the fabric. They felt so soft and natural that I wanted to suck on her nipples but it was impossible with her dress on.

Jane told me to get behind her and put my cock in, so I got in position and entered her from behind, pulling her knickers to the side, staring down at Tatainia's beautiful, naked, hairless pussy. Reaching forward I started stroking her clit with my thumb as Jane's hand was going deeper and faster.

Suddenly, Tatainia arched her back moaning and trembling, she had a huge orgasm and was jerking on the sofa as we both stared down at her. Jane kept easing her hand in and out slowly... then Tatainia started squirting...! It was incredible and going all over Jane, so I held my hand over the flow and rubbed her clit faster making her cum a second time as she jerked and trembled for a good 30 seconds before calming down.

My cock was still inside Jane and I kept pumping in and out slowly, but I could sense that Jane was also about to cum, so I moved my hand from Tatainia to Jane's clit and rubbed it faster, pushing my cock in deeper with each thrust until she moaned and collapsed on top of Tatainia.

As I pulled out, I held Jane's tits from behind, her nipples were like little sultanas and Tatainia was laying back watching me and smiling.

I asked her if she enjoyed having sex on the ecstasy and she sort of moaned while saying,

"Oh God... It amazing... I never feel that when cum before and so sorry for carpet all wet... but... Jane... you make... me wet myself when I cum... Oh My God, I need get more."

Jane was still laying across her but looked up and giggled,

"Yes, they make you want more and more and after the club we are still making love and playing for hours."

Jane had started fingering her again, saying she felt so fucking horny, and Tatainia had opened her legs wide, holding them apart with her hands behind her knees.

"Finger her sexy butt babe... like we watched her husband do in the club last week...!"

Jane pulled out and moved to her butt, one finger slipped in very easy so she tried two, then three fingers went in, four were a little tight so I offered her more gel and she lubed up her hand again. This time she made a point with her fingers and thumb and pushed her whole hand right in.

Tatainia let out a really long moan then told us,

"He like fuck me there, he also like put fist in me but his hand too big for pussy, but Jane... Oooohhhh.... Hand in pussy and in arse... it all inside... My God... it feel so good... please wait... and then push deeper."

Jane waited while Tatainia got used to her whole fist in her arse, then slowly, Jane started pushing in and out again. Tatainia opened her legs even more and looked down to see how much of Jane's hand was inside her butt. Jane was in well past her wrist and edging in further, it was nearly half way to her elbow. I looked at Tatainia rolling her head around in, I can only imagine as pain and pleasure, so I went round to rub her clit while Jane stared in disbelief at her whole hand and forearm sliding in and out.

"I gonna cum again... AAAAAHHHH... I cannot stop...!"

Tatainia started squirting again so I rubbed her bud softer as her warm pee squirted out all over the carpet.

Jane eased out and Tatainia lay back holding her pussy, still panting from her third orgasm. Jane seemed to need more so I told Tatainia to move over a bit and let me lay on the sofa. I told Jane to straddle me and get on my cock, then told Tatainia to get on my face so I could taste her beautiful sexy smooth pussy.

As she got up, she took her tights and knickers off completely and lifted her leg over my face. It was so beautiful... Jane was riding my cock and I was holding Tatainia's butt cheeks over my face alternating between licking her pussy and rimming her well stretched little anal starfish.

I wanted to try my own fingers in her butt, so pushed a couple in... she let out a long moan and pushed back obviously wanting more, so I pushed all four together and slipped inside... stretching her anus as she moaned out even louder... Jane's hand was now between her legs, rubbing her own pussy and clit... I pushed hard but it felt so fucking tight... then her sphincter muscle opened and Tatainia screamed... I was in her and Jane started to jerk and cum... She grabbed Tatainia and shuddered as her climax took over. My fist was completely inside Tatainia and I felt her anal muscles gripping then relaxing. As they relaxed, I pushed in a bit deeper... this made her go all tense and then she begged,

"Please make cum again... Please... please, my husband, he try do this... but cannot get hand all inside like you... his hand too big...!"

I was in up past my wrist and she was moving up and down herself. Jane had finished cumming and slipped off my cock so Tatainia leaned forward and started wanking my cock into her mouth... It was all sticky and covered in Jane's juices and what looked like white cream.

She looked up at Jane and said,

"I never feel this horny before... I need too much, can I suck he cock... he cum in mouth, I want taste him... he have whole hand up me... My God... incredible...!"

Jane comes round to see me with my hand up her arse then asked,

"What do you want me to do babe...?"

"Help me make her cum again, play with her tits and pussy while I do this."

We were doing all kinds of things to each other, I even had three fingers in Jane's arse but she was far too tight for any more. Jane stood over Tatainia and offered her pussy, so Tatainia fingered and licked her for a while then went back to wanking me into her mouth.

I was nearly ready to cum, so told Tatainia... Jane kneeled down next to us and they took turns sucking my cock, then Jane pushed a finger in my butt and sent me over the edge and shooting my cum in Tatainia's mouth. She absolutely loved it and sucked me dry.

We all relaxed and lay back to recover.

Chapter 5

Webcam fun

Jane asked Tatainia what time she had to get home and she said her babysitter stays the night and her husband said he wouldn't be back till after midnight, so no need to rush back.

The time was only 3 o'clock and we had the rest of the afternoon and whole evening so I asked Jane what she wanted to do? We were all laying there naked and still feeling nice and horny from the sweets we took a few hours ago.

"How about we check out to the dogging place near the lake, it's only 30 minutes from here and we can see if there's any action, only problem is, it's the afternoon and not much happens until it gets dark."

I know... let's look on that webcam site and see if anyone wants to watch two sexy girls with a guy... You ever done that Tatainia...?" Jane asked.

"I no mind, I feel... so... nice and... I feel like lay in bed and play," she replied.

"OK, let's take the computer upstairs and we can all lay on the bed and see who's available to web cam with."

The girls went into the bathroom for a shower together while I set up the computer and logged on to the swinging heaven website, then opened up the chat rooms. There were about 120 people in chat and few other web-camer's. Most of the participants showing their webcams were fat old men and one was a Transvestite dressed up as a dominatrix, another was a young couple in their mid 20's.

When the girls came back in they jumped on the bed to see what I'd found. Tatainia was surprised at all the old guys wanking their cocks and the chat was like waiting for paint to dry... absolute rubbish and how they could even talk such crap to each other was well... beyond me... what was the point.

Jane seemed to be interested in the young couple so we started to watch them and turned our cam on. I told Jane to get a couple of the eye masks she sometimes used when we went to the clubs, so she and Tatainia could stay anonymous, I wasn't worried about myself, so just operated the computer and chat if anyone asked us anything.

Tatainia had put her tights back on and sat there topless showing her lovely sexy tits and Jane was wearing her clubbing mini skirt with no knickers and also topless. As soon as we turned our cam on, all the stupid messages started to come through... I read a few out and then saw one from the young couple.

They asked what we were into and if we enjoyed group sex and mutual fucking on cam? I replied that we did like group sex and went to various clubs. They then asked, What we were into again? So I told them most things... They then told us to watch them... and if we wanted, to direct them what to do.

Sounded fun, so we started watching them with our cam still sharing to everyone in the chat room. They started by the girl getting on all four's and the young guy fingering her... then he was lubricating up a big glass Fanta orange bottle and pushing it in her pussy while his other hand was fingering her anus.

Jane was laying back caressing her tits as was Tatainia but also with half her hand in her pussy. The girls seemed to enjoy watching this couple so I let it continue. Then a message came through asking if we wanted to go private as they couldn't do everything they wanted with all the other people watching.

I asked the girls and they said OK, so we all went private and they asked us to move our webcam closer so they could see the girls pussy's better. I pulled Jane over and got her to suck my cock while Tatainia got on all 4's like the girl on cam and started pushing her hand inside herself again. I told Jane to go help her and moved around so I could reach under Tatainia as Jane was behind her fingering her arse. Suddenly their the web-cam went off, it looked like they exited the chatroom. The girls just giggled and joked at what we just saw and I suggested we look at some more cams and find something else.

We got a message from the transvestite dominatrix, asking if we wanted to play?

I said OK, so he started telling us to do things while he got his huge cock out and was wanking it close up on cam.

"My God... LOOK... it's huge,"Jane said giggling.

Then she asked Tatainia if she ever had a cock that big before? She surprised us by telling us her husband was big like that, but he only liked to fuck her in her butt as her pussy was too small, she said he couldn't get it in deep enough...!

The tranny on cam told the girls to get on top of me and for one of them to sit on my face... It was all going OK until he told them to tie me to the bed...! That's when I told them, I didn't think it was a good idea, but they laughed and said,

"NO... let's see what he makes us do... don't worry babe were at safe at home...!"

Jane went off and came back with some of my neck ties from the wardrobe. The tranny told them to tie my wrists to the bed posts, then told them to leave my legs for now and just do my arms. I was unable to move my arms and must admit, I was a bit worried to say the least.

Jane also came back with some more sweets and gave Tatainia a couple and took two more herself. She offered some to me so I thought, what the fuck, if I don't, they will still be high and I won't, so I let her give me a couple with some water and the tranny on cam messaged and said he saw what we just did and he approved.

We'd already switched to private and Jane was messaging him back as he asked questions.

“He asked where we lived... shall I tell him...?” Jane asked me.

“Well... tell him Milton Keynes... that’s not too far from here, just to be safe.”

Jane messaged him back and he replied saying he was in Watford. We were actually nearer to Watford but I didn’t want him to know that.

He started getting the girls to show him their pussies close up on cam and then make me hard by sucking me and then sitting on my face. Then he wanted Tatainia to get on my cock and ride me... This was going to be nice I thought and Jane even helped her by holding my cock while she lowered herself down. Her pussy was fucking amazing and she made love to me using her pussy muscles to relax and contract.

Jane was OK and enjoying herself and when Tatainia had made herself cum, Jane jumped on and did the same. All the time the tranny Dom was ordering them to do things while wanking his huge cock and telling them how he was going to let them watch him hoot his load and asking them if they wanted to try a real cock...!

Jane was really getting into it and did things I never though she would do, like pee in a glass for him while he watched close up, then he made her bend over and have Tatainia lick her pussy and anus.

However, when he got Jane to do the same to Tatainia, Jane started fisting her again and the tranny got really excited and told to girls to watch as he shot his load all over his stockinged legs. Soon after, I got the girls to untie me and we exited the private cam session.

Then we came across a link for local dogging forums, so I had a look and the last message posted was from a guy with a young Indian girlfriend asking for any other couples in the area looking to meet to watch them. I fired off a quick reply saying we were a couple with another girl friend and were in the area. He responded immediately asking for a safe place where we could all meet up?

I told him we could meet at a car park near the zoo in

Whipsnade, gave him the location and then told the girls to get showered and dressed we were going to meet a young Indian guy with his girlfriend.

Chapter 6

Dogging at Whipsnade

Jane and Tatainia were cuddling and kissing next to me, but were soon off the bed looking for something to wear and get ready, so I went in the bathroom first while they were sorting out what to wear. When I came out, they went in together and after about ten minutes, I had to call them to ask if they were ready...?

No answer, so I went upstairs to find them snogging on the bed and still not even dressed with clothes strewn all over the bed and floor. It looked like they were trying on some of Jane's clubbing gear and then started having sex again. Not that I minded, but I was feeling the second round of sweets kicking in and wanted to go out to see some live action and hopefully join in with the girls. I told them to hurry up as we were supposed to be meeting this couple, so they giggled and jumped off the bed.

On the way in the car, I put some house music on and Tatainia was cradling Jane's head while Jane was caressing and sucking on her tits in the back. I had my cock out and was wanking it slowly as I drove. Luckily the traffic was minimal and we arrived at the car park in about fifteen minutes. There was only one other car parked up so we parked next to it, but I realized there was just a single guy in the car who was just sitting there. He looked over to us and smiled, probably thinking, his luck was in as usually there weren't many doggers out in the daytime.

The girls were sitting up and looking around outside, asking me questions and then Tatainia said she needed to pee. I told her she would have to go in the bushes or behind the car, but she said she couldn't because of the guy next to us.

Then another car pulled into the car park and parked right next to us. My phone rang and sure enough, it was the young Indian couple. I told them there was a single guy in the other car but they said, no problem, could they come sit in our car as theirs was too small for five people? I said OK and hung up the phone, told the girls and Jane said she would jump in the front with me and poor Tatainia was looking a bit strange as she still needed to pee.

As the Indian couple got in, we noticed the girl looked really small and skinny.

We all introduced each other and he told us his girlfriend loved sex and was only eighteen. She was wearing a thin flowery dress and was virtually flat chested except her nipples were sticking out.

I asked them what they liked to do? and he replied, they liked to be watched and he liked to see his girlfriend being touched by strangers. He then told us she loved the taste of cum and couldn't get enough. She sat there looking all shy and nervous and then her boyfriend told her to open her legs and show us her pussy.

She did as she was told and lifted her dress so we could all see, she had no knickers on and was completely hairless, not shaved as her pussy looked really small and just the top of her slit was visible.

My cock was twitching and Jane was already squeezing it while we watched the Indian guy part her legs. Tatainia held the girls hand and asked her if she was OK and she responded by nodding her head.

The young guy then opened her dress at the front and exposed her tiny little tits and puffy long nipples.

Tatainia then asked us again where she could pee?

Jane said,

"Just pee on the floor in here, I've done it before and we can watch," she giggled.

The Indian guy looked all excited and said,

"Yes please, can we watch. Mina also can do pee and she will do with you...Can you do Mina...?" he asked her.

Tatainia couldn't wait and told us she was going to pee, so opened her legs and started squirting onto the floor in the back of the car. Mina stared and then reached out to touch the stream and held her hand over Tatainia's pussy and started rubbing her.

Tatainia looked surprised but still let out a long moan, as the small Indian girl massaged her pussy and clit while her pee streamed out. Then Mina started to go... she tried to manoeuvrer her body so her stream aimed at the floor between Tatainia's legs but it was going everywhere.

Tatainia reach out and rubbed the little Indian girls pussy, just like Mina did to her. It was so horny to watch and my cock was rock hard. Jane was kneeling on the front seat leaning forward so her bum was sticking out. So I slid my hand up her skirt and fingered her up the side of her knickers.

The two girls in the back were still touching each other but had both stopped squirting. Tatainia seemed to be well turned on and willing after taking some more sweets and her breathing was like, long sighs and rolling her head, eyes closing as the sweets kept giving her waves of pleasure.

The Indian guy asked me if she was OK, as it did look a bit weird so I told him we'd all had some ecstasy earlier and it was Tatainia's first time and she seemed to really like it.

He asked if we had any more as he would like to try some with his girl friend.

I told him I did, but that it takes an hour to kick in, but he wanted some anyway, saying we can still play. I gave them a tab each which they excitedly took then Tatainia had Mira lay down on the back seat with her head on her boyfriends lap as she was stroking her legs and pussy.

He was playing with her puffy red nipples that looked like he'd been working on before as they were quite swollen, her dress was wide open and I was pushing my fingers into Jane from the back as she'd parted her legs to help me get inside easier.

I'd discovered that taking sweets somehow made people, guys included, enjoy deep insertions, be it fingers, dildos or other objects. Whereas it hurts if you try to do it normally, but on the sweets, there's no pain and the muscles seem to really relax making it really easy and with Jane, I could normally only get two fingers in but on sweets she could take three and four easily, and even moan for me to push harder. I had four fingers in her now and she was pushing down onto my hand.

Tatainia was trying to get three fingers in Mira but she was so small and tight it wasn't possible. Mira was moaning away as she must have really liked it, and then I saw the guy from the other car peering in the window.

Jane also saw him and told Tatainia, so we all watched as he wanked his cock by the window while watching the show we were giving him in our car.

The Indian guy told his girlfriend that he was going to ask him if he wanted her to suck his cock? I looked at Jane as he opened the rear door and got out. The guy looked startled and I thought he was going to run away, but the young Indian guy said something to him, and then he was getting in the car, while the Indian guy stood outside and told his girlfriend to suck his cock and make him cum.

Mira turned her head and took his short fat cock in her mouth. He was looking at us all in the car as if he also, couldn't believe what was happening but Tatainia continued fingering Mira and even reached out and fondled the old guys cock and balls as well.

She was so fucking sexy and turned on, I wanted to play with her as well and Jane saw I was getting really hard and as luck would have it, suggested I fuck Tatainia from outside. I couldn't believe she just said that, so I asked her if she was sure?

"Yes babe, this is so naughty and I want to see you fuck her...

do it for me babe."

I jumped out and walked around to the rear door, opened it and told Tatainia to step out and keep doing what she was doing to the girl.

Tatainia stood there with her legs parted leaning into the car still fingering the Indian girl as I parted her cheeks and just had to get in there and lick her anus and sopping wet slit. She was dripping, so I pushed a few fingers in, just like I did with Jane, then stood up and rubbed my cock up and down her slit and plunged in. It was fucking incredible, and as I started fucking her, I saw she was fondling the old guys cock again and so was Jane...! Both of them were wanking him as Mira occasionally licked and sucked him as they offered his cock to her little slutty mouth.

The old guy was about to cum and I wasn't surprised having 3 girls all playing with him at the same time. He started to ejaculate and Mira missed the first spurt as it ended up on her little flat chest, but she soon clamped her mouth onto his cock and milked the rest in her mouth.

When he finished, she let go and swallowed it all licking her lips. Tatainia fondled his cock a bit more saying she wanted more, but he was already soft and not responding, then the old guy slipped out the car without saying a word and was gone.

The Indian guy got back in and Jane asked him to get his cock out for Tatainia. I was still fucking Tatainia from behind and watched as the old guy drove out the car park. Jane was fondling the Indian guy and Tatainia was trying to suck him.

He said how we were all crazy, and if this is what the sweets do, he'll definitely want to get some more. We all laughed as his girlfriend started moaning and sighing under Tatainia.

I couldn't cum but was really enjoying fucking Tatainia and had her tits in my hands, pulling her back onto my cock.... Then another car pulled in the car park.

"Shit.... It's a family with 2 kids in the back...!"

I pulled out of Tatainia and she quickly got back in the car as I walked round to the drivers side and jumped it. Obviously we'd have to stop play or drive somewhere else. The Indian guy said he knew somewhere nearby and it wasn't far, just a mile up the road.

"Follow me," he said as he jumped out and went to his car.

His girlfriend Mira was still laying virtually naked on the back seat with us, so we all sat up and tried to look normal as we followed him out of the car park. He drove along for about two miles and then called me on my phone and said,

"I had to drive past as there were 3 cars parked in there."

"Never mind. Let's go back to our place, it's only 10 minutes from here,"I replied.

He slowed down and let me pass. Jane was laying back with her eyes closed so I asked her if she was OK?

She said she was just enjoying the tingly feelings.

Then I asked Tatainia about Mira the Indian girl?

"She's lay down and smiling... so must be feel nice also. I so horny though, I never so horny like now... today... and... I need... I don't know."

"I know how you feel, I could never sleep like Jane can after we'd been to the club, and played all evening, then played on the way home in the car from London, then we'd have sex in our bed or on the sofa. Then Jane would want to sleep but I couldn't... I had to go watch some porn on the computer downstairs and sometimes, I even went out again to find some dogging action at 5 am! but always came home disappointed, but ... couldn't stop playing with my cock."

Mira started talking,

"I feel all warm and waves of... something... something making me shiver but it's really nice."

"Stroke her legs or something Tatainia, the sweets are kicking in now, I think we need more guys to satisfy you girls today...!" I sad jokingly.

"What about "Gary," Jane said.

"I think he's too far away and he will be with his wife and kids on a Saturday afternoon... Maybe Dennis though... I could call him and ask...?"

"We can call Dogboy" Mira suggested.

"DOG BOY.... Who the hell is Dogboy...!"

Jane leaned over and whispered,

"Oh My God... what she talking about...?"

"So is that a friend of yours...?" Tatainia asked Mira.

"Yes... I like all kinds of things, guys, girls, old men, tranny's and I like Dogboy cos he can cum a lot."

Tatainia and Jane were really interested and asked her to tell them more but we were nearly home.

Mira then said said,

"Dogboy's really big and Raj likes to watch me make him cum in my mouth and then he helps him to fuck me... Can we get Dogboy for me today please... I feel so sexy and I could get Raj to call him... Can I please...?"

Chapter 7

Dogboy

We pulled into our driveway and walked quickly into the house, Raj pulled in behind us and followed us inside.

Mira immediately asked him,

"Raj... can you call Dogboy, I want to play with him...?"

We were all silent and couldn't believe what she was asking, I looked at Jane and shrugged my shoulders and even Tatainia gave us a surprised raised eyebrows look. Her boyfriend saw our reaction and told us she must be feeling really horny as she'd never asked that before.

So I asked him straight, if they'd ever done it before and he said,

"Well, yeah... my mate and me did get her to do it with him, sort of put on a show for us. At first she didn't want to... but after he got hard and she tasted his spunk, she sort of liked it. We only did it twice and it must be your sweets making her so horny."

"Probably...!"

"I can call him if you want...?"

Jane and Tatainia were sitting with Mira, asking her more details so I sat with Raj and also tried to find out more.

"Well, she likes cock and especially the taste of spunk, and she can't go out alone, cos she can't drive, so I take her in my car.

Setting her up with Dogboy was my mates idea, he knows him and everyone says his cock is massive and he cums… well he cums bucket loads… Anyway, my mate said we could try it with Mira… Well man… she liked it so we did it again the next weekend."

We heard some moaning and looked over at the girls, Jane was kissing Tatainia and Mira was between her legs with her skinny little hand all the way inside Tatainia's pussy…!

"Look Raj, she can take my fist, I want to try… can you call him please…?"

I looked at Raj and he asked me if I wanted to see her with a really big cock?

"What do you think girls, do you want to see little Mira here do it with a guy with a really big cock…?"

"Jane looked at me and said, up to them I don't mind."

Tatainia was moaning and rolling her head around with her eyes closed again and didn't answer, Mira was pushing her fingers in her other hole with her other hand and because she was so small, her whole hand slipped in really easy.

"OK, go call this Dogboy character, this is something I want to see."

Jane called me over and got me to join in with them, she asked about Raj, so I told her he'd called his mate, but she said no…. she meant does he play…?

I told her I didn't know, then Mira said,

"Yes he likes to play and let's me suck him after we go dogging."

I was behind Jane and she had hold of my cock again, I was caressing her tits and then asked her if she was still feeling horny and wanted me to put it in? She said, no not yet as she wanted to watch Mira make Tatainia cum.

We both played with Tatiana's tits and I rubbed her clit while

Jane was trying to hold her head still so she could kiss her mouth. She truly seemed to be in heaven with both her holes filled and eventually orgasmed when Jane sat on her face and rubbed her pussy on her mouth. Mira had pulled out and was laying on the floor trying to get her own fist in her little pussy...!

Jane said she'd get the gel as that would help and when she came back, smeared some on her hand and tried to get three fingers in Mira's little pussy. Surprisingly they slipped in, so she tried four and again her little pussy was taking them, probably because Jane's hands were pretty small. Then she tried with her thumb as well. Mira started panting and told Jane to wait... but was also clearly enjoying it from the sounds she was making.

Then Jane was inside her and Mira gripped her wrist, telling her to hold her to still so she could get used to her little womb being stretched. Tatainia came over and kneeled next to us so I put my arm around her and pulled her close, slipping my hand down and playing with her from behind.

Raj's phone rang and he told us his mate was outside, so I told him to go open the door. His mate came in and said hi to everyone and must have been around twenty like Raj and all smiles as he saw the three naked girls and myself on the floor playing with Mira.

When the girls saw him, they all stopped play and got up, he was really fat and Jane and Tatainia sat together on the sofa just staring at him. I went to sit next to them on the arm and Mira stayed sitting on the floor, then Dogboy went over to her and sat on the floor next to her.

This was really weird as he was definitely the fattest 20 year old I'd ever seen, at least 25 stones and I'm sure we were all thinking the same which was, how the hell could she have sex with such a fat guy, she looked so tiny compared to him and why was she so excited and asking for him!

He said hello to Mira and asked if he could watch and maybe join in if she was OK with it? We didn't know what that was all about, but it seemed like they had all done something else together before.

"No, I got Raj to call you cos we all want to see you try to do me again...!" Mira replied, then a big smile appeared on his face.

Jane and Tatainia were holding hands and watching intently as Mira opened her legs to let him have feel with his fat pudgy hand, then he was snogging her as she started to pull at his belt and undo his trousers... It was so funny as he was like a huge beached whale and she was about a third of his size, pulling away at his trousers and then she was kneeling down pulling them off his legs. He just lay back on the floor smiling, and then Mira jumped on his legs and pulled the biggest, fattest cock out of his pants we'd ever seen in our lives...!

"See... it's huge and he cums a lot...and I mean like... really loads" Mira said giggling while pulling his pants off.

He pulled his own T shirt off and just lay there stark bollocks naked. Mira straddled his face and started wanking his cock. It must have been at last 10 inches long and pretty fat, a bit like a big flaccid zucchini, and it wasn't even hard yet...! He was already licking away between her legs and it looked so funny seeing them both together. It wasn't long before he started to get hard and his one eyed monster grew to about 14 inches and at least as fat as Jane's arm.

Mira was slurping and licking away at his bulbous head and we were amazed she could even get her mouth around it...!

Shit this was so horny to watch and even Raj and his mate had their cocks out and were wanking. I noticed Jane caressing Tatiana's breasts again so went over and sat next to them so Tatainia was in the middle.

No way could Mira get that inside her, I thought to myself.

She started squeezing his balls, then wanking it with both

hands, it didn't take long before he was spurting his sperm into Mira's mouth. She yelled he was cumming and we all watched in amazement how she took most of it in her mouth and was swallowing as much as she could. But she had to pull off to breath and swallow and her little brown face was covered in it... she even had it in her eyes and hair.

Mira's boyfriend Raj started cumming and moved in so Mira could have his jizz as well. She sat back onto Dogboy's face, licking her lips as Jane and Tatainia stared with open mouths, then told her that was so naughty and what was she gonna do next...?

Mira went over to the armchair and climbed up and leaned over the back. Dogboy got up and kneeled behind her and continued licking her arse and pussy for a bit while Raj asked if we had any lubricant?

Jane looked at Tatainia and said,

"No way... he can't fuck her...!"

"My husband big... but not that big... I not know."

"Jane, Go get the gel, I can't believe this...!" I asked

Chapter 8

Tatainia

Jane came back with a tube of gel and handed it to Raj who gave it to Dogboy. He smeared it between Mira's legs and then his own cock. Everyone was just sitting there in awe not believing their eyes. If he put that inside her it would reach up to her heart.
He smiled at us all and started rubbing the head of his one eyed monster up and down Mira's little slit. Mira was squealing like a pig as he started pushing the head inside.
Then she screamed,
"OOOhhh... It's in me.... I can.... It doesn't hurt like last time... OOOhhh I feel so tingly and hot... it's not like last time... He's in me...!"
We were all staring and even Jane and Tatainia had stopped playing with each other as they watched. Dogboy looked so overweight it was like a freak show but Mira was actually loving it and had reached under herself to grope his big balls hanging down.... I could see now how he got his nickname Dogboy, he was crouched over her and fucking her really fast just like a dog. But his cock could only go in about 7 or 8 inches.
"Give me the lube," Dogboy asked Raj.
Raj handed it to him and he squirted it onto Mira's little bum hole. I looked at the girls and they were just staring open mouthed, none of us could believe he was going to try to fuck her in her tiny little butt.
He pulled out slowly and her pussy was gaping wide, then he pushed the head to her anus and to our surprise, it went in...! He had his big fat bulbous cock head in her butt... Mira was

gripping the sofa with both hands and her head was down as if she was in pain. Raj went over and asked her if she was OK, then came back smiling and said,

“watch this.”

Dogboy grabbed Mira’s little hips and started to fuck her arse, slowly at first but he was soon going in and out faster and somehow, her little anus was stretching wide enough to take him. She started moaning and shouted for Raj to come over, so he jumped up and stood in front of her as she started sucking on his cock.

“This girl should be called Dog-girl not Mira,” I joked and everyone laughed.

His cock was about ¾ of the way in and she was somehow taking it.

Raj then said to me,

“She has a very loose arse and loves to play with big dildos at home... I can’t satisfy her with my cock it’s too small...! “

Mira starts to wail and cum and pushes Raj away.

“FUCKING HELL... she nearly bit my cock off...!” Raj screamed.

We all started laughing but Mira was jerking like she was having an epileptic fit.

Dogboy held her still and slowly eased his cock out and Mira collapsed on the sofa panting. Tatainia jumped up and surprised Jane and me, it was like she couldn’t wait to get involved, she went over and kneeled next to Mira and grabbed Dogboy's cock.

“It more big than husband... I must try.”

Dogboy pushed it straight into Tatainia’s pussy and she moaned like someone being impaled on a spike, then he was nearly half way in, bucking away really fast as she was holding it to stop him trying to get it all in. She started wailing it was too big and we could see her pussy was stretched to the limit.

“But it doesn’t hurt, it feels... OOOhhhh my God... I can feel... deep inside me... Fuck my arse... yes my... can go deep... husband do and I can take... In arse please,” Tatainia said all excitedly.

Dogboy pulled out and squirted the lube on her anus while smiling at us all watching him perform. As soon as he entered her, Tatainia was like a wild animal... wailing and moaning and pushing herself back onto the massive phallus that was going deeper and deeper in her back passage. She started to cum and her body was trembling and jerking but Dogboy held her tight by the hips and continued to pump into her.

"Wow... This girl is fucking amazing... she can take it all and I'm gonna cum in her.. can I cum inside her...?"

I looked at Jane and then Tatainia screamed out,

"Yes... in me... do inside... no pull out... in me please."

He was bucking away like crazy then let out a long deep guttural moan you would not believe, he sounded like a bloody werewolf or something. Shooting his spunk deep inside her and sweating profusely. Tatainia moaned that she could feel him cumming in her arse and we all watched as he was almost all the way into her arse as she gripped the back of the chair.

Jane moved over and sat next to Tatainia stroking her hair, she was also jerking and trembling and seemed to be having multiple orgasms...!

Tatainia eventually lay still and looked up,

"Please him out... him off me please... I cum too much... it so good but cannot... I no more... he too big me."

He pulled out and the creamy grey spunk dribbled out of her gaping orifice.

She looked up and told us she was OK and said, it was "amazing experience" and then asked Jane,

"Are you go now to try...?"

Jane responded by saying,

"No fucking way."

I'd never heard Jane talk like that before. Tatainia's phone started ringing and we all stared as she jumped up and staggered away trying to find it. It was in the kitchen so she jumped up naked and went to answer it.

When she came back she said she had to go home as her husband was coming back early with his friend. Jane told her to go and have a shower and we'd call her a taxi.

While she was in the shower, Raj, Mira and Dogboy also said they were leaving and thanked us for an interesting afternoon.

As Tatainia left, she hugged us both and said thank you for a great day and could she call us later in the week to find out about the club next week...

I hope you enjoyed this story.

If you like my writing style, and stories about Husband or Wife sharing, Wife watching, BDSM, Cuckold, Swinger and Fetish clubs, Dogging and many other fetishes...

Why not check out my other stories on Amazon and sign up to my newsletter to get the heads up on all my new releases.

Dante X

Authors Website – Contact and Newsletter sign up

www.DantesErotica.uk

Lost My Wife in the Fetish Club

Cuckolds and Swinging Couples

by Dante

Contents

Introduction

Chapter 1 - New Fetish club

Chapter 2 - Guy with a Hungarian wife

Chapter 3 - Guy with a Hungarian wife

Chapter 4 - Jane tells us what happened

Chapter 5 – In the car

Introduction

At the time we'd been married about 2 years, I was in my early 40's and my wife Jane was 27 and from the Philippines. We'd been introduced to the club scene by a friend of mine about a year previously and had been attending various fetish / swinger clubs every month or few weeks if there was a special event going on... We both loved it and had progressed to same room sex with other couples and even let them touch and play with us. However, we hadn't gone all the way and actually swapped partners or let any single guys fuck Jane in the club... Jane has a nice sexy slim body, UK size 8 and about 110 Lbs, 4' 11" tall with nice long nipples on her shapely 34b breasts. She's never had any children so as you can imagine, her body is really petite and sexy.

Barry my mate, mentioned that there was a new club in London he'd been told about and was going on Saturday evening to check it out and did we want to come?

I said we probably would, so long as Jane was up for it, which I was sure she would be. So we arranged to go up in his car this coming Saturday. When I told Jane, she was also keen to go and saw is as a good reason to go buy a new outfit, as most of the fetish clubs have a strict, no street wear dress code and everyone must wear either, sexy gear, rubber, leather or BDSM gear.

Chapter 1

New Fetish club

On the night, we had a couple of sweets (ecstasy) each, like we usually do an hour before arrival. Jane ended up wearing a white mesh body stocking with her nipples sticking out of the mesh... It was also crotchless... so she wore a short black skirt to cover her nicely shaved pussy. My god she looked so fucking sexy and even Barry commented that all eyes would be on her at the club. I wore my usual small black leather shorts with a front zip and a skin tight black Lycra T shirt. Barry had similar shorts and a gladiator style chest harness made of chains.

When we went out to the car, I noticed Barry's wife was not with him and he told us, they had a row and she refused to come out that evening... Barry then told us he often went out alone as she was always getting moody in the clubs lately and never wanted to let anyone touch her or play with other couples...

So off we went with me and Jane in the back of his Mercedes whilst he drove. On the way, I could see he'd adjusted his mirror so as to be able to see Jane in the back so I decided to give him a bit of a show. I started to hug and play with her tits while we were on the way. During the hour or so drive to the club, I managed to finger Jane and make her cum whilst Barry was watching in the mirror and this turned me on even more.

We arrived at the club somewhere in central London and it was like a typical London pub on the street level with another 2 floors above and a basement area. This is where they had set up a playroom with all the usual fetish type accessories, swings, whipping racks and various other BDSM play things. There was a couples only room which was virtually pitch black inside with a girl guarding the curtained doorway, making sure only couples went inside. Then there were stairs going up and down at both ends of the club. On the 1st and 2nd floors were loads of rooms and different themes. There was a cinema room with a big screen showing hard core movies. It was really interesting with so many rooms and themed areas to explore.

After we got a couple of beers from the bar, Barry went off to look around and we did the same exploring all the different play rooms. The place was packed as we had arrived at about midnight and there must have been at least 80 to 100 people packed in... It was mostly single guys but about 15 other couples were wandering around or playing in rooms or corners with groups of guys looking on.

Chapter 2

Guy with a Hungarian wife

One couple started to chat with us and Jane seemed to really like them. The girl was blond with a perfect figure and Hungarian, about 25ish and her partner was about 40 and English like myself. They were chatting away to Jane, then said something to her... when all of a sudden, she grabbed my hand and we started to follow them upstairs. They led us through the crowds and eventually to a small room which had a double bed. There was actually no room to stand and we all had to clamber on the bed, then they pushed the door closed.

On the way to the room, I tried talking to Jane and asked her,

"Where are we going babe?"

She just replied that they, the couple said to follow them.

I then told her,

"Well you know what they want to do don't you?"

She looked at me and said,

"It's OK, we don't have to do anything."

I was really shocked at her naivety but in we went... No sooner that the door was closed, Jane was on her back and the girl was touching her tits and stroking her hair. Her partner and me, just sat on the bed and watched them for a bit and then I saw, that he had started stroking Jane's leg...

He nodded for me to touch his wife but I was more interested in watching Jane snogging away with this girl she had only just met. The girl was clearly fingering her while they were laying together snogging on the bed.

The door kept opening and closing as people were looking in to see if any action was going on inside. Then another couple and several single guys were crowding the doorway trying to see what was going on in our tiny little room. The guy had now positioned himself between Jane's legs and was going down on her with his tongue, while his partner continued to kiss my wife on the mouth. Jane was just laying back letting them this guy lick away between her legs... Her head was rolling from side to side as he was obviously doing something to her she was enjoying.

I positioned myself near Jane's head and the girl was reaching over and squeezing my cock, so I opened the zip and let it out. Jane looked up at me when she saw what I did, so I asked her,

"Are you OK?"

She just smiled back and said,

"Yes for now."

The girl then lay over the top of Jane and was sucking my cock while Jane was trapped under her and the guy was licking and fingering Jane. I was sure Jane was nearly cumming and the girl was working on my cock with her hands and mouth making me very close to going over the edge as well...

Then I saw the guy was kneeling up between Jane's legs ... He was about to fuck her ... but Jane saw what he was going to do and was holding him back with her hand. She somehow pulled herself out from under the girl and told him that she was not ready to go that far.

Although she was enjoying the fingering and licking, we had both agreed that we wouldn't go all the way with anyone, just watching and some playing, so long as we both felt comfortable.

Jane turned herself towards me and I managed to get between her legs and was amazed to see her pussy was gapping open... I'd never seen it like that before... Like this guy had been fingering her with all his fingers or trying to get his whole fist inside her. She was soaking wet and as I touched her pussy my two fingers just slipped inside as if this was a totally different pussy and wife!

The guy seemed a bit put out and asked me, if he could fuck her?

So I had to tell him,

"Sorry mate, afraid not as we're both a bit new to the scene and never gone all the way."

I then got down between Jane's legs and was kissing her pussy while I saw the guy was kneeling at Jane's head and she was wanking his cock whilst his wife was alternating between sucking his cock and snogging Jane. A few minutes later... I got up and kneeled between Jane's legs and pushed my cock inside her. I was so turned on with the sweets we took earlier and watching her bringing this guy off with his wife watching. They then both watched as I fucked her in front of them.

The room was only the size of a double bed and another couple had somehow squeezed in and were on the bed...! Then there were about 3 guys inside the doorway reaching in to grope the new girl with her man.

There was hardly any room to move and this new couple had started to play with us as well... I was about to cum and as this new couple started groping Jane's tits and I just couldn't hold back any more so shot my first cum of the evening inside Jane... She was still wanking the guy that wanted to fuck her... So after I pulled out, she continued wanking him until she made him cum... He shot so much, it went all over her tits and on her face...

I pulled Jane up and as we tried to exit the room but hands were groping Jane from all directions, mainly the guys in the doorway... We managed to get out and went to the bar downstairs where we could grab another drink, rest and reflect on what just happened and decide where to explore next in the club.

Chapter 3

Jane disappears

I told Jane I wanted to use the men's room and asked if she wanted to go as well? She said she didn't... so I said to wait here I'll be back soon.

I was only gone for 5 minutes but on my return Jane was nowhere to be seen. Where the hell could she be I thought... Maybe she went to the ladies after all, so I wandered back upstairs to the toilets and hung around for another 10 minutes. Still no Jane... so I decided to go back to the bar and see if she had come back. Nobody there, but Barry was there chatting with a group of guys, so I asked him if he'd seen Jane?

He said,

"Yes mate, she was chatting to a couple about 10 minutes ago over there."

He pointed to where we were sitting...

"But she's not there now."

I was starting to get worried... So off I went again to try to find her. There were so many people and it was hard to get through some of the play areas as guys were wandering around in packs like wolves. I saw a group of them in a room and tried to push through and saw that there was a couple or well, a female being split roasted with hands groping her all over. The husband was probably in there somewhere as well.

Most of the rooms were occupied and had guys trying to get in while other rooms had closed doors with action going on inside. I made my way back to near the toilets hoping she had made her way there to find me... but still no Jane.

The cinema room was nearby so I went inside and saw 3 couples laying on sofa's playing with each other while watching the movie and about 15 single guys all wanking near the couples and a few were being allowed to play with them.

I then thought I heard some moaning that sounded just like Jane, but I couldn't see her anywhere in the room. On my way out I saw there was a gangway leading to I supposed another room but it was blocked with people and I couldn't get through. I started to look around in other rooms and for at least 2 hours... I went through the club, I don't remember how many times, on all levels looking for Jane. I was going out of my mind and eventually I was back at the cinema room. I managed to squeeze through all the people, crowding in the doorway that I couldn't get into before. It led to some stairs that went up to an area above the cinema where there were a few padded benches and like an open balcony area where you could still see the movie playing down below.

There were also some cubby hole areas with mattresses inside, each contained 4 or 5 people with action going on. Then there were people crowding around watching or leaning in and trying to grope the players. But with so many people and mainly guys up there, I couldn't see in all the cubby holes or what was going on...

Then I heard it again... that distinctive moaning that I knew was Jane... She's was in there somewhere... but where... I tried to push through but it was heaving with mainly male bodies all trying to get closer to whatever was happening in there.

I eventually squeezed through to the front and saw a guy with his wife being well fucked by two guys and he was holding her hand as these two black guys, one underneath and the other on top fucking her pussy and arse at the same time. Another 3 guys had climbed in the raised cubby hole area and were wanking and groping the woman being fucked.

Then I heard Jane moaning again... So I pushed my way out and went to another area in the corner and saw about 10 guys all crowding round someone getting fucked in the middle. I pushed my way through and could just see beyond another 4 guys that a girl was on her back on a large padded corner bench and all the guys were taking turns with her.

Yes it was Jane... but she was just laying there almost lifeless, being used and seemed to be drunk or something.

As I struggled to get to where she was I saw at least 2 more guys fuck her on this bed in the corner, as one finished and had cum inside her... another jumped in and took his place... She looked like a rag doll as all the guys close enough were mauling and groping her. One guy was trying to get his cock in her mouth while another was fucking her pussy but she was... well... unresponsive... as if she was totally knackered or only semi conscious.

I managed to get to the front and was not only really pissed off, but wondering... how the fuck was I going to get her out of there? I was kneeling next to the guy inside my wife and just as he finished, I got between her legs and pushed my own cock inside her. She was so fucking loose and dripping with cum I could hardly feel anything and Jane still didn't even know I was there!

She was totally out of it and her head was rolling from side to side as she moaned. I tried to pull her up... but two guys were pulling her back down, they wouldn't let her go... They were all groping her and one guy was telling me to hurry up as he wanted to get in next.

I pushed him aside and said,

"No man, This is my wife and she's coming with me."

He laughed and said,

"No way man, she's been here for two hours now and there's still a load more guys need to fuck her."

I was so fucking angry that the guy must have sensed it and started backing away... I remember pushing him and he must have known I was deadly serious. I grabbed Jane's hand and pulled her up. She saw it was me and started to plead,

"Help me... Help me."

I managed to get her up as two guys were trying to pull her back down and another was fingering her while I was trying to pull her to her feet. Eventually I got her up and pulled her through the mass of bodies. On the way out of the room and down the stairs she couldn't stand up or walk properly, she was falling over as if she was drunk or had been drugged.

Chapter 4

Jane tells us what happened

In the cinema room downstairs, I sat her in the corner and tried to talk to her but she was totally out of it. Her skirt was gone and her body stocking was ripped to pieces, her tits were hanging out and her crotch area was totally ripped open. She had sticky cum all over her hair, face and body, her pussy was all red, swollen and puffed up.
About 15 minutes later, I saw Barry and told him I'd found her and we needed to go home. It was about 4.30 am and he said, OK, meet him downstairs he will get our coats. In the car as we were driving home I started to find out what had happened.

Jane was just laying there in the back seat with her tits exposed and her legs open. Poor old Barry was trying to drive through London and look at her at the same time. She managed to tell me, that the same couple we met at the beginning, and went in the little room with had come into the bar while I went to the men's room. They'd told her to come and see the cinema room which was near the toilets and that she could wait for me there.

As Jane was waiting outside the toilets for me, the couple disappeared into the cinema room and all of a sudden, a group of guys grabbed her arms and pulled her into the passageway that led to the room above the cinema.

She said, she struggled but couldn't stop them and she was

being groped and fingered as they carried her up the stairs. Once in the room the guys were all over her and she said she was fucked over and over again. Every time a guy finished another was inside her. She was turned over and fucked in the arse and was double fucked with a guy underneath and one in her arse several times.

She also said they made her drink something and after that, she felt really strange and couldn't remember where she was... like she was in a crazy dream. Then she felt all relaxed and someone made her cum with his fingers and she remembered squirting all over the floor.

Then she said,

"They kept making me drink this blue drink... and they turned me over and it hurt at first but then..."

"What do you mean babe?"

"Well it was hurting at first... when he did it in my bum... but when the next one did it... I started to feel really... I don't know... but it didn't hurt any more... One of them was holding my head and pushing his cock in my mouth... and then he cum all over my face... Then this guy was making me wank his cock while another was inside me... and the guy who made me wank him was huge."

"What do you mean huge babe .... How big?"

"About the size of my arm."

"What!"

"Yes... it was so big babe, my hand couldn't go round it and then he told the guy fucking me, to move over... so he could get inside me next. I was scared and didn't know where you were... I was worried you wouldn't be able find me up there... but they kept taking turns and making me cum and I couldn't get up or stop them."

She continued,

"He got his big cock head in and then he was holding me

down... another guy was groping my boobs and another one was wanking on my face. He could only get about half of it in me as it was so big... I'm too small down there. He kept pushing and trying and then I think he cum inside me and pulled out. But I couldn't get up... so many hands all over me... then another guy was in me and I started to cum again."

While Jane was telling us what happened, I was really concerned and pleased she was OK but I was also, so turned on and getting hard.

Then Barry said, "My god, how many guys has she had?"

"I don't know mate, but she was missing for about 2 hours and she said she never left that room. Must have been about 30 or more!"

"Fucking hell mate, is she OK?"

She smiled at me and said,

"I'm OK now but it was really scary with you not there."

Jane had been squeezing my cock as she told us what happened and I was rock hard in the back of the car. I saw that Barry had also pulled his cock out and was wanking slowly as he drove along.

"Fuck me listening to that makes me so horny." he said.

"Me too mate..."

Jane just lay there and opened her legs more as I started to stroke her swollen pussy.

"Are you still horny babe?"

"Yes... I still feel all weird and my pussy is tingling."

"Someone must have spiked her drink with something and with the sweets as well...!" Barry said.

Jane leaned over to suck my cock, so I told her to better be careful cos poor old Barry here hadn't had any action tonight... too many single guys there.

"Oh really Barry, didn't you play with anyone tonight?" she

asked him in a sort of daze.

“No, just watching... couldn’t get in on anything.”

“Hey babe... I know you’re still horny cos I know I am... Why don’t you sit in the front so Barry can watch us play on the way home? We don’t want him crashing the car trying to watch us in the mirror back here.”

“Really, you want me to...?” she replied.

Chapter 5

In the car

With that I leaned over and reclined the passenger seat down, so Jane could climb in the front. Once in the front seat she was laying down in her ripped body stocking with legs closed covering her pussy area with her hand. I was stroking her hair and tits while she stared at Barry stroking his big wide cock.

Barry wasn't really long, probably about 6 inches but he was definitely twice as wide as myself.

He looked down at Jane and said,

"My God, is your pussy OK, it's all red and does it hurt after all those animals did that to you?"

"Show him your pussy babe, go on don't be shy."

She moved her hand and parted her legs slightly so he could see...

"That's it babe, let him see how swollen and red it is."

Barry looked down and stared at Jane laying there with her pussy on show and legs parted.

"What do you think mate... she looks beautiful doesn't she?"

I ran my hand down her belly and fingered her as he drove along watching.

"Fuck me mate, she's stunning."

Jane was still watching Barry play with his cock as he drove then he said to her,

"My God... you look so fucking sexy Jane... can I touch?"

She looked at me for approval, so I said,

"Go for it mate... I'm sure she's OK with that after all the action she's had tonight."

I sat back and stroked her hair and he moved his arm over and started to play with her tits and erect nipples. She closed her eyes and moved her hand down her belly and started massaging her clit and moaning softly as he fondled and stroked her in the passenger seat.

I was now wanking again in the back as I watched her playing with herself and Barry caressing her tits. Then I saw his hand move down and slip his fingers into her swollen little slit as she moaned and closed her eyes.

"Fuck me mate, she's so wet and loose down here, and I bet they didn't wear rubbers...!"

"No mate, I'm fucking sure of that.... when I found her, she was covered in cum and I even saw two guys cum inside her before I could get her out."

She then leaned over and grabbed hold of Barry's cock and wanked him while he drove us home... It was only a few minutes before he shot his load all over her hand. He thanked her as she lay back in her seat and then we both continued playing and fingering her all the way home.

After Barry dropped us off, you can imagine, we fucked like rabbits in our bedroom until we fell asleep in a 69... only to start again as soon as I woke up staring at her sexy little hairless slit... still swollen and puffed up from her first unplanned gang bang in a club.

I hope you enjoyed this story.

If you like my writing style, and stories about Husband or Wife sharing, Wife watching, BDSM, Cuckold, Swinger and Fetish clubs, Dogging and many other fetishes...

Why not check out my other stories on Amazon and sign up to my newsletter to get the heads up on all my new releases.

Dante X

Authors Website – BLOG - Contact – Comments and Newsletter sign up

www.DantesErotica.uk

Touched by a Stranger

2 short stories about Cuckold wife watching

by Dante

Contents

Story 1 - In the Cinema
Story 2 - The Coach trip

Story 1

In the Cinema

As I have already outlined Jane and myself in previous stories, I will jump straight into what happened. Jane was only 26 at the time and was still quite shy as we'd only been married for about a year. She'd attended a few London Fetish clubs with me, so was getting used to the fact that I loved watching her getting touched up and I suppose I was becoming a real cuck.
Anyway, what happened was, I'd seen a good video online and it was all about this girl in Japan whose boyfriend had not turned up for her date to the cinema. She decided to go in and watch the movie alone rather than go home, and consequently, gets touched up by a guy sitting next to her and then groped by other several guys... and ends up getting fucked by a whole group of guys at the back of the theatre.

I really wanted to take Jane to one of these sex cinemas but couldn't find any in our local area so started asking around on a few swinging and dogging forums. After a bit of research, the closest cinema that showed sex movies was in Soho, Central London or we could jump on an Easy jet flight to Amsterdam for a long weekend. Out of all the forums, it was pretty clear that Amsterdam was the best place by far. So I told Jane what I'd found but she said, she had no idea what actually went on inside these type of cinemas. I did tell her it was a bit like the playing in the clubs and she hesitantly agreed to go and check them out but she made me agree, that we would come out if she didn't like it.

As the flight we booked was only a couple of weeks away, I got her curious and excited by telling her, sometimes people go to cinemas like the London clubs and play with each other in the back row while watching a hot movie and sometimes get watched by another couple or maybe single guys.

She then surprised me by saying,

"But I've never been to a big Cinema before..."

Jane had only been in England about a year and came from a small island in the Philippines.

"Well, why don't we go to the movies tonight in Bedford? You can see what it's like and there's a new 18+ horror movie showing and who knows, maybe another couple playing in the back row." I said smiling.

"Really" she said, and jumped up and hugged me...

"Can we, what should I wear?"

"Well how about your long black coat as it's a bit cold and a fairly long walk from the main car park, and maybe your short silky skirt... the one you wore to the club last month with the creamy blouse that has buttons at the front. Maybe we can play a bit at the back as it's pretty dark when the movies on."

"You want to play in a normal cinema, you said not much happens in the local cinema...!"

"Well I don't know to be honest as I haven't been for years myself."

Jane got dressed and we jumped in the car. As we entered (I think it was a vampire movie), we headed for the back row and sat in a corner. In the back row were 5 empty seats at the end so we took two of those with me nearest the wall and a couple of empty seats next to Jane.

Jane still had her coat on so I told her, she would be more comfortable if she took it off and placed it over her legs or the empty row of seats in front of us. I scanned the theatre and counted about 25 people, mostly couples or groups and a few single people dotted around.

As the movie started, the lights went down but surprisingly it was still pretty light, even at the back... but as soon after the movie started, I noticed this guy, fairly well dressed, about 50ish coming down our row from the aisle.

As he got close, he leaned over and asked,

"Are these seats taken?"

I answered, "No they are free."

So he takes off his jacket and sits right next to Jane. Jane looks at me and I shrug my shoulders as if it's normal and she goes back to watching the movie.

He had his jacket on his lap and I was watching him out of the corner of my eye. Jane's blouse was quite low cut and I could see into the top and her tits were well on show but she did have a low cut bra on as well. So he must also be able to see what I could see from his side. Jane was staring at the screen as it was a new experience for her seeing such a huge screen as the only other cinema she'd seen in England was in the Fetish clubs and they are just fairly small dark rooms.

Just as I suspected, he started to casually look down her cleavage and I could see he kept watching me at the same time. This is gonna be interesting, I was thinking to myself. I just stared straight ahead and pretended not to notice him staring at Jane's tits.

I couldn't see his hands as they were under his coat but I did see his right leg was really close to Jane's left leg. Sure enough about 10 minutes later, Jane whispers in my ear,

"The man next to me keeps touching my leg with his leg...!"

I leaned over and whispered in her ear while still staring ahead,

“I think that’s why he sat next to you babe. He wants to play like in the club.”

“What, in here...! How can he play in here...?” Jane whispered back.

“Don’t look down now, just keep looking at the movie but I think he’s already playing with himself under that jacket on his lap.”

Jane looks at me and says... “Oh My God I don’t believe you...”

A few minutes later and Jane whispered again,

“Yes I think he is, can we change places?”

“Listen Jane, we’re going to a sex cinema in Amsterdam soon and this is similar except most of the people in here are only interested in the new movie. Well nearly everyone, this guy must do this all the time.”

The guy just stared ahead at the screen as we were talking and didn't move his hands. I said to Jane,

“Babe, just let’s see what he does, it could be interesting and then we can fuck and chat about it at home later...”

Jane started giggling,

What...! You want me to let him touch me?, and you’re going to watch him like you did last month and make me pretend I’m alone in the club so you can watch the guys chat me up and stuff."

"Yes babe, I'm gonna pretend to be really into the movie but I will be watching out of the side of my eye OK?"

I grabbed her hand and squeezed it then placed it in my lap so she could feel my growing erection. She gave it a quick squeeze then gave me a naughty little smile. Then she whispered in my ear...

"My God babe...,You're hard already, you're really sick you know..."

"I know babe, just pretend I'm really into the movie and let's see what he does next. If he says anything to you, just smile or answer but pretend I don't know what he's doing."

A short while later, Jane squeezed my hand, so I had a quick peek. His leg was touching Jane's and his right hand was moving under his jacket. It looked like he was touching her thigh.... Jane stared straight ahead as if nothing was wrong and then the guy got really bold and started rubbing his hand up her leg again... He then turned and smiled at Jane.

I assumed that Jane had smiled back as she reached for her coat that was on the back of the chair in front and placed it over her lap as if she was cold. The guys hand was still moving and Jane was gripping my hand tighter. He must be touching her under her coat ... my god, this guy was either very brave or knows women love being naughty or whatever.

Jane moved her coat so it was also covering my lap and reached for my cock again. It was already hard as I knew Jane was letting this guy touch her leg under her coat. Still staring ahead, she parted her legs a bit and I could see the bulge of his hand under her coat at the top of her thigh.

Fuck me it was so horny, I was also trying to look ahead but also down at what was happening with Jane as well. Jane gripped my hand again, it was like her little signal that the guy was doing something else to her. Did I hear her sigh? She squeezed my hand again and then I could see he was between her legs.

I leaned back a bit so he couldn't see and whispered to Jane,

“Are you OK?”

No response as she was sitting really upright and then she lay back and turned her head and kissed me on my ear.

“He's fingering me” she whispered.

I looked down and she obviously had her legs open wider than before and was sort of laying back in her seat with the coat covering up whatever he was doing between her legs.

Then I saw the guy turn to Jane and whisper something in her left ear.

She turned to me and said,

“He knows you are watching, he wants me to unbutton my blouse so he can see my tits more.”

I was thinking what to do so... I simply reached over with my right hand and undid a couple more buttons on Jane's blouse and pulled it open slightly so he and I could see her beautiful sexy tits better. He looked directly into my eyes, nodded and smiled. Jane was still looking ahead at the screen but I noticed her eyes were closed and she was being seriously fingered. The guy then reached inside her blouse with his free hand and into the top of her bra and started fondling her tits. I looked around the room to see if we were being watched but as we were in the back row, nobody seemed to be watching.

I also reached over and started fondling her right breast and Jane opened her eyes and looked directly at me with a look of shock and pleasure. I pulled her tits out of the bra and the guy looked at me and smiled again. His hand was in her blouse and fondling both tits so I placed my hand under the coat and unzipped my jeans. My cock was throbbing so I grabbed Jane's right hand and put it under the blanket. The guy had obviously seen what I did so he whispered something to Jane again and she turned to me and said,

"He wants me to touch him like I'm doing to you...!"

Suddenly she moaned and grabbed his hand with her left hand under the coat and held it still as she started cumming and trembling in her seat.

"He made me cum, he's got 3 fingers in me, Oh My God...."

She panted in my ear.

Jane calmed down and I watched as the guy moved her hand under her coat over to under his coat. Fucking hell, she was holding my cock in her right hand and must be holding his cock in her left under his coat.

He started fondling her tits again and Jane slowly started wanking my cock and him under the coats. I put my other hand down under her coat to feel her pussy and it was so juiced up. She was moaning again and the guy had leaned over and was sucking her nipple and then his hand was back between her legs. I pulled my fingers out and let him have another good feel and couldn't hold back any longer ... I started to cum and Jane wanked me faster as she realised I had gone over the edge.

After I finished, Jane concentrated on the guys cock and was cradling his head to her tits as he was clearly trying to finger Jane to her second orgasm. Just as she cums again... I could hear the guy moaning into her tits as he also shot his load under his jacket.

I have no idea what the movie plot was about but we both got up and left shortly after.... saying our thanks to the old guy. We fucked like rabbits all night after that session and Jane says she's really looking forward to our long weekend in Amsterdam next week..

Story 2

The Coach Trip

It was a beautiful summer weekend and Jane and I had decided to go to Brighton on the National Express coach for a short break. When we boarded the coach it was virtually full, so Jane ended up sitting next to this oldish guy, probably in his 60's. I was in the seat opposite Jane with the aisle between us.
Now Jane is 26, fairy small, petite and from the Philippines. One of her best features apart from her innocent look is she has really shapely 34B breasts and nice little rose bud nipples that stick out when aroused. And on this trip she was wearing a white flowery cotton dress with a low cut neckline with buttons down the front. Her bra was very thin and her nipples were showing through slightly making her look really sexy.

I could see that the old guys eyes lit up as she sat down next to him and as I sat in the seat opposite he probably had no idea we were travelling together. The journey started and after about 15 minutes we were on the motorway M25 and I noticed he kept looking at Jane's tits. Jane looked me in the eye and giggled so I winked and smiled then sat back and pretended to nod off to sleep.

Now Jane knows I love to watch and we've had a few sexy clubbing experiences where we have had some soft swing sex with other couples and once with a few single guys where we let them play with us, fondling her tits and stuff, we even let one guy finger her in the corner of a dark cinema room at the club once.

So as I was sitting back and slyly watching, I saw the old guy rubbing his leg next to Jane and Jane was letting him. I will now let Jane continue the story because I couldn't see what was actually happening, but Jane told me all the details after we got off the coach in Brighton, and we couldn't wait to check in to our hotel. We fucked all afternoon as she told me all the details of how the old guy made her come several times on the coach.

Jane's account –

The old guy started pressing his knee and leg next to mine and then as I didn't move my leg away, he started rubbing it up and down. I wasn't sure what to do but it was sort of making me feel horny. He wasn't attractive or anything but he was just making me feel aroused. When I looked at you and you smiled and winked at me, I felt it was OK and decided to let him continue and see how far he would go.

When I looked down to his lap he had a blanket over him and I could see he was playing with his cock under the blanket. He even saw me looking and just continued, so then I looked him in the eyes and he smiled at me. Now I know I should have moved my leg away and give him a dirty look but my eyes went back to his lap and I couldn't move my leg.

Oh My God he was rubbing his left hand up my thigh and it felt so naughty... I was sure he must have been thinking that I was alone on the bus and I just let him touch my leg. After a few minutes of letting him rub my leg, I smiled at him and said,

"You shouldn't be doing that you know."

He smiles back and said,

" You have the most beautiful face and breasts young lady."

Then he moved his right hand over and cupped my right breast and gave it a squeeze.... I felt so horny and it was so naughty, he moved his hand back down under the blanket and started wanking his cock again.

I was getting wet babe and I couldn’t help touching myself for a second, then realized we were on a coach and you were sitting opposite me. I knew you couldn't have seen what he'd just done but I saw you looking at his lap while he was playing with himself. He was still stroking my leg with his left hand and then he whispered in my ear,

“Can you help an old man out here? My wife died several years ago and I have not had the pleasure of intimate relationships or sitting with a beautiful young woman for many many years...”

He then took my hand and placed in under his blanket.... Babe, his cock was out and it was huge. As I put my fingers around it I realized it must be really wide as my fingers could only go half way around it. He pulled the blanket up more so it was nearly up to his chest and then moved it over me also, to hide what he was making me do. I started exploring his cock and rubbed the head with my finger tip and he was already leaking pre cum so I rubbed it all around the head of his cock as he just let out this long sigh and said,

“Yes good girl, good girl.”

I then felt his left hand slide up over my thigh and up under my dress in between my legs. I was trembling as he inched his way up slowly caressing me and sort of teasing me. Then he reached my knickers and said,

“Oh my dear girl ... what lovely smooth legs you have and I feel your knickers are already damp...”

Oh My God... I nearly cum there and then.. and I wanted him to finger me, but he just rubbed my inner thighs and ran his finger up and down the outside of my little white panties over my clit and feeling my slit. I knew you were watching but you couldn't see under the blanket so I thought, OK I can tell you all about it later. His cock was throbbing in my hand and getting even bigger so I felt around a bit more and then got my hand down into his trousers and found his balls. Wow what huge balls, he was like a horse babe... I squeezed them a bit then he pushed his finger inside my knickers and rubbed my sticky wet pussy juice up and down my slit. Then he pushed two fingers inside me and started frigging me very fast. Oh My God, I cum within seconds and clamped my legs shut and held his hand down on my pussy till I calmed down and my pussy stopped pulsating... It was so strong and unexpected.

That's when I realized you must have seen something, so I looked over and saw you playing with your cock under your blanket and smiling at me. Good job the guy sitting next to you was asleep. Jane started giggling.

Anyway, he started rubbing and fingering me again but more slowly and exploring in my wetness. I opened my legs again to give him easier access and started stroking and pulling his cock again under the blanket. He managed to get two fingers in me and was whispering in my ear again.

He was asking me "If I had a boyfriend and did I like him fingering me like that?"

I said "Yes it's nice and I'm married."

"Really young lady! and what would he do if he knew you were being fingered my an old man on the bus?"

"I don't know, why don't you ask him?" and I started wanking his cock harder. "He's sitting next to me here and wanking his cock watching us..."

The old guy looked shocked but then a big smile appeared on his face and he said,

"My my, you two are swingers and he's a cuck."

"We're not swingers but we do like to play in the clubs and now on the bus" I giggled.

"So why don't you ask him if he likes the show?"

That's when I asked you if you mind the old guy touching me and you said,

"No babe please carry on and tell me all about it later."

and I told you his cock was huge and I was holding it under the blanket and you said....

"Fucking hell babe can you show me?"

"So what did he say?" the old guy asked me.

I told him, He said it was OK and he wants to see your cock. That's when I looked around to make sure nobody else was watching, then reached down and pulled the blanket back to see myself and show you his massive cock. After I saw his cock I felt really naughty babe, I didn't know if you saw it.... but that's when I leaned down and started sucking him off. I could only just get the head in my mouth so I wanked him while cupping his balls and squeezing them. The old man just held my head and whispered,

"Your husband is looking at me and I think he is about to come dear."

He then pushed my head down harder and I started to gag and cough so he let me up a bit. Then he said,

"Carry on girl, I'm going to cum soon."

I went back down on him and he pushed his hand down the top of my dress and started fondling my tits inside my bra and then he started ejaculating in my mouth... I kept wanking his cock slowly as he filled my mouth... I didn't want to swallow cos there was way too much, so I sat up and kissed him on his mouth and gave him all his cum back. Giggling... This shocked him a bit but he soon started to lick his lips and we had a sticky wet passionate snog with his cum dribbling down both our faces.

His hand was now back between my legs and he had about 3 fingers in me and I was about to cum again and he was trying to kiss me again, but I didn't want that and felt a bit embarrassed kissing an old guy on the bus, someone might see us. So he started whispering in my ear again.

"Your husband knows I'm fingering you and he's watching my hand under the blanket between your legs... Open your legs a bit wider young lady... let him see you're letting an old man finger his young wife on the bus. Yes that's it... open them wider now."

Then he pushed another finger in me and my legs were wide open. I didn't even care who could see... I just needed to cum again. He was forcing all his fingers and thumb inside but he couldn't get his fist in as my pussy's too small but when he whispered to me...

"I think your husband is cumming now, his eyes are closed and he's smiling...",

It sent me to heaven and I grabbed his hand while I cum again and babe... I peed all over his hand and the seat. Oh My God... it was so naughty and the bus was full.... Then you reached over and grabbed my hand and said to me,

"That was amazing babe, do thank the gentleman and let him get cleaned up, we are approaching the bus station soon."

As soon as we got off the coach you started asking me what happened and to tell you how it all started. I started to tell you and you waved to a taxi so we got in and headed for the hotel. And you were so worked up... you pushed your hand up my dress and was feeling my pussy in seconds and the taxi driver was listening and watching in the mirror.

“Come on babe, I can’t wait, tell me what he did?”

As I started telling you the taxi driver was smiling and watching me in the mirror. That's when I told you,

"How can I tell you here, the driver was listening.”

Back to me telling the rest of the story.

“You don’t mind, do you driver...?”

“No mate, I see and hear all sorts driving a cab.”

So Jane carried on telling me all the intimate details as the driver watched us in the mirror. I started fingering Jane and kissing her neck knowing the taxi driver was getting as turned on and trying to see what was going on in his mirror. I unbuttoned Jane's dress and started squeezing her tits and made her nipples hard.

“Fucking hell babe you really wanked his big cock under the blanket on the coach?”

The taxi driver was staring in the mirror in disbelief....

“Then you let him finger you and you squirted all over the coach seat ... Open your legs babe...”

I pulled her knickers to the side and said to the driver...

“Fuck me driver, her pussy is fucking soaked, look at this...”

The driver tilted his mirror down to see Jane laying back with one tit exposed and hanging out of her bra, legs wide open with me exposing her bare shaved pussy to the driver.

He nearly lost control of the cab and so I said,

“I ‘m going to take her to the hotel and fuck her now. So did you like looking at her tight little pussy and tits mate?”

"Fucking Ace..." he replied as we pulled up at the hotel.

I hope you enjoyed these two short stories

If you like my writing style, and stories about Husband or Wife sharing, Wife watching, BDSM, Cuckold, Swinger and Fetish clubs, Dogging and many other fetishes...

Why not check out my other stories on Amazon and sign up to my newsletter to get the heads up on all my new releases.

Dante X

Authors Website – BLOG - Contact – Comments and Newsletter sign up

www.DantesErotica.uk

Asian Wife went with her Dad's Friend

A Cuckold story

by Dante

Contents

Chapter 1 – Sexting with Jane

Chapter 2 - Newbies in the club

Chapter 1

Sexting with Jane

I just can't sleep or stop playing with myself.... My wife just called me from the Philippines and told me one of her dad's friends had turned up and taken her out in his pick up truck.

I'd better back track quickly and explain what happened. We live in the UK and she got this phone call last week saying her father was really ill and in hospital. She said she had to fly home to be with her mum as it was very serious and they were fearing for the worst. So we booked her on a flight to Cebu ASAP and she flew out 3 days ago. I couldn't go, because of work commitments and such short notice so she went alone.

Anyway, we were in touch via Whats App several times a day and either message each other or do a video call. Well, she tells me yesterday, that her father's best mate fancied her and he kept coming on to her at the house and the hospital. Now we are not full on swingers but we have had quite a few group play sessions at the swinger / fetish clubs and do play as a couple. So I told her to do what ever she felt comfortable with, on the condition that she tells me everything later....

You have to understand, we have this game we play in the clubs or a crowded pub or nightclub. I love watching her flirt with strangers and we pretend, she's alone and she tells them she's married but alone that evening and I just watch from somewhere else in the club.

Now my missus Jane is 28 and a real looker, slim and a small size 8 figure with beautiful 34 B tits with very sensitive nipples. If fact, as soon I or anyone I let touch her tits, she goes into a sort of sexual dreamland and starts moaning and getting wet. It's really amazing cos she goes all weird and can't stop from touching herself and eventually masturbating herself to orgasm.

I'm Dave and 20 years older than Jane and I have to admit, a real cuck I suppose. I get so fucking turned on when I see a strange guy coming on to her and when he touches her leg or waist and then touches her tits and she starts to melt into the situation it makes my gut turn over and I get so fucking hard and want to see her get fingered and played with and sometimes even get fucked.

So back to what's happening, she's over in the Philippines and about an hour ago told me this old friend of her dad's, gave her and her mum and 3 sisters a lift home, in his pick up truck, after the evening hospital visit. She was texting me what happened because her mum and sisters were in the car and when they arrived home, he told them all, he was taking my wife back to his house to meet his wife.

Apparently, that was just an excuse to get her alone and away from her family.

I was waiting for the next message and my heart was beating so fast, my palms were wet and my cock was already twitching. I couldn't wait, so I sent her another quick message.

"Hey babe, you OK, what's happening?"

A few minutes later she messages me back,

"We're driving and he keeps telling me how beautiful and sexy I am, he says he wants to take me to the beach road view point. I'll update again soon."

That was the last message about 30 minutes ago and I need to know what's going on. My cock is out and I've been wanking and waiting and going out of my mind thinking, what the fuck is going on...

I send another message, "Hey babe, can you call me via Whats App and leave the phone on in the car somewhere, so I can listen in?"

"LOL.... Yes OK, but you call me as we're driving and I will answer and leave it on. He touched my leg and said he knows I'm married but he fancied me since I was 16! Then he got my hand and put it on his cock. What shall I do babe, he wants me to have sex with him?"

I rang her straight back but it went to some stupid message saying unavailable!

Shit... Maybe she's not in range, no signal... Fuck. I have to call her again. This time she answered, but she seems to be sounding all strange.

"You OK babe, you sound strange?"

"Eerier... Yes I'm OK... we're just driving home... from the hospital... with my mum and sisters..."

I immediately knew, she was telling me "old news," as he was obviously listening and didn't know, that I already knew he was alone in the car with my wife, so I asked her,

"Have you... you know... touched his cock yet?"

She responded, "Yes babe... and I 'll tell you how Dad is tomorrow OK. So call you later or in the morning, love you."

She pretended to hang up but I could still hear the road noise and him talking to her in Tagalog or whatever the native language is called. I could hear they were driving along and then I heard her sigh and knew he must have touched her tits or her legs as I recognized her sounds. More sighs and moans and then I heard it go all quiet and the engine switched off.

I am... as tense as fuck and my cock is rock hard.... Silence... what's going on... I can hear some moving around and then more moaning and sighs.

What the fuck is he doing to her...? Is she letting him finger her...? Is she touching his cock...? Fuck me, I need to know what's going on, it's driving me nuts, making me feel so fucking horny. He must be kissing her or has his hand in her blouse as she only makes those sounds when her tits are being touched or could he be between her legs and fingering her...?

Something was said in Tagalog and my wife replied to him in English,

"Oh my god, please No, I'm married".

Then she repeated it again in Tagalog. He said something back, that I couldn't understand and then a few minutes later...

I hear her slurping and gagging!

Fucking hell, he's making her suck his cock. My gut is going round and round and I am about to cum but I managed to hold back.

Another 5 minutes and I hear more movement and then she whispers into the phone, (which must be near her head),

"I'm on the back seat and he's between my legs licking my pussy... oooohhhhh"

She is moaning away and I could tell, she was about to fucking cum! Then she yelled,

“Oooohhhh yes... push deeper, oooohhhh yes deeeeepp-peeeeer”.

Fuck me, I exploded and cum, I couldn’t hold back. My wife is being licked out and fingered by this friend of her dad’s and I am listening in live!

She then starts panting and screaming

“Yes, yes, fuck me hard, Oh ... fuck me harder.”

Then suddenly, she lets out this really long loud moan and I could tell, she must have cum and he must have had his cock inside her.

The phone goes dead.

What the fuck, She must have turned it off. Why? What’s going on now? So many questions? Then I get a message.

“We are driving again, he said he wants to get some drinks and go somewhere, text you later.”

About 20 minutes later, she messages me again.

“Hi babe, I'm at a house and he has 2 friends here, we're having a drink and his friends are already drunk... he's telling them I am his second wife LOL... they're all laughing and I'm sitting on his lap. He's got my blouse open and flashing them my tits and... he's telling them to come and have a feel.”

“Fuck me babe, are you safe with 3 guys all alone...? I’m really worried now.”

“No don’t worry babe, he’s my dad’s friend and very protective of me. He knows I'm married and I told him we play in the club's and stuff... It got him all excited. He asked me if you let anyone make love to me, so I told him we play around, touching and stuff but only made love with a few couples, but babe... I'm feeling really drunk and ... and ... and ... they're all touching my tits babe and he's just letting them!"

My cock was rock hard again as I read her message, so I replied saying

"OK babe, but please be carefully with 3 guys in a strange house."

Two hours later and I'm going out of my mind, after sending several more messages with no answers... I eventually receive a message.

"Hi babe, sorry but couldn't message, I OK but they all make me do stuff and I so drunk. Can't remember much. They pass me around table, all touching me, tits and my bum, then fingering me and made me sit on one guys cock while they take turns to lick my pussy and feeling my tits. Take turns putting cock in my mouth. Then they put me on a table and all 3 playing with my tits and putting their cocks in my mouth. Then they all took turns doing me on the table one after another, many times ... Oh babe, please ... you still love me, I sorry ... they make me do things. Cannot think now. So tired. We talk tomorrow, tell you everything I remember Xxx."

I was wanking like a man possessed and cum again before I even finished reading the message. The next morning I received another message saying she was back at home and would call me later... This put my mind at rest and I knew she was safe. But she's there for another 8 days before her flight home... Whats gonna happen over the next week with her dads friend... He's not going to stop now, not after she... well last night... fuck, how am I gonna get through another 8 days...

Chapter 2

Newbies in the club

I can't just wait in the house and read her texts, it's going to drive me crazy... I'm gonna go to the fetish and swinger club tonight... I usually only go with Jane but with the time difference and stuff, she will still be sleeping... but it's Saturday evening here so I'm gonna go alone and see if I can get into some action and play then chat with her in the morning... I called a mate of mine who's also into the clubbing scene with his wife and asked if he was going to the club this evening and he said yes they were both going.. So I told him I was coming alone as Jane had to fly home for a week. Then I sent a message to Jane telling her I was going, just in case she messaged me while I was there and no phones are allowed in the club.. She'd probably see the message when she woke up in about 4 hours time...

"Hi babe... So you going to the club without me then..."

"Sorry babe, did I wake you up....Yes I'm meeting Pete and Gale there as well. What you doing today... or are you going out anywhere with your dads friend again tonight?"

"I'm going to the hospital again today and will be with my sisters and mum. Rene told my mum he will pick us all up and take us in his truck again.. I'll tell you if anything happens babe... And... you going to tell me what you do at the club to-night too?"

"Of course babe... no secrets... I tell you everything but are you going to go with him again then... Rene?"

"I think so but have to be careful cos my mum and sisters... you know.. it's really different here.. they are all religious and stuff... Anyway babe... have a good time xxx"

In the club I was standing at the bar chatting with another couple we knew and had played with before... Just chilling out and watching the couples and single guys arriving and wan-dering around.

Then they walked into the club... it was obvious they were newbies as they wandered around and explored all the differ-ent areas and rooms, holding hands and watching various couples playing or fucking in threesome's and mini orgies in a couple of rooms. After about an hour of wandering around, I saw them again in the play room with a small group of people crowding around them. The girl seemed to be really nervous but her boyfriend told a few of us standing close by, that she was a bit embarrassed but wanted to show off her tits for the first time.

She was white about 18 or 19, slim and sexy, white blouse and black mini skirt. The boyfriend was about 22, also white British and he said that no touching was allowed... unless she agreed ... but as it was her first experience of exposing herself in front of guys, we could wank and watch or fuck in front of her if we had a partner.

He introduced her as his long-time girlfriend of 3 years and told us, she gets really turned on seeing guys staring at her tits in the pub or walking in the park or town and they'd just heard about this swinger club from a friend.

He told me, she had this urge to get them out and make guys wank while they watch her. He then asked her if she was ready... and then unbuttoned her blouse as she just stood there looking really shy. He let the blouse slide off her shoulders and placed it on the bar. She looked a bit scared but also wide eyed as a couple of guys had already got their cocks out and were stroking them in front of her making sure she could see.

The boyfriend reached behind her and clipped her white bra and slowly exposed the most amazing looking breasts for a young girl. They were quite big and about 36C but also had a heavy curvy shape with up turned nipples. When she leaned forward they hung down and were really shapely and beautiful.

The boyfriend started to stroke and squeeze them and her nipples got hard and erect like 1/2 inch long pencil rubbers. She still had her short black skirt on but he then took her by the hand and led her through the crowd of about 6 guys and 2 couples to the door... It looked like he was going to parade her through the club and let everyone see her.

I followed them, as did a few more single guys and we followed them into the bar area where a few people were dancing. He led her over to the dance floor, where she started to dance with him. He made her face a couple dancing and we watched as her beautiful tits were bouncing with her movements and to the music. There was another girl with a guy dancing, but she was only wearing a low cut red bra and tiny red G string. They were both staring at her stunning bouncing exposed tits so she shyly covered them with her arms, but the boyfriend moved her arms away and stood behind her.

The couple moved in closer and the girl stroked her arm... then whispered something in her ear. She looked around at her boyfriend and he nodded, the girl then stepped closer and started snogging her and touching her tits.

Fuck me this is gonna get interesting, I was thinking. So I and another guy moved in closer to get a better look. It was quite dark in the corner of the dance floor, and the guy with the girl in the red bra and G string was also feeling his girlfriend up between her legs, while she was snogging the young girl.

After a few minutes they led her to an even darker area where we could only just see them continue the playing with her tits and snogging. I managed to squeeze in as close as I could behind the couple and watched her rub the young girls lower belly, then went down to suck on her left nipple. The boyfriend was holding her up as she seemed to go weak at the knees and the girls hand was now stroking her thighs and moving up under her skirt. The young girl looked nervous but was also really turned on and with the couple really close... and a hand between her legs... Then her boyfriend was also feeling her other exposed breast...

Wow this was horny and I now had my own cock out, as did another guy next to me. The young girl was being fingered now, as she was holding the shoulders of the girl in front fingering her and then I noticed, she had her eyes on my cock... so I moved to the side a bit so she could see better... Then I saw the boyfriend also with his hand behind her fingering her from the back. She must have had a finger in her butt and the girl in front's fingers in her pussy... she then parted her legs a bit more.

As I watched and kept showing my erect cock to her, the boyfriend and girl in front frigged her till she orgasmed and nearly collapsed. Her boyfriend held her up and as soon as she started cumming and the girl in front went down on her knees and then turned her head, so she was directly under her pussy and started licking her. Her partner moved in front and started fingering her again.

I nearly cum myself as I watched this couple working on the girl. Other guys were now moving closer and the boyfriend was having a real problem with stopping them all trying to grope her breasts. The girl between her legs noticed what was happening so also stopped licking between her legs and got up. They then all walked away holding hands as the other couple followed them.

Shit... was the action all over... I thought, but decided to follow them again.

They all went into the cinema room and sat on a corner sofa. The room had about 6 guys all sitting around by themselves wanking and watching the movie on the big screen. The young girl sat next to the other girl and the guys were at each end. The young girl looked up at the screen and stared open mouthed at the hard core action being shown. The boyfriend was already playing with her tits from his side and the other girl had her hand on her thigh while also watching the movie.

Single guys were already moving in closer, so I positioned myself right on the arm of the sofa. Her tits looked amazing and I could see the boyfriend was really getting into showing them off to all the guys gathering around. One guy tried to touch again but was quickly pushed away by the other girl who then started caressing her other breast.

One hand was still rubbing her inside thigh and the young girl was staring at all the guys playing with their cocks in front of her, almost blocking the movie screen. One guy leaned over and asked,

"If she wanted to watch him come?"

They all looked at this guy who was standing directly in front of them and after a few more pulls on his cock, was ejaculating all over the floor. The other girl reached out and wanked his cock for a bit longer and then her boyfriend got his cock out and she started to play with him next to her at the same time. The young girls boyfriend pulled her down so she was laying across his lap and I could see her reaching for his cock. Her legs were open and the other couple moved position, so as she was able to get between her legs and pulled her G string to one side and gave us all a flash of her beautiful shaved slit.

Then she was fingering her again as all the guys were crowding round, wanking and watching. My cock was now quite close to the young girls head as I was perched on the arm of the sofa, I kept it hard by wanking slowly by her face and she kept looking at it while playing with her boyfriend's cock. Her boyfriend said something to her then nodded towards my cock and to my surprise, she reached over and started to squeeze it. I moved my hand and let her play while she went down on her boyfriend and took him in her mouth.

A few minutes later and she was wanking me seriously and staring at it... then her boyfriend pushed her head towards my cock... Fucking hell, she's gonna suck my cock. I lay back as she took me in her mouth and tasted, I was sure, her first strangers cock. I placed my hand on her back and asked the boyfriend, If I could touch her? He smiled, so I slid my hand round to play with one of her tits. Well, they were so soft and beautiful and her nipples were long and hard. I couldn't help it and started to cum... She just held my cock tight as I pumped my seed into right into her mouth.

The boyfriend looked shocked, and so was I... but even more so when she pulled off my cock and went straight to his mouth and started snogging him. I could see this was new for him too as she had a mouth full of my cum and was now showing him what a dirty slut she had just been.

I was still playing with her tits, with no resistance and she was laying back now with her legs wide open. The other girl, still licking away between her legs and several fingers in her pussy and ass.

"I really need you to fuck me now...", the young girl whispered to her boyfriend.

He said, OK and pulled her up so she was now straddling him on her knees. The other couple could see what she wanted to do, so got into the same position next to them. Holding her ass up, he slid straight inside her. I touched her back again to see if it was still OK to touch... She looked over and smiled at me, grabbed my hand and placed it over her tit then started to ride him.

I was now fondling both her tits while he fucked her... or more like she was fucking him. There were another 3 guys standing right behind her who also tried to touch but their hands were quickly brushed away by the boyfriend. Then one of guys started shooting his load all over her back. Surprisingly, She didn't even stop... so the other two guys were looking at each other wondering if they could do the same. They wanked a bit longer then another started to cum over her back and the girl, it seemed, was telling her boyfriend what they did while still riding her boyfriend's cock.

I was still playing with her tits and then she cums really loudly and slumped down pulling his head into her tits as if exhausted. The other couple next to us, were being groped by the guys and she started wanking one of them off... This guy was quite short but had a real monster of a cock and as soon as he came, the girl pulled his cock into her mouth and even her boyfriend joined in and was sucking it in turn with her.

What a great night.

On the way home I started to wonder what Jane was going to tell me later and I was going to have to tell her all about my nights experience in the club...

I hope you enjoyed this story.

If you like my writing style, and stories about Husband or Wife sharing, Wife watching, BDSM, Cuckold, Swinger and Fetish clubs, Dogging and many other fetishes...

The FULL LIST of all my other stories can be found on my

Amazon Author page

www.Amazon.com/author/danteserotica

Or on Amazon search for: DANTE X

Register on my website to get the heads up on all my new releases and sample excerpts on the blog.

Website: www.DantesErotica.uk

Dante x

Sex, Drugs and Wife Sharing

In the Fetish & Swinger clubs

By Dante

Contents

Introduction

Chapter 1 – A surprise visit

Chapter 2 - Fun in the Fetish Swinger club

Chapter 3 - Our first fetish club

Introduction

As you may already know from reading my other books, my writing style is more like a diary or blog of events rather than a "fictitious story," with a beginning middle and end. I like to keep the story line flowing without all the irrelevant details and padding like many other authors.

Over the years, I've written many erotica stories... Some are purely fictional and some are true stories of actual experiences with only the names changed to protect the people involved. This story is also totally factual and is about, how it all began.

Let me start by saying, I have never had any negative experiences in the Fetish and Swinger clubs or taking recreational party drugs like ecstasy (street names E's, molly or sweets) or joints (ganja, spliffs, weed etc,)

My Filipino wife Jane and I were totally new to the Fetish club scene in the UK and never ever taken ecstasy before. We were introduced to the highly erotic lifestyle, clubs, after parties, sweets and dogging here in London and our very first experience of taking sweets was in Club Rub, a Fetish / Swinger club.

Jane was my second Asian wife and we'd been very happily married for about a year and living back in the UK. Previously I'd lived in and out of Thailand for about 10 years and experienced some amazing things and people... So after divorcing my crazy gambling, money wasting Thai wife of 7 years... I'd seriously had enough of Thai girls and all their stupid attitudes, scams and bullshit and decided to try the Philippines.

I'll get into that a bit later but first I want to tell you about a funny thing that happened shortly after our exposure to sweets and the fetish club scene.

About 6 months after we started using sweets in the clubs, an old friend of mine, of whom I used to live and work with in Thailand a few years previously, had moved back to the UK with his new Thai wife.

Now this guy, used to do lots of crazy things and told me many, many stories of his Thai wife issues, drug running escapades, and even diamond smuggling.

He even tried to get me to do a "diamond run" with some Russian mafia type dudes he used to work for. Apparently, it was transporting diamonds in a false bottomed suitcase... I asked him if we could actually prove it was really diamonds and not drugs or something else? But he told me, it didn't work like that and the job was to carry the bag through the airport and there was NO chance of opening it to check what was really inside!

I declined, as it was Thailand to Italy and I didn't want to risk getting arrested in Thailand... especially if it contained drugs and not diamonds... Getting caught with ANY type of drugs in Thailand is seriously not funny and I've heard several stories of people I know personally that ended up in jail. One was even stitched up by his long term girlfriend (in collusion with the Thai police), he ended up paying millions of Baht, in bribes for promises of release but the extortion continued for over a year before he was eventually released.

The payment for transporting the false bottomed suitcase would have been US$10,000.

A while later he told me another courier had done a runner with his false bottomed suitcase of "diamonds" and had a contract on his head... Apparently he ran away with the suitcase (value was supposedly several million $ in diamonds..) No idea if the guy got caught, killed or managed to keep the hoard.

So lets jump into the story and what happened...

Chapter 1

A surprise visit

A month later, my mate turned up at my home in London and told me he was going to do a runner with a load of Ecstasy pills he was transporting...! He said he came in via the Euro tunnel and they (the pills) were strapped to his body.

I looked at him in disbelief, until he stripped off in front of me and his waist, back and both arms and legs were huge and wrapped in cling film. When we peeled it all off, we were looking at 2 large packs (waist and back) and 8 smaller packs (arms and legs) of Ecstasy pills, of which I estimated was between 50,000 to 100,000 pills.

He said he had to go underground and hide for 6 months and "Could I look after them or sell them for him...!"

The going rate in the club's was about £5 a pill but I didn't know anyone I could approach, I only knew my mate who introduced us to the club's and always got my sweets from him. I did end up selling quite a lot at wholesale to another mate because he knew a lot more people in the clubbing scene, and we also got to use them ourselves for free. Best of all, the quality was fantastic, the best you could find anywhere.

Six months later, my drug runner mate surprised me again and arrived at my door again. This time he was doing another run from Amsterdam to Heathrow...! Some people are just nuts and can't live a normal life...

Which has just reminded me of another interesting story I have to write down when I get time.. All about this Spanish guy Pedro I met in the UK. What a story.... He used to be a drug courier between Columbia and other S. American countries. Married a Brazilian hooker and had a couple of kids with her... They are now divorced but he was really pissed off because his daughter of 16, still living with his ex, was also a becoming a hooker...! Back in Spain he told me he used to run hookers out of several apartment buildings and then I met him in the UK, he was living with 5 Spanish girls... all hookers and none of them spoke any English at all... He'd brought them in from Spain and got them jobs as lap dancers in this strip club, they were making £700 + per day... each. His cut was £200 per girl per day. The problem was, they all used drugs at work and also when they were at home, cocaine mainly, he said they used to drive him nuts with all their arguing and fighting between themselves. They were so fucking sexy though... his personal (stripper) girlfriend was only 21 and had a face and body to die for... I will have to do a totally separate story on him and the girls later.

Anyway, back to the story... My mate told me, he was all strapped up with pills again, just like before in the cling film and was just about to board the plane, when he noticed, everyone was being searched and hand patted down, they even had drug sniffer dogs at the gate...!

He realized there was no way could he get through without being caught, so had to go into the toilets and remove all the drugs off his body and left them in a locked toilet cubicle at Amsterdam airport.

And when stopped by the airport security, because the sniffer dogs made an obvious play for him, he was searched and questioned, but luckily for him nothing was found and they had to let him go.

When he arrived at my place, he was worried to death that his bosses wouldn't believe he had to dump his consignment at Amsterdam airport again... I believe that was the same excuse he used for losing the hoard 6 months ago...!

Anyway, I gave him 50% of the proceeds of the last consignment, that my other mate who had connections in the club scene had sold.

So off he went again and the next time I heard about him was about a year later, when someone told me he was in jail in Canada.

However, I still had this amazing free supply of sweets for my own use. Then about a year later, I received a message... He told me I was to give all the remaining pills to some guy who turned up and took them up north for him, he was still in jail but needed the cash...! He'd somehow done a wholesale deal with someone.

To be honest, I was glad to be shot of them but obviously kept back a good supply for my own use. So that's how we ended up using the sweets. We'd take them most weekends, whether we went clubbing or not, and that's why they're mentioned in so many of my other stories. I had a free supply and absolutely loved them. And they were nothing like most other drugs that made you go off your head. On the sweets, I was able to walk around town, act quite normally and even drive my car with no adverse affects. Definitely not the case if ever I smoked ganja, no way could I drive normally.

Jane also enjoyed taking the sweets for the first year. However, if you take too many, the next day was not that pleasant, they made us feel really drained and tired and I found, I couldn't do any hard physical work. Jane then stopped taking them after a year or so as she said she didn't like how she felt the next day.

I suspected a different reason, Jane was a very shy and reserved Filipino girl and had no previous experience of boyfriends, clubs, bars or the fetish scene. Her background prior to our marriage was living at home with her parents and 5 siblings, university educated and never smoked, drunk alcohol or even been in a bar before.

However, when she was on the sweets she became a totally different person. See all my other "Asian wife" stories for the erotic details.

Chapter 2

Fun in the Fetish Swinger club

Anyway, one evening, (I think this was the last time she actually took them), we were in a club and my mate had turned up on this particular evening without his wife. They'd apparently, had an argument so he came out to the club alone.

That night I shared Jane with my mate and we were both playing with her... She was playing with both our cocks and even sucked his cock when he asked her... At one point she was straddling him on a bench seat while I was playing with her butt and tits from behind. She was wanking his cock as he was fingering her and sucking on her tits.

She leaned over and told me, he'd asked her, if he could put his cock inside her...?

We'd agreed not to go that far (soft swing and play only) and because she was friendly with his wife, she felt guilty so slid off him before he could put it inside her.

Then a bit later, she led me to another play room, holding my exposed cock and told me the following day, he was fingering her from behind as we were all walking along in the crowds.

In the play room it was quite dark and I remember turning her to face him, she was wanking both our cocks as he fingered her to orgasm standing up while I caressed her tits from behind. And a bit later, we had her laying down on this bench and he was sucking on her nipples and playing with her tits while I was fingering her with two fingers quite fast.... Suddenly she orgasmed and jerked like I'd never seen her do before and squirted up in the air for the first time. It was truly incredible, she squirted so much, it was going all over her belly and tits and I had to hold my hand over the gushing stream so as it went over her legs and the floor. If it wasn't so dark, the whole room would have seen her cumming and pissing up in the air.

So I think the real reason Jane stopped taking the sweets was because she became too uninhibited and horny... or maybe the best description is, willing to do anything while using the sweets. Although we used to bring it up and talk about what happened while making love... and it used to make her cum really quickly... I think she felt too guilty about what we did that night with my mate.

Sadly, I now have to buy my sweets like everyone else and the quality is rubbish compared to the stash I had from Holland. Just two - four pills were more than enough for a great evening at the club. But the rubbish on sale these days... I've taken as many as 8 and had virtually zero (nice ecstasy effect) all you feel like is like being a drugged up zombie...

Chapter 3

Our first fetish club

This is the story of what happened the very first time we went to a fetish club and was offered some sweets. Jane was dressed in a black silky short dress, G string and black hold up stockings. No bra and the top of her dress could be pulled down to expose her beautiful breasts and sexy 1/4 inch nipples when aroused. But back then, Jane was quite shy and reserved and although she was really keen to go to the club... it was a bit of a mission to get her dress up like that.

I wore some skin tight rubber shorts, as advised by my mate that I bought at a fetish / BDSM gear shop in Camden market, London. A black Lycra T-shirt and black motorcycle boots. Everyone in the fetish clubs are dressed up and you can't get in unless you do.

We'd never been before and were amazed to see all the different types of people and everyone was wearing some kind of leather, rubber or BDSM type gear. The club was called Club Rub and held monthly in a pub in Houndsditch, Central London and the layout was on 2 levels... The main drinking area was on the ground floor and the basement area was set up as dance floor with another bar, a separate BDSM play room with all kinds of racks and play equipment. Then there was another curtained off area in a corner called a couples only room that we were told would be full of couples later, playing and having sex with each other.

There were several TV monitors showing hard core sex movies on the basement level but not in the main bar upstairs.

People were of all ages... from mid 20's to a few over 65's and some girls were already walking around topless and or in very skimpy revealing outfits.

We had arrived at 10.30 pm and met up with my mate and his Thai wife. That's when he asked us if we had ever taken sweets? (Ecstasy). We said no and he told us that most people in the club use them and they make you want to dance, feel really nice and relaxed and make you feel horny.

Jane and I had a brief chat and decided to try them, so he gave us a couple. We only took one each and started wandering around the club, looking around and generally people watching.

About an hour had passed and nothing had happened, we still felt the same but were still excited with all the weird people and near naked girls and guys wandering around in the club. My mate then said, one sweet was probably not enough so gave us another couple, now we had taken 2 each....

Thirty minutes later and I felt this intense wave of pleasure and a really nice tingling sensation all over my body... Jane said she felt the same and up till this moment, she was the most shy person you would ever meet. I remember I put my arm around her and as we touched each other... the feeling was amazing ... like a very weak electrical tingling which made you sigh with pleasure.

I slid a hand inside her dress top and she actually let me cup her breast and squeeze her nipple without stopping me in embarrassment.

Her tits even looked and felt different... like the skin seemed softer... and Jane trembled as I caressed them... I was thinking how absolutely beautiful they were... with her erect nipples curving up like little coat hangers... 34B on a sexy Asian 25 yr old girl that never been pregnant... They were truly stunning tits...

She just closed her eyes and sighed as she let me caress them inside her dress right in front of my mate and his wife.

They were also both touching each other while dancing and smiling as they knew exactly what Jane and I were experiencing for the first time on the sweets.

I remember easing down her dress top and exposing her tits even more... to the delight of my mate who commented how beautiful they were.

Then I remember, running my hand down her back and cupping her bum cheeks, sliding up her short dress and fingering her from behind.

It was like nothing Jane or I had felt before. She was sighing and kept closing her eyes and hugging me and nearly collapsed on the floor in pleasure.

Now normally, she would never let me near her little bum

hole, but I remember she was squeezing my cock at the front through my rubber shorts and her other hand was going down inside the back of my shorts. I couldn't even believe she was doing this in front of loads of people.

My hand was up the back of her dress and as I was feeling her bum... I pushed my finger in her little anus and she did the same back to me... The feeling was out of this world and so intense.

Jane had never done that to me before and also never let me do that to her but at that moment we were both fingering each other in the butt and it felt amazing.

We looked at each other... both smiling and eased our respective fingers out. She then pulled my shorts down at the front and released my cock... squeezing and cupping my balls... right in front of my mate and his wife!

I started playing with her tits again and had both out on show with several guys and couples close to us giving us admiring looks.

The most amazing feeling was when my cock was released and Jane was just touching it lightly.... then squeezing and wanking it... then pulling my balls out and squeezing them too. I was rock hard and my cock felt like it was throbbing and tingling. Her touch and even my own, made it feel so electrifying. I wanted to keep touching it or have Jane play with me as it felt so different and I was so fucking horny it's hard to describe.

Anyway, her tits were exposed and she didn't even try to cover them up. Probably because lots of other girls were walking around virtually naked and several couples were having sex in corners or nearby with single guys crowding around them. The time must have been past midnight and the place was literally packed.

The pub wasn't huge, each of the 2 floors were probably only 30 x 60 meters and about 250 people were packed in. Techno music was playing loudly and the dance floor area downstairs was also heaving and we could barely squeeze through the crowd. Jane was even getting groped by single guys wherever we tried to walk.

She still had my cock out and led me through the dancing crowd to the play area and couples room. This is where we saw couples seriously playing, people were tied up and getting whipped, girls in swing seats being fucked or groped by groups of single guys.

I remember us hugging each other in a corner, I was fingering Jane, trying to make her cum and these guys kept groping her arse and tits. We fended them off... and said NO and then they moved away.... The whole scene was so new to us and we were yet to learn the rules...

Then there were all the strange shapes and patterns when we closed our eyes. We would be sitting on some cushions in a dark room and listening to the music with couples making love right next to us.... and when I closed my eyes... it was like I was in the matrix...

Back in the dance area everyone was dancing together like sardines in a can... Jane's tits were still exposed, in fact the whole top part of her dress was down around her waist now and as we danced, my cock was sticking out with Jane constantly grabbing it and laughing.

Several single guys were dancing very close to Jane and kept trying to touch her tits and butt, so we moved over to some chairs at the side of the room. As we sat there, I started caressing Jane's legs and tits and right next to me was a stunning Korean girl wearing... well virtually nothing really. She had these long white sexy legs and her small but shapely tits were exposed... smaller than Jane's but longer nipples. When she got up and crossed the room, I saw she was only wearing a tiny silver G string.

However, as she walked away into the darkness, the ecstasy made my vision really clear but weird... it was like being in a 3 D video game and I saw her skin change from really smooth... to all scaly... like snake skin... Like she was shape shifting but it was all so erotic and from the back she looked totally naked.

Jane was wanking my cock again and the waves of pleasure were overtaking me so I closed my eyes and watched all the silver colored fine grid like patterns forming all around me in the darkness.

The Korean girl came back and sat next to me again, fuck she was so tall, slim and beautiful, her English husband was on her other side. Both were now watching Jane play with my cock and smiling. I wanted to touch her leg as it was virtually touching mine but I didn't want her to move away or get offended so I just enjoyed what Jane was doing.

I couldn't even believe what happened next...

Jane got down on the floor between my knees and started sucking my cock. I was so shocked but also so excited... I held her head and then reached down to caress and play with her tits. As I opened my legs a bit wider, I felt the Korean girls leg pressing against mine, she was smiling and watching Jane while her husband was playing with her tits.

We actually became good friends with the Korean girl and her husband as they were at nearly every club event we attended over the next 2 years and we all had some really interesting group fun together.

They were also both really into Jane as she was Asian like the Korean girl but more than anything else, they liked to play with Jane's tits... and I had a thing for the Korean girls bum... it was so perfect and she used to let me squeeze it while we were all dancing together or in a dark corner while watching some sexy action in a group.

Her husband seemed to get really turned on whenever he saw me touching her as he would often ask me (after he saw me grope her bum) if she let me finger her...?

A lot more happened on that first night but not to repeat myself here, you can read all about our clubbing experiences in my other more in depth stories.

At 4 am the lights came on and everyone was getting dressed in their street wear to go home. I distinctly remember standing directly behind the Korean girl on the stairs while queuing up to get our bag and coats on the upper level. Her bum was directly level with my face and I had such a hard job not to just reach out and kiss or caress it.

On the way home, we were still buzzing from the sweets and the night felt so young. All the way home, I had Jane's tits exposed and was fingering her as she just lay back in the passenger seat moaning and pulling my hand in deeper... but her pussy was actually quite small and tight so I'd never been able to get all my fingers inside her.

However, the sweets seemed to make her want to force my fingers in... She even let me finger her ass again as she put her feet up on the dashboard and opened her legs wide. I had one finger in her pussy and one in her ass...

My cock was also sticking out and exposed, twitching all by itself as we drove along, I would keep squeezing it and wanking it or Jane would reach over and squeeze it.

Somehow, we got home OK and the sweets were still making us feel so fucking horny.... It was amazing. As soon as we got in the bedroom, we were naked in a 69 position in no time and I was licking and eating Jane out like never before.

She tasted fucking incredible, a really naughty, sexy taste and smell. I remember trying to force all 4 fingers in her and instead of the usual "stop... please... it hurts", She was actually egging me on and asking for some gel to get more fingers inside her.

She even started to like having large insertions pushed inside her while on the sweets. Also her nice little ass was now part of our sexual pleasures and what a beautiful tight little bum she had.

It wasn't long before we started to play with other couples and occasionally let one or two single guys join in the soft play with us... I particularly liked it when we would pretend that Jane was alone and I would watch to see what happened from a distance... Jane would sit at a table or in somewhere alone, while I watched from somewhere near by... Single guys and sometimes even couples would approach her and come on to her and sometimes, she would let them touch her tits or legs and then I would walk over to join them... At first they would be surprised but when they realized we were a couple and up for some fun... everything was good and we would let them join us.

In fact many times after we came home from clubbing and Jane was exhausted and wanted to sleep... I would go downstairs and watch some porn for a couple of hours beating my meat some more then go up to bed to sleep.

The sweets I found out later actually make it harder for a guy to orgasm and many guys complain that they cannot get a hard on when taking them. My answer was to take a Viagra pill with my first 2 sweets and then later in the evening I may take another Viagra with another two sweets but never more than two Viagra. Because my erection would last nearly 3 days LOL. I have been doing that for 10 + years now and it still works just fine.

So that was our first experience and the clubbing continued for the next year or so. Now because I had such a ready supply of the sweets, I started taking them occasionally in the evenings... I would pop one at about 7 o'clock and they would start working by 8 and they would make me so horny, we would make love or watch a sexy movie or I would get Jane to play with me...

But it was never as good an effect as in the club's, as the music and atmosphere were not at home.... And as Jane was not taking them with me, (week nights) she would fall asleep and I would end up popping another 2 at about 10 o'clock.

This would keep me feeling really horny till about 4 am or until I cum watching the porn, whereby I would get back in bed and sleep. So after Jane was asleep, I would be downstairs watching porn and abusing myself. Some times when I was feeling really horny, I even went out in the car to a local dogging spot.

However, I never engaged with any doggers at that time as there was never much going on.. I only ever saw older single guys in cars and I was not into guys. In the main I just sat there watching and playing with myself while sitting in the car...

But the best dogging experiences came a few months later, when Jane and I would drive to a dogging spot on the way home from the clubs....

I hope you enjoyed this story.

If you like my writing style, and stories about Husband or Wife sharing, Wife watching, BDSM, Cuckold, Swinger and Fetish clubs, Dogging and many other fetishes...

Why not check out my other stories on my

Amazon Author page

or sign up to my newsletter to get the heads up on all my new releases.

Dante X

Authors Website

BLOG - Contact – Comments and Newsletter sign up

www.DantesErotica.uk

Cuckold Sexting with a Shared wife

Asian Girls Erotica Story

by Dante

Contents

Introduction

Chapter 1 - I sent Jane a text

Chapter 2 - Another story about her sister

Chapter 3 - Her Dad's friend

Chapter 4 - Jane gets caught

Introduction

Jane was 25 and in the Philippines when we met. I was 42 and over the next 4 years we were very happy and had some great times at many Fetish and Swinger clubs in the UK. I must admit though... some of the horniest experiences of my life were with Jane... But then things took a turn and she now lives with another guy... However, we still chat and things are going well for us both and here is a very horny sexting session we had recently.

Chapter 1

I sent Jane a text

The other night, I was feeling horny as usual and in a drunken moment sent Jane a text...

Me: Hi Babe, How you doing? Saw you was with your daughter and Colin and your sister Rey last week on Facebook.

Jane: Yes we were on holiday for 3 weeks visiting my family. Long time no contact. So are you happy now? and where you living?

Me: I'm living in Thailand again... been here for a few years now.

Jane: You must love living there again with all the stories you told me about your last ex wife and what you did together.

Me: LOL, well its been a long time now babe and many more stories to tell but I keep thinking about you and when we used to go to the Fetish clubs in London.

Jane: I think about that too but it seems so long ago.

Me: So are you still having problems with him?

Jane: No not really, he's a good guy and dad but we don't do anything together. I just see my friends and he works in a warehouse every night.

Me: So he's in a warehouse now?

Jane: Yes... a few years now.

Me: Don't you have a part time boyfriend then... if you're so unhappy with him.?

Jane: No... What about you?

Me: No, I don't have girlfriend. I'm very happy with my wife but the only problem is... She doesn't like sex.

Jane: LOL me too, I don't remember when we last had sex together... He's weird and just not interested.

Me: Same same, I just watch sexy movies or play with myself thinking about you and what we used to do in the clubs in London.

Jane: I just see my friends and look after my daughter now. My sister was asking about you when we were in the Philippines last month.

Me: Really... Why is that babe?

Jane: I think she fancies you...

Me: Well babe, I did think about linking up with her up after we split up, as I knew she fancied me.

Jane: What do you mean?

Me: Well, you know what she did one evening after she came home from work?

Jane: No! what did she do?

Me: Well you were in the kitchen and she came in your mum and dads house and sat opposite me in the arm chair and we started chatting. She'd just split up with her boyfriend and was living at home with her new born baby.

Jane: Yes I remember, so what did she say?

Me: Nothing I can remember but she was wearing that really short skirt and tights and her tits were huge and leaking milk and she was so small, 21 years old and so sexy...

Jane: I don't understand. So what happened?

Me: Well she was sitting opposite me and I remember her opening and closing her legs?

Jane: What!

Me: Hey it was not me... she was coming on to me! Are you getting jealous?

Jane: No, So what happened...?

Me: Well she was sitting in the armchair in front of me and was parting her legs so I could see right up her skirt. She was doing it on purpose and looking me directly in the eyes. I knew she saw me looking and it was turning her on. Her tits started leaking again and she covered them with her hands but opened her legs wider as she looked around to see if anyone was watching. I could see up her short skirt to her little white knickers and pussy.

Jane: What happened next...?

Me: I reached down and touched her leg but your dad walked in the room and saw what she was doing and sent her upstairs to change.

Jane: You dirty bastard. So you fancy my sister then...?

Me: No but at the time it was really horny and she was always rubbing her leg against mine when we sat together.

Jane: She has a new boyfriend now but still asks me about you.

Me: What I want to know is... What have you been doing cos I know you told me a couple of years ago you were not happy with him.

Jane: We had a lot of problems cos he's so jealous. So now, I do my own thing and he does his.

Me: So where are you now babe,

Jane: At home

Me: And are you alone?

Jane: No, I'm on the computer and he is watching TV.

Me: My wife has gone out for the evening with her friends. Can you send me a picture please?

Jane: What sort of picture? I know you... you dirty bastard...

Me: Send me a shot of your tits or go to the bathroom and send me a pussy shot... hmmmmmm

Jane: I can't do that, he's sitting on the sofa opposite me.

Me: Do you get turned on when we chat like this?

Jane: Yes

Me: Do you remember when we were in the club in London and my mate gave us some sweets (Ecstasy) and his wife was not with him that night.

Jane: When you asked me to let him play with us and I sucked his big fat cock. LOL

Me: Yes and he told me a year later you were letting him finger you while we were walking from room to room in the club.

Jane: OMG... I don't remember much because we'd taken the sweets and I was so turned on...

Me: Remember when there were 5 guys crowding around us and I had your tits out and legs open and was fingering you as that old guy stepped forward and cum right in front of us?

Jane: Yes and Gary's cock was so wide I couldn't even get my hand or mouth around it...

Me: You getting wet babe? Bet you're rubbing your pussy now?

Jane: He keeps looking over at me so I can't... I'm by the computer.

Me: My cock is so hard now chatting with you. Go to the bedroom and send me a picture of your tits please?

Jane: OK but I want to see your cock then.

Me: Did you get the pic?

Jane: Hhhmmmm Yes. You look so big and why is it all sticky... are you using gel?

Me: Yes and I had a couple of sweets so feeling well horny. Just seen your pic... Oh babe your tits are still amazing and your nipples are hard. What about a pussy shot babe?

Fifteen minutes pass and then a picture comes through with Jane sitting on the bed in tights and no knickers with her legs open.

Me: What happened?

Jane: He nearly caught me taking a pic of my pussy so I told him I was taking a shower then going to bed.

Me: So you gonna play while I tell you another true story? Get nice and wet and then send me a pussy shot. But you have to tell me a true story as well... OK?

Jane: OK, you know I love hearing your stories but not the made up ones. Tell me a true story.

Chapter 2

Another story about her sister

Me: Are you shaved or hairy now?

Jane: Shaved... Tell me about what else you did with my sister?

Me: That evening when your dad caught her flashing me her pussy up her short skirt, I was coming out of the shower and she was in the hallway so I let my towel fall open and she stared at my cock. She just couldn't look away...

Jane: You dirty bastard... you were teasing her LOL.

Me: Yes I wanted to show her I was interested but you were always around so couldn't do anything at the house. So remember when she called you a few days later and said she was going to be late home and I was in town?

Jane: Yes I remember

Me: Well, I saw her at the print shop she worked at in the mall just before she finished and offered her a taxi ride home with me but when we were in the taxi, she snuggled up to me and was getting all touchy feely... so I put my arm around her and she pressed her tits into me and held my hand. Next thing was, she said, can we go to the viewpoint before we go home. That's when she rang you.

Jane: OK... go on...

Me: I started to touch her tits with my other hand and she started kissing me on the mouth.

Jane: What... she really fancied you then!

Me: And I'd got a hand in her blouse and she was trying not to let the driver see what we were doing. Then she told the driver to go to the viewpoint instead of home. Anyway I carried on snogging her in the back and the driver was smiling and watching in the mirror. Then she said, the driver is watching us... so I told her it was dark outside and in the back of the car, I'm sure he can't see anything so we carried on. She was getting really turned on and I had her blouse unbuttoned and had my hand inside her bra playing with her swollen tits. They were huge and her big nipples leaking milk. I started sucking one and slid my hand down over her belly and she just grabbed my hand and said ...NO the driver will see.... I said, don't worry he doesn't know you and it's more fun with someone watching. She giggled and said ... What you want him to watch us!

Jane: So you were doing my sister in a taxi and you love being watched LOL! Here's another pic coming... I'm in bed and soaking wet you dirty bastard...

Me: So I put a hand on her knee and opened her legs a bit. She had that short skirt on with black tights. I got my hand between her thighs and started sucking on her nipple. She started moaning so I kissed her on the mouth again and I got my hand on her pussy and was rubbing it over the tights. I remember it being so fucking hot and she was squirming around. The driver must have had a hard on cos she had her legs wide open and I was inside the top of her tights and going into her soaking wet hairy pussy.

Jane: She's so hairy down there LOL... Did you get the pic? God your making me so fucking horny. What did you do next?

Me: Wow love the pic ... your pussy is so smooth... I loved shaving it for you.. God... I want to eat it now. Hhhhmmmmmm

Anyway, Your sister was letting me finger her and was laying across the taxi back seat with her legs wide open and then taxi pulled into the car park of the hilltop view point. Find a quiet spot I told the driver. He parked up and turned off the lights and engine and turned around to see what we were doing.

Your sister was about to cum as I had two fingers in and was fingering her quite fast, I was trying to make her squirt like you did when I used to do that. Then she said... He's watching us OMG. I said calm down and let's give the poor driver a good show and started snogging her again. I told her... Lets show him your tits and opened her blouse and pulled her bra up.

The driver stared open mouthed and said mama mia she is beautiful. How old is she sir? 21 I answered, and she has just had a baby... look at all the milk coming out. I squeezed her tits and milk was squirting out and I just told her to relax and motioned for him to touch them.

Jane: You let the taxi driver touch my sisters tits!

Me: Yes babe LOL you know what I like.... Threesomes and watchers..., and I know you have your fingers in your pussy now .... I want you to push a finger in your arse as well, imagine I am there doing it to you like before.

Jane... What happened next?

Me: I let the driver play with her tits and she just closed her eyes and let him while I went back inside her tights and fingered her some more. She started to really like it so I pulled her tights down some more and she tried to stop me. But the driver was leaning over and sucking on her tits... anyway I managed to get her knickers and tights down to her knees.

Jane: You bastard... you made me cum but don't stop...

Me: The driver was looking at me parting her legs so I nodded for him to touch her legs..... then he went higher and touched her pussy. Your sister just jerked had another orgasm as soon as he put his finger in her.

We let her calm down a bit and for the next 20 minutes, she was letting us do whatever we wanted to her. I peeled off the rest of her clothes and we had her naked on the back seat with legs wide open and taking turns to finger fuck her and then I got undressed and made her 69 me with her on top so I could lick and taste her pussy while the driver played with her tits. The driver had his cock out and was trying to get her to suck him but she wouldn't.... she did wank him though and he cum all over her tits and hand.

Jane: Is that a true story?

Me: Of course... ask your sister. Tell her I told you all about it and I'm sure she will admit it, to you anyway, it is all true... It happened a couple more times but that can be for another time. Now it's your turn. I want you to tell me a true story so I can stop texting and play while you make me cum.

Chapter 3

Her Dad's friend

Jane: I don't know many true stories. I only have one really but can't talk about it... as it's too ... well ... not right I suppose. I never told anyone but suppose I can trust you so here goes.

When I went back to Cebu in September, I went alone and left him and my daughter at home as I had to go do some important stuff with lawyers and stuff, for the house I bought for mum and dad.

Me: Just sent you another cock shot... Like it? So what happened then?

Jane: It was with my dad's friend.

Me: What! you went with your dad's friend! How old was he? Tell me all the details. Did your dad know? Sorry...

Jane: LOL I knew that would turn you on. He is about my dad's age 59 or 60 and always flirting with me when my dad was not around. He saw me in Robinson's mall and asked me to go for a coffee with him.

Me: So your dad did not know anything?

Jane: Of course not.... he would kill me....

Me: So what happened?

Jane: Well he asked me if I wanted to go out that evening to the casino, you know the one in the big hotel we went to together.

I said OK but just for a few hours or my dad would ask loads of questions cos he knows I'm married but alone in the Philippines and night time!

Me: So how did you meet him? My cock is so hard babe... are you in the bed now and making yourself wet?

Jane: In my dressing gown on top of the bed and yes my pussy is shaved and really wet you made me cum twice. So I met him outside Robinson's at 4pm and he picked me up in his 4 x 4 truck. I was wearing a low cut beige dress and skin coloured tights and my uplift bra. He was always looking at my tits so I wanted to tease him. As we drove to the casino he kept touching my arm and telling me how beautiful I was and did I like casinos...? I said yes... what are we going to play?

He said... Can we play a game?

What sort of game? I asked him. Well what if I give you 10,000 pesos to play blackjack any game you like. If you win and you come out with more than 10,000 pesos, you can keep all the winnings.

What if I don't win and lose your money? Then we go to a hotel and you let me fuck you.

Me: And you agreed?

Jane Of course... I was bored and wanted to get out from my family for one evening. So at the casino he let me try all the different games and after about 30 minutes I had lost about half of the money LOL. Then we went to play roulette and I won a lot back... but then lost it all shortly after. He kept buying me drinks and I was feeling really drunk and he kept putting his arm around me and touching my tits and bum.

Me: So you knew he was gonna fuck you then?

Jane: Well I had no choice... so I had another drink and he had to hold me up as we left the casino. He drove to a hotel and we went to the room and I just fell on the bed. He started to undress me and I remember him kissing me and he had his hand in my tights and fingering me.

Me: Fucking hell babe... he was your dad's mate. Shit I'm gonna cum but want to hear what happened next.

Jane: I know but he would not stop and he had my buttons undone and my tits out. He was fingering me and sucking on my tits and I was so drunk... I just let him do it. Then he pulled my bra off and my tights and knickers so I was laying naked on the bed. He got undressed and when I saw his cock it was huge.

Me: How big babe?

Jane: Bigger than you and really fat... about 10 inches. I tried to wank him with one hand but I needed to use two hands, but I was so drunk. He tried to make me suck him but I couldn't get it in my mouth. His cock head was too big.... so he turned me around and started licking and fingering my pussy again and he made me cum and I squirted a bit in his mouth... He puled away and watched it coming out... it was going all up in the air and over the bed..

Me: Fucking good story Jane, so what did he do next?

Jane: He made me kneel on the floor bent over the bed like a dog and was licking my bum and pussy again and then tried to get his cock inside me. OMG I'm cumming now...

Jane stopped texting for a few minutes then resumed

Me: Fucking hell Jane, did you just cum again... how are you texting and playing with your pussy as well.... God you're so fucking sexy... So he got it inside you then?

Jane: Yes and it hurt at first but he held me down and just kept pushing and telling me to relax... then he got it in. He fucked me for 2 hours in all different positions and made me wank him into my mouth as well. I was so drunk I just let him do it.

Me: Great story Jane. Is that all...?

Jane: Well not really cos he wanted to see me again a few days later and said he would take me to dinner and a Lady-boy show at a big hotel.

Me: Did you go?

Jane: Yes but he had already booked a room there and his friend turned up for dinner after the show.

Me: And what happened then babe?

Jane: Well he said his friend had just got divorced and he wanted to help him out. So he invited him to his room with me and I though we were just going to talk with him....

Me: Are you kidding me. You went to his room with another guy!!

Jane: I know... I'm a bit stupid sometimes, I should have suspected something. Anyway they both started kissing and touching me and...

Me: What happened next babe?

Me: Jane are you still there?

Chapter 4

Jane gets caught

Fifteen minutes go by and then I get another message from Jane.

Jane: Can't chat now. He came in and saw me playing with myself and started shouting.

Me: Where is he now?

Jane: I don't know.... downstairs I think.... He's coming back.

I didn't text back but 20 minutes later my phone rings.

Me: What happened Jane?

Man: Who is this?

Me: It's Dave, I suppose you're Jane's new husband Colin!

Colin: Yes and I was watching her playing with herself on the bed and messaging you.

In the background... I hear Jane shouting at him "give me my phone back" He shouts back at her... not till I see what you two have been saying. Phone goes dead and I am getting worried for Jane. Another 20 minutes and my phone rings but its a video call.

I answered it and...

Jane says – He's read all the messages and seen the pictures I sent you, my open legs, tits and my pussy and your cock pictures. He said if I don't do what he says now he will kick me out and take custody of my daughter...

Jane was Sobbing and crying....

ME: So what does he want you to do...?

Colin grabs the phone and says – not her... both of you. I want YOU to watch what I do WITH HER while “YOU” (he shouts) Tell us another fucking so called true story.....

He holds the phone camera towards the bed and Jane is laying naked and crying.

Colin: I’m gonna set up the camera so you can see the bed and I want you to do the same cos I want to see you as well.

Me: Fucking hell mate. Take it easy... don’t hurt her she looks really upset.

Colin: UPSET – How do you think I fucking feel after reading about you and her and her fucking her dads friend and his fucking mate!

Me: OK calm down, Let me just get a beer and set up the camera on the desk.

I grab a Budweiser and go over to my sofa.

Colin: OK, I want to hear a story about what she did with you....

SHOUTING AT JANE – What one shall we get him to tell us away Jane?

Me: I know one... when we went to a fetish club in London and she well both of us were high on E’s.

Colin: Yes she told me you made her take Ecstasy and do things to her in the clubs.

Me: Firstly mate, I never made her do anything! and we both took E’s for the first time together, about a year into our marriage when we were both introduced to the clubs.

Colin: Whatever... I don’t give a fuck... so tell me the story and no fucking bullshit OK?

Jane had stopped crying and was drinking a coke from a glass bottle and by the bed were some sex toys and dildos...

Colin: I am fucking angry as fuck but never been so turned on as I am tonight after seeing her fingering herself and reading all your fucking messages. So I want to see what it's like with a threesome on the video cam. Open your fucking legs you slut and let Dave here see your little shaved pussy again.

Me: Fucking hell mate she still looks tight and how she got her dads mates cock in there is amazing. I used to love making her squirt when she comes.

Colin: Squirt! I've never seen her do that.

Me: Well me too until she took Ecstasy and we had sex in the clubs or the car on the way home. Let's get her worked up a bit and then I will explain how to make her cum and squirt ... You better get a towel on the bed or we can do it while she is standing up in front of the phonecam.

Colin: – Jane.... Play with that dildo while Dave here shares another story.

I watched as Jane started pushing a flesh coloured dildo in and out of her pussy. He was laying next to her.... fondling her tits and they are both watching me on my cam. I am naked on my sofa and start telling him about how I made Jane squirt for the first time in a Swinger Fetish club.

"We'd taken a couple of sweets each (E's) and were walking around the club checking out the different rooms... watching couples and sometimes groups of guys playing with couples. Anyway we were in this dark room and some guy standing next to Jane was wanking his cock right next to her. She told me he kept rubbing it on her arm and hip so I told her to let him do it a bit more and let him touch Jane.

We were horny as hell and I was fingering her from behind and Jane was wanking me as we watched these three couples fucking through a glass window. The room we were in was pitch black but this guy wanking next to Jane was trying to... get us to invite him to play. Jane told me he was rubbing her arm so I got her tits out and nodded for him to have a feel.

He started playing with her tits and I was still fingering her from behind so I whispered to Jane.... To have a feel of his cock.... She was a bit hesitant but reached down and he let go of his own cock so Jane grabbed it and started stroking him.

So now she was playing with both of us while me and this guy were exploring her tits, bum and pussy."

Jane was now being fucked in a spoon position facing the phone camera and I could see Colin's cock going in and out while they both listened to me talking... They in turn were watching me play with myself while telling them the story on my phone cam.

Back to the story.

"This guy was now rubbing Jane's bum and legs so I moved my hand away so he could explore between her legs. Jane just stood there and told me he was fingering her and she was gonna cum.... I told her... "let him bring you off babe" and I started squeezing her tits and nipples and kissing her on the mouth. Suddenly Jane started moaning really loudly as this guy had two fingers in her from the front and was frigging her really fast.

She moaned in my ear she was cumming ... and then said "oh no he 's making me pee." I slid my hand down to her pussy and she was squirting all over my fucking hand and the floor. It was the sexiest fucking thing we had ever done. When Jane calmed down the stranger guy thanked us for letting him join in and he left the room. We then went for a walk about and ended up with 3 guys watching me fingering Jane in a dark corner while they all crowded round us and groped Jane's tits and arse as I made her squirt again like the guy showed us in the dark room earlier."

Talking to the phone cam –

Me: Jane looks ready to cum so why don't you make her squirt for us both...?

Colin: What do you want me to do?

Me: Get Jane to stand at the end of the bed with her pussy facing your phone cam. Now open your legs Jane and let him finger you.

You need to push 2 fingers in from the front and start frigging her fast with your fingers in as deep as you can.

That's it.... Keep doing that and she will cum and squirt but when she starts to pee... Keep your fingers inside and keep moving them fast.

Jane couldn't hold back as she remembered the story and was watching me wanking and cum at the same time on my sofa. She started gushing all over his hand and even when he did stop.... she continued pissing all over their bedroom floor.

Colin: Fucking hell Jane, you're so fucking turned on... and if these stories are true, why don't we make love any more...! Maybe we need to go check out these clubs or do you just like sex with other guys?

The phone cam goes off and I wonder what's going to happen between them now....

Jane messaged me the next day and said... After he turned off the phone he was like a man possessed, he was like an animal and fucked her all night long..... and now he wants them to start going to the clubs together....

I hope you enjoyed this collection of stories.

If you like my writing style, and stories about Husband or Wife sharing, Wife watching, BDSM, Cuckold, Swinger and Fetish clubs, Dogging and many other fetishes...

The FULL LIST of all my other stories can be found on my

Amazon Author page

www.Amazon.com/author/danteserotica

Or on Amazon search for: DANTE X

Register on my website to get the heads up on all my new releases and sample excerpts on the blog.

Website: www.DantesErotica.uk

Dante x

Sample of Dante's books available on Amazon and Audible.

Steppingley Manor (Private Members Club) series

Steppingley Manor

Dantes Erotica - Private Members Club

Dantes Erotica - Yasmin's Abduction

Waterworld Thailand - The Girl on the beach

The Navigator - An Erotic Sailing Adventure

Bangkok and the Vampires of the night

Japanese Escort

Transsexuals and Katoys in Thailand

Dogging with Dave

Sex, Drugs and Wife Watching in the Fetish & Swinger clubs

Japanese Girlfriend who loved the BDSM Fetish Lifestyle

Ladyboys - 10 different stories

British Indian wife 2 book set

Asian Wife Series of 14 books

Erotic Story Collection 1, 2, 3 and 4

The Man on the Train

The Man in the Park

Dangerous Game – Wife watching and sharing

The German Inventor

Living on a boat

The Landlords Tales

Swinging and Wife Sharing

The Arrangement

Shonie's Watersports Parties

Jinn - An Egyptian Adventure with Erotic Supernatural Horror

Adult Theatre Lover – Cinema Groping with Strangers

Erotic Lucid Dreaming – A technique for seduction

Abduction and Escape (Two book series)

Sexless marriage led to our naughty game

Revenge on the Bitch

Abducted and Addicted in Hong Kong

Fat Bastard Seduces my Wife

Something about Jasmine

Full Title List on www.Danteserotica.uk

Made in the USA
Monee, IL
03 July 2025

20421128R00184